A Game for Eagles

By the same author

THE PLEASURE GARDEN

THE DOWNHILL RACERS

WARLOCK

MARDIOS BEACH

CORPUS OF JOE BAILEY

SO MANY DOORS

A Game
for Eagles

by Oakley Hall

William Morrow and Company, Inc.

NEW YORK  1970

For Dennis Murphy

A Game for Eagles

(1) MONDAY

TRAILING the black limousine with its white, Federal District, Diplomático license plate, I felt as inconspicuous as a fire chief in my red Corvette. Through the rear window the woman's veiled head was visible, regally immobile. This was my first, preliminary toe-wetting in a brand-new bag of Caribbean émigrés, counterrevolutionary organizations, and the fluctuations of the stock of La Compañía Azucarera de Santa Cruz—the Big Sugar, as my father-in-law called it.

No snowy volcanoes could be seen today. The Valley of Mexico was swamped in eye-smarting mist. The capital was Americanizing itself at full bore, with *supermercados* and laundromats, *Time* magazine and Sears Roebuck, Ford Big Job trucks, anxiety-level traffic and smog. Ahead out the Calzada de los Misterios I could dimly make out the hill among higher hills, where—I had learned on yesterday's Grey Line Tour of Mexico City & Environs—the peasant Juan Diego had witnessed his miracle. It was easy to deduce from her black veil that the Dark Angel of Santa Cruz was paying a visit to the shrine of the Virgin of Guadalupe.

The limousine swept into the plaza before the Basilica, made a lordly U-turn through a snarl of taxis and streetcars, and halted. The veiled woman passed in through a gate, and I hustled for a parking place.

I was still disconcerted by the tilts of Mexico City. The capital had been built upon the bed of the great lake of Tenochtitlán, and had an infirm base; many buildings leaned, sidewalks buckled, and old churches foundered by the bell tower corner. Now as I hurried through the gates into a huge, stone-paved area, I was confronted by the Basilica, with its yellow dome, careening off to the right, while an adjacent structure tilted left, like vessels on either side of an ocean wave.

Penitents approached the doorway of the Basilica on their knees, a broken line of them making painful progress across the rough stones. A young man was accompanied by a friend afoot, who carried his shoes for him; an Indian woman, in a cheap black-and-silver rebozo, had her stockings rolled to save them, but the Dark Angel did not concern herself with torn stockings or scuffed shoes. Even on her knees she had a monumental quality; straight-backed in her black dress and veil, hands crossed on her breast like a figure from a Medieval tomb, she slowly advanced across the stones of Guadalupe. Beneath the veil a glimmer of eyes showed.

I strolled along the line of penitents to the steps of the Basilica. Inside, dim figures continued to move toward the altar that gleamed white and gold by candlelight. There was a heavy odor of burning wax, of dust and damp and humanity. A representation of the Virgin gazed down in compassion on communicants kneeling at the rail, on tourists wandering and whispering, on a small boy making water in the shadows of a pillar base.

The floor slanted as I moved down past a life-size bleeding Christ with lacerated knees, past ranked candles and coin boxes, and carved marble testimonials. As an executive and troubleshooter for American Ventures, Inc., I gave the place high marks as a well-managed commercial establishment. . . . And then, feeling a cheap cynic from the cynical Colossus of the North, I went on outside to gaze at the humanity on view, while the Dark Angel of Santa Cruz inched her way along.

I joined a small circle of spectators around an Indian with a cage of performing birds. For a coin, a canary hopped to a tiny rack of rolled slips of paper, selected one, and the proprietor passed it to a fat-faced girl. She giggled and crumpled it before her girl friend could see. *"¿Señor Americano, la fortuna?"* the Indian asked. I gave him a peso and a scrubby yellow bird drew a roll from the rack.

EL AMOR Y LA MUERTE, SIEMPRE JUNTOS. CUIDADO CON UNA EXTRANJERA HERMOSA. I wandered across the street for a beer, and considered my fortune; the togetherness of love and death, the danger from a beautiful stranger. Or maybe *extranjera* meant foreigner. When I returned to the Basilica, my veiled lady had made considerable progress.

I did not follow her inside, and finally she reappeared, limping down the steps with her skirt covering what must have been the ruin of her knees and stockings, hands folding the veil back from her face—a younger-than-I-would-have-thought face, shaped from some very dark, very smooth-grained wood, a hawk nose with flaring nostrils, pale eyes, full lips. She was a beautiful stranger and a foreigner, and she had an air of tragedy about her.

The limousine U-turned across the plaza for her, she let herself in, and the long Cadillac drifted away from the curb like an ocean liner leaving the dock. I had one more glimpse of her fiercely lovely face as she turned in profile to glance out the rear window—a Cruceño combination of Eleanor Roosevelt, Jackie Kennedy, and perhaps Florence Nightingale; the daughter of Senator Anastasio Herrerro, and with him relevant to the changing of regimes in the island Republic of Santa Cruz.

The U.S. Embassy was located on Mexico City's Sunset Strip, a white lampshade crouching on bathtub legs, with the black and white monolith of the hotel María Isabel towering behind it, and the rush of Reforma traffic in front of it. I circled blocks until I found a parking place, and walked past a fence of two-by-two steel palings and up the steps beneath the lampshade. Thomas Murdoch to see the Deputy Chief of Mission: I was immediately VIPed into Mr. Herbert Justin's office.

The DCM rose from behind a desk as large and bare as a ping-pong table, and came out past an American flag on an eagle-headed staff to shake hands, a slight, graying, slightly balding man in a gray suit. "So you're Clipper Armstrong's son-in-law."

I nodded and smiled, he smiled and nodded and jingled the change in his pocket. We sat down on two Danish modern chairs.

"That's quite a sunburn," Justin said.

"Cruising down through Mexico with the top off."

"Red face, blond hair, and blue eyes. Quite an all-American color scheme. And you're here representing American Ventures for Armstrong?"

I said that was correct. He had a way of nodding as though to an interior monologue. "Well, we are at your service, of course," he said. "Anything we can do, and so forth, and so forth."

"I'm interested in the Organization of American States conference down here next week," I said, and he nodded. "In what American policy toward Santa Cruz is going to be," I said, and he frowned. "The Flores government has expropriated the railroad, and now they're after the sugar industry," I said, and he sighed.

"I'm afraid I can't help you on matters of policy. John Doane Finch will be coming down as our ambassador to the OAS—extraordinary, plenipotentiary, and all the trim."

"The Great Liberal himself," I said.

"It might be useful if I introduced you to the Great Liberal's very good friend, Mrs. Jenny Gray. She's in residence down here, an artist. Quite an attractive young woman."

"I'd also like to meet Senator Herrerro and his daughter."

"Sometimes it's difficult to gain an entrée into these Latin American families," Justin said.

"What's he like?"

"Best of a bad lot. The Dark Angel is much admired in the Republic, however: the daughter." He cocked an eye at me. "And you are interested in the émigré army up in Jalisco?"

"I'm more interested in Herrerro at the moment."

"He may be leery of Americans. There were rumors we had a hand in the murder of the old dictator—the Protector." He squinted at me with his lips pursed. "I don't happen to remember Thomas Murdoch in the national tennis rankings, do I? About ten years ago?"

I admitted it, pleased. Justin also looked pleased. "Herrerro's a tennis buff. I'll see if I can't get something worked up. Why don't you come over to my place for a drink this evening?"

I was to call him Herb. I was to let him know anything he could do for me. Everyone was always glad to do anything for Clipper Armstrong.

Herb Justin lived in a residential district called Polanco, on what could have been a street in Pasadena, in a nineteen-thirties Pasadena house behind a wall topped with broken glass. Inside the wall was a green lawn and a turquoise swimming pool, hedges and clipped trees. Herb was sitting beneath a striped parasol with Mrs. Justin, whose yellow bikini revealed unpleasant facts of middle age. A girl with long hair was swimming a slow backstroke in the pool.

"What a very blond, very handsome, tall young man!" Faye Justin said, giving me a limp hand to shake. "And married to the wealthiest girl in America!" she added, wide-eyed.

I pursed a smile in return. Herb assumed a blankly weary expression. The swimmer was coming out of the water, tossing her long hank of wet hair over a shoulder. She wore a blue-and-white checked bikini that revealed only pleasant facts. This was the American artist Jenny Gray, the friend of John Doane Finch, and an access to the corridors of power; she turned pink with the awareness that I couldn't keep my eyes off her body, donned a pair of glasses, black-framed and severe, but no more clothing. She had prematurely graying hair.

We were served Margaritas in frosted glasses with salted rims, and pumpkin-seed kernels. I nibbled and sipped and over the rim of my glass watched Jenny Gray's spectacular body with the line of fair hairs dropping from her tautly-lidded navel toward the promised land. Yes, she loved Mexico City. She had been here a month, painting like mad in her studio in San Angel. San Angel was a suburb; it was pleasant there. Yes, she would appreciate being driven home after the party, she had come in a taxi. When Jenny had gone to change her clothes, Faye Justin pried into my business in Mexico.

Two men arrived together, with introductions and a

new round of Margaritas. Sandy Brody was a reddish, freckled pipe-smoker. Dr. Ibis looked like a caricature of Teddy Roosevelt, and talked like a caricature of a middle-European psychiatrist. The subject of tennis came up, all the men seemed to be tennis players, and Dr. Ibis offered to include me in a game with some friends; the name of Anastasio Herrerro was never mentioned. All had been smoothly stage-managed, but there was tension in the air. Ibis contributed to this with conspiratorial winks, and Brody with a manner of pausing before speaking as though even platitudes had to be checked by teletype with higher authority. Herb had a degree of cool I admired; I liked the DCM.

At twilight Jenny and I set out for San Angel. The top was off and beside me in her bucket seat she fingered leather and chrome, dials and shift lever, brushing a hand at wisps of her hair that frayed loose in the wind. "Such an urgent, potent, *excessive* car," she said. "There must be a theory that cars match their owners. Like dogs."

I explained that the designers of the Corvette had had a mako shark in mind, not a dog, and she laughed. The friend of John Doane Finch was frank and appealing, with her high-cheekboned face guarded by prim spectacles, and the hem of her tight, striped, silk dress fluttering above her knees.

"I'm afraid I enjoy the men's conversations more than the women's," Jenny said. "What were you saying about hamburgers? Doesn't twenty percent chuck and eighty percent plate, and six percent soybeans add up to a hundred and six percent?"

I explained the proportions of the Red Tower hamburg mix. "I work for a corporation that buys struggling companies, shoves them over into the black, and sells them for a profit. Red Tower is a chain of what's called junk-food stands."

"What did *you* do?"

"Persuaded small entrepreneurs they could become rich capitalists by putting up money for a new Red Tower, which they manage themselves. The company lends them money at a hefty rate of interest, and supplies market research and advice."

"Are you *good* at it?" Jenny asked in wonder. "Do you *enjoy* it?" I was annoyed to feel myself flushing.

A horn honked and a small black Mercedes roadster whipped past. Dr. Ibis was at the wheel, a hand raised in greeting, the brim of his panama buckling in the wind. His taillights flicked into the lane ahead of us.

"I don't like shrinks," Jenny Gray said in a suddenly coarse voice. "I especially don't like shrinks I run into wherever I go."

"Do you run into Ibis wherever you go?"

"Maybe it's just that he's so . . ." She couldn't decide on a word.

"Excessive?" I asked, and she laughed and laid a hand on my arm for a moment. She was going to be one of those women with whom I had instant rapport. She began to talk about herself. Her home had originally been Mount Vernon, Iowa not Virginia, but she had lived in New York, Paris, Washington. She had worked for UNESCO. She liked to pilot a sailplane, to snorkel, and dance, and she loved painting. She had been a diving champion who had missed going to the Olympics because of mononucleosis. She had been married twice, widowed once, divorced once. She did not mention John Doane Finch.

"Right at the next corner for the Casa de la Fuente," she said.

"What's the Casa de la Fuente?"

"It's where I live."

I guided the excessive car through dark, bumpy lanes

between curving walls. Jenny stopped me where there was a little light from a lantern over an arched gateway. I opened her door, and then the gate. Inside was a patio dimly lit by orange bulbs, with feathery shadows of trees and shrubs pushing in from the darkness.

I asked if she knew of an apartment for rent.

"There's a studio apartment open here," she said. She did not invite me to come in, perhaps feeling the same restraint I was, flaps-down after too quickly getting along too well. "Good night, Murdoch," she said. "Thanks for the ride home." She crossed the patio with her silk skirt swinging and tightening over her bottom, a quick catch of muscle in her calf, a breast profiled as she turned to wave good-bye. She became a moving shadow among shadows.

I drove home to the Hilton, unsheathed my Olivetti, and typed a report of my first days in Mexico City for my boss, C. E. Armstrong, American Ventures, Inc., Armstrong Savings and Loan Building, Beverly Hills, California, U.S.A. I had scouted the Dark Angel of Santa Cruz. A tennis game had been arranged so I could meet her father, Senator Herrerro. I had made the acquaintance of the mistress of John Doane Finch, that famous man, who was the Chief of the American delegation to the Organization of American States conference in Mexico City next week.

I arranged to have the brown envelope delivered to the early bird Aeronaves de Mexico flight to Los Angeles, and went to bed. But as soon as the concentration of making out the report was relaxed, I recognized that the strain with which I had driven home from San Angel was still on hand. I lay in the dark calling up memories of Eloise Armstrong Murdoch, who, if she were not the wealthiest girl in America, was certainly the most desirable, with the spacious skies of those

great, nearsighted orbs, her shining hair like waving
fields of grain; our happy and uncomplicated sex life
with its bombs bursting in air.

But I was being prodded by that familiar devil Ex-
tramarital Lust.

(2) TUESDAY

I REREAD the telegram from my beautiful wife over a Hilton breakfast of bacon and eggs and weak American coffee, a cute Mexicana waitress with a boyish hairdo hovering by. GOOD LUCK MY DARLING TAKE CARE LOVE ELOISE. I was Eloise's darling so long as I took care to please her father, the Clipper, and made my own luck. I wondered why she had chosen to send me this particular message, and thought of the canary picking from the tiny rack an item concerning love, death, and beautiful strangers.

Over second coffee I pictured my wife with her father in the study of the great house in Bel Air, with the green phone and the two black phones on the leather-covered desk, and the color TV in the French Provincial cabinet turned on, but with the sound down, if all were quiet, or turned up to drown the gargled agonies of Mother Eloise upstairs in her narcotized incarceration; the Clipper pacing pigeontoed up and down the room while Daughter Eloise lit a cigarette when she already had one burning in the ashtray. It was pleasant that they were worrying about me on my dangerous mission, Eloise impulsively telegraphing a message of love and caution.

I couldn't see that anything was particularly danger-

ous about my mission. It was only another troubleshoot
for American Ventures. Last year Red Towers, this year
Big Sugar. It required my presence in a foreign country
and involved foreign elements, but the nut of the situation was still a company with undervalued stock. What
was the difference between a chain of junk-food stands
facing bankruptcy, and a sugar company with expropriation hanging over it? I would pull Clipper Armstrong's
chestnuts out of the fire for love and money—the love
of my wife, and the kind of money that made Corvettes, and penthouse apartments, and country club
memberships, not luxuries but necessities. For a long
moment I mused on that most expensive luxury of all,
my wife.

Following this I went shopping and spent 2100 pesos
on tennis gear, including two Dunlop tennis rackets
strung to sixty-five-pound test with the best lamb gut.
It was a total satisfaction to be able to buy two tennis
rackets on my expense account. Of such is the kingdom
of heaven.

At two o'clock I met Dr. Ibis at the Sports Club at
Chapultepec and we hit balls at each other on one of
the clay courts. Pudgy, with sparse fair hair, steel-
rimmed glasses, and a smile like a mouthful of white
dominoes, he scrambled all over the court whacking his
big, top-spin forehand that sent the ball bouncing errat-
ically off the clay. It was a mighty shot, and I told him
so.

"Ah, but you are the very fine player, my friend!" he
said, stopping to mop his steaming face. "Yes! We will
deal severely with these opponents. Then we will
change partners, eh?" He gave me an overblown wink.
"Ah, here they arrive!"

The Senator Anastasio Herrerro, father of the Dark
Angel, cousin of the late Protector, was very old. He
wore white flannel trousers on bandy legs, a long-

sleeved tennis shirt, a long-billed cap. He resembled
one of those Negro jockey hitching posts, though he
was not so dark as his daughter. His spotted face, with
a goat's pale slash of pupil, was continually smiling and
nodding. As a former senator he was a depressing
statement on the past of the Republic of Santa Cruz,
and even more depressing as the best of a bad lot and
prospective strongman. His partner was a tall Mexican
pro with legs covered with black sphagnum moss. Herrerro only hit balls that came directly to him, giggling
as he dealt out trick spins, cuts, and drop shots. His
partner solemnly stroked deep, steaming drives.

Playing the pro for points, and Herrerro to make him
look good, my partner and I immediately ran into trouble, and Ibis made a series of bad-line calls. I offended
him by offering replays. But I soon realized that Hairy-
legs was a machine hitter—never a shot that couldn't
be anticipated—and I began poaching the big drives at
net. Ibis and I walked away with the set, and we
changed partners, Ibis and the pro, Herrerro and me.
The Senator and I had a fight on our hands, with Ibis'
line calls and Herrerro's habit of belatedly ticking balls
that came past him at the net, but covering three quar-
ters of the court and puffing desperately at the altitude,
I managed to keep us in the match.

At five games up, the Dark Angel of Santa Cruz
appeared. All in white, carrying a white parasol, her
hair caught up in a frilled boating cap, she floated into
the court like a cloud. Her impassive dark face was
shaded by the parasol as she sat watching our play like
some Caribbean Renoir lady.

My game is profoundly affected by a money match
and beautiful spectators, and with three big shots and a
lucky flub of Herrerro's, we broke the pro's serve. In
the final game I served two aces, beat the pro in an
exchange of volleys, and on the fourth point set up one

of Ibis' big forehands and sprinted in to catch it at the
top of its arc and powder it for game and set. Ibis
dropped his racket to clap, Herrerro clapped, and the
Dark Angel patted white-gloved hands together.

"Ah, Señor Moordoak!" Herrerro burbled. "Such
very fine play-ing, señor! Come, you will meet my
daughter!"

But the Dark Angel was not much interested in
blond, red-faced, show-off American tennis players. She
did not offer me her glove, but she smiled at the Mexican pro and rose, monumentally, turning her parasol in
her hands. She was as tall as I.

Going back to the clubhouse, Herrerro took an Ancient Mariner grip on my arm, his monkey-face peering
up at me from under the bill of his jockey cap as he
flattered me rapid-fire. I congratulated him on having
played intelligent tennis.

"It is all one has left, señor! Do you know how old
this very old man is? Seventy-nine years of age! Already
it is too old for anything but for watch. But! I have the
so beautiful tennis—*corte*, señor! So gold the color, so
white line. You will come to my house in Lomas de
Chapultepec and play with my daughter Aurelia, eh?"

"Your daughter plays tennis?" I tried to picture her
in a tennis outfit, heroic-sized, but it would not come.

"But not enough, señor! Do you think she is beautiful, my daughter?"

"Very beautiful," I said, and he bobbed and nodded
with enthusiasm. As we arranged a game for Saturday,
at Herrerro's, the Mexican pro glanced back at us
gloomily, Ibis with a fat-mouthed, conspirator's leer.

When I returned to the Hilton there was another
telegram for me. This one was not a message of love
and caution, but of stern duty: MEET AL REP POLICE
PLAZA CAHULA JALISCO TOMORROW TEN AM AMVI. "AL"
was the Army of the Liberation of the Republic of

Santa Cruz, "REP" would be its representative, CAHULA was in JALISCO, where the émigré army was in training at the Hacienda Rodríguez, south of Guadalajara. "AMVI" was American Ventures, Inc. From my room I telephoned the hotel travel agent for a reservation to Guadalajara, a little short of breath at the altitude and with the major action beginning. I was informed that there was a fiesta on in Cahula, a very fine, very ethnic one, with dancers, fireworks, bullfights: I had chosen well. Leave Mexico City 8:00 A.M. Arrive Guadalajara 9:30. A car and chauffeur could be engaged at the Guadalajara airport, from which it was less than an hour's journey to Cahula.

I had popped a Seconal and was dozing off over *Time* magazine, when a many-buttoned bellhop arrived with another telegram: REMEMBER DARLING YOU ARE MORE PRECIOUS THAN ANYTHING TAKE NO CHANCES LOVE ELOISE.

(3) WEDNESDAY, I

THE most aggressively available of the chauffeurs at the Guadalajara airport was a young man with a bronze complexion and a great mole on his right cheek that twisted his face into an expression of wry good humor. "Call me Chuy, huh?" he said. He wore a hairline moustache, a blue yachting cap, and a shirt open at the throat to reveal a Saint Christopher medal. He stamped cowboy boots impatiently.

"Where's your bags?" he demanded. "You don't even have a briefcase? Where you want to go, Tiger? Tlaquepaque?"

"Cahula."

"We eat dust," Chuy said, pushing his cap back on his head. We went outside. "Hey, that's a dirty trip to Cahula. You like these hick fiestas, huh? Where's your wife, Tiger? You want to check some rough stuff when we get back from Cahula?"

I said I would be flying back to the capital tonight, and Chuy presented me to his limousine, which was polished to a brilliant black gloss. It was an aging Buick with chrome portholes evenly spaced not merely along the hood, but on the doors and rear fender as well, so that the car appeared to have been grommeted for lacing.

When I had been seated in the rear, Chuy started
the engine with a sound like machine guns firing underwater. He jockeyed out of his parking place, the
machine guns increasing in volume, and we turned
right onto the highway. I gripped the passenger strap
and tried to compose myself for the hour's trip to
Cahula, to meet the Al Rep. "Where you from, Tiger?"
my driver asked.

I said I was from Los Angeles.

"I used to live up in East L.A. I had a woman there,
she ran a place that sold tacos, tamales, stuff like that to
take out. Last June immigration caught up with me. I
didn't try going back. I was sick of that woman, and I
had plenty money."

We were running along a black-topped highway
through gently rolling, grayish-brown landscape. We
passed an Indian leading two burros laden with terra-
cotta pots, and a motorcycle policeman haranguing the
driver of a ramshackle truck he had pulled over to the
side of the road. In the cop's holster was an ivory-
handled .45 with the hammer cocked.

"Do your cops always carry their guns cocked?"

"Always, yeah," Chuy said. "Faster to shoot. They
like to shoot. Just like your cops."

"It would be good if he didn't fall off his motorcycle
with that pistol cocked."

"Be good if he did. He blows his balls off."

"You don't like cops?"

"I don't like cops that chew up poor old Indios in
their poor old trucks. And the *ricos* go past fast as hell
in their Cads and Mercies."

"Is there a lot of that?"

In the mirror his face stiffened. Then it relaxed as
though the mole were a spring loading that kept him
smiling. "Yeah, but it's better," he said. "Everything's
better. Coming back from eight years in the States I see

how much better this country of mine gets. It's slow,
but it *moves*—you know what I mean?"

"What moves?"

"The Mexican *revolución*. It's not like the *revolución
norteamericana* that went up, big show, bam! In the
gringo way, and then everybody forgot about it. This
revolución down here goes pretty slow sometimes, but
it's alive, it *moves*, it's not finished yet."

"Congratulations," I said, irritated with revolutions
and comparisons.

"Yeah, thanks," Chuy said. "Well, here's where we
eat dust, Tiger." He swung off the highway where a
small sign indicated: CAHULA, 6 KMS. The road was dirt,
and the windows and windshield immediately turned
impenetrably tan. Chuy switched on wipers which
stirred the dust like fine talcum. It seemed to me he
drove much too fast for the visibility.

Inside the dust-shrouded car General Galindo's émigré army seemed a bad idea, and the salvation of the
Compañía Azucarera de Santa Cruz of little interest. I
wished I were back in the States where the revolution
was dead.

All at once we burst out of the dust into bright sunlight, a grassy field. Beyond a low serration of adobe
walls the bell tower of the church of Cahula was visible.

"Someday they'll pave that bad road," Chuy said,
with a booster's faith in Mexican future perfection. He
locked the Buick carefully against the imperfect present. We trod the grass in company with neatly dressed
Jaliscans from many tour busses. The street entering
Cahula was cobbled, crowded, and lined with stalls sell-
ing Coca-Cola and orange pop, peanuts and corn kernels in newspaper cornucopias, dusty pastries and dubious candies, dethorned cactus paddles, bolts of
striped cloth, plastic dishes, clay pots, melons and
oranges, and papayas in pyramids. I stopped to watch a

penitente writhing with a crown and necklace of thorns. Naked and dusty and bleeding, eyes rolling whitely, he swayed and chanted, while a group of tourists, my countrymen, photographed this excess of Mexican faith.

"Say, how do you like this nut?" one of the men called to me. As we walked on, Chuy, with his face screwed up severely, said, "Always you guys make jokes about what you don't understand."

"Do you understand?"

"No, but I don't make a joke, either. I remember on TV up in the States when a guy burned himself up with gas at the UN, remember that guy? They said he did it for the publicity. In the States you think everything is done for the bad reason."

Just then we entered a large plaza, one end of which was dominated by the stone facade of the church. Nearby were tables and chairs, and a large temporary structure made of palm fronds, with the signs: CERVEZA, TACO, TAMAL. It was five minutes after ten by my watch, a time of tension by my pulse.

A bullfight poster decorated an adjacent wall. A giant matador in a magenta suit revolved before a mastodon of a bull; SEIS COLOSAL TOROS/GANADERÍA DE FRANCISCO RODRIGUEZ. "How far is that bull ranch from here?" I asked. "Hacienda Rodríguez."

"Not so far," Chuy said. "But it's not the hacienda of Don Francisco any more." His face was perfectly blank. "You going there, Tiger? There's bad men there."

I shrugged. He asked when I would be coming back. I said I hoped by dark.

"So what if you don't come back from these crazy Cruceños, what am I supposed to do then?"

I gave him a hundred pesos on account. When I glanced back he had seated himself at a table beneath

the CERVEZA sign, with the yachting cap pushed back
on his head.

From the direction of the church came a tinny too-
tling, a fast drumbeat. The increasing crowd parted
around a barefoot peasant who lay face down in an
orange puddle of vomit. Before the church, the crowd
had congealed, and from the black tulip of a loud-
speaker fastened high on the stones came a squawking
intrusion of sound, a recognizable tune—the secular
"Green Eyes." I started as a rocket exploded golden
balls against a dark blue sky.

Two shabby policemen scowled from a doorway,
above which was the wooden sign: POLICÍA. Just past
them, leaning like a flying buttress against the wall, was
a thin man in a tan Italian silk suit. He wore outsize
sunglasses that effectively hid most of his pockmarked
face. A snap-brim hat covered his forehead, a cigaret
jutted from the corner of his mouth.

"Murdoch?" he said in an American voice.

I nodded and the AL Rep separated himself from
the wall, squashing his cigaret under his foot. He indicated with a twitch of his head that I was to follow
him, and moved off through the crowd, sprung-shoul-
dered in the tan suit. I trailed behind him, on my way
to scout the possibilities, the pros and cons, the costs
and the problems, of buying an army for Clipper
Armstrong.

(4) WEDNESDAY, II

BEYOND Cahula the road wound among low hills and then headed like a ruled line through sagebrush into arid distance. The transportation this time was a dusty Toyota with a buggy whip antenna and a two-way radio in which a small ruby eye glowed. The radio remained silent except for an occasional buzzing, like an imprisoned fly, and this chauffeur, whose name was Mickey, spoke little. At regular intervals he replaced the cigaret like a fixture at the corner of his mouth. He said he was from Miami, his accent was scratchy New York, he wore a gold ring set with a red stone, and he had a theatrical menace about him. Perhaps he was not the only Dade County hood in the Army of the Liberation of the Republic of Santa Cruz. How did a mercenary soldier differ from a hired gunman, after all? In profile this mercenary had a pointed face, like a rhinoceros with a calcium deficiency.

"Where are the bulls?" I asked. There was no sign of life on the plain.

Mickey shifted his cigaret from one corner of his mouth to the other with marvelous skill. "What bulls you mean?"

"Isn't this a bull ranch?"

"I haven't seen no bulls."

A shrill buzzing I thought at first was the radio grew swiftly louder, and Mickey peered out the window and in the mirror. A cruciform shadow fled past. The plane came into view ahead, a small twin-engine waggling its wings. "The Big Guy," Mickey said.

"General Galindo?"

He rolled down the window, spat, rolled it up again, and turned his dark glasses on me for a moment. "Nagh!" he said.

It was stifling in the cab of the Toyota. A long fat tail of dust rolled out behind us, and presently I noticed a tan scared-cat's tail standing where the airplane had landed. I thought I could glimpse scattered, dust-colored buildings, a tiny splash of red on a flagpole. There was a staccato sound, distant but urgent; firing. I felt a rise in my adrenalin count. Mickey nodded disinterestedly when I asked if it was machine gun practice.

The dun cubes of buildings became larger, red tile roofs showed, the flag of the Republic of Santa Cruz hung on the windless air like a bloody shirt. I was developing a negative bias against the Army of the Liberation. Usually my first impressions turned out to be the most accurate.

Another trail of dust became visible, another moving vehicle preceding it. A dusty olive-drab truck with a canvas cover turned into the main road ahead of us, and a fine talc of dust sifted into our cab as we began to catch up. My first glimpse of General Galindo's assault force was of brown faces peering back from beneath a canvas hood.

We followed the truck through an arched gate where three soldiers lounged in green paratroopers' uniforms, highbooted, dark foreheads decorated with fatigue caps, automatic weapons slung over shoulders. We rolled into an enclosed area the size of two football fields where there were more soldiers sloppily drawn up into squad lines. Mickey headed straight toward two small evergreens in wooden tubs and a sentry pacing beneath the sign: COMANDANTE. Two Toyotas were already parked there, one with a white star on the door.

Mickey halted in line with the other vehicles and we got out. Down to our right was the flagpole with the drooping red-and-blue banner. Barked commands echoed across the hard-packed area. Lighting a cigaret, Mickey indicated the doorway beside the sentry, who had come to attention.

In a large office three men waited, two standing, wearing the green paratrooper uniforms, the third seated in a leather chair. This was a big, Latin-handsome young man wearing a tan cashmere jacket, checked slacks, and brown-and-white saddle shoes with fringed bibs.

"Señor Murdoch!" cried one of the soldiers, a plump man with greasy hair center-parted, and a major's gold leaves on his lapels. "Gallegos!" he said, cracking his heels together. Standing at attention, he extended a hand. I shook his hand. "Señor Murdoch!" said Major Gallegos. "I present to you—" He cracked his heels again, and turned toward the other officer. "The General Galindo!"

The General Galindo was of medium height, with sad eyes set in dark saucers of flesh, a downturned mouth and blue chin framed by his moustache. His bald head was creased like a washboard, on his lapels were silver stars.

The young man in the chair stirred, and I caught a locked glance of communication between him and Mickey, who had remained in the doorway. I leaned across the desk to shake hands with the general. "Señor," I said. "Señor!" Galindo said. His eyes looked tired as they appraised the man who had come to appraise him.

"Señor Murdoch!" the major was barking again. "I present to you—" He pivoted. "The Señor Cisneros!"

The man in the chair must be Mickey's Big Guy. He had long curly hair, a hairline moustache, a chin cleft as though by a hatchet. He did not rise to shake hands, his heavily fringed hypnotic eyes staring into mine as his big hand gripped my hand harder and harder, to the edge of pain, before it relaxed. I had not been checked out on this one, but whoever he was he seemed to have the qualities Clipper Armstrong was shopping for, more than Herrerro, more than Galindo.

Galindo spoke to the major, who said, "Señor Murdoch! You have come from the investors of the sugar company of Santa Cruz to the Army of the Liberation. The General Galindo makes you welcome!"

The general and I bowed to each other. Mickey leaned in the doorway with a cigaret in place and his arms folded. Cisneros said, "Did you bring any sugar with you, Sugar Company?" He grinned, but he emanated a hostility that could have been cut into bricks.

Galindo was frowning. The major stood very stiff and bright-eyed. Both of them seemed dominated by the younger man, and Mickey seemed to be owned by him. Tensions crackled. The general spoke in Spanish again.

"Señor Murdoch!" the major said. "You will see a demonstration of the Army of the Liberation of the Republic of Santa Cruz!"

"Three thousand American a day," Cisneros said, again freezing the two officers. "An army needs an angel," he said. He laughed long, harshly, and without amusement, while Mickey chuckled.

The general moved from behind his desk, bowing again to me. We followed Galindo outside, blinking in the heavy sunlight. The army was drawn up in three companies on the far side of the area. An officer stood at attention just beyond the tubbed trees. As Galindo appeared, he screamed an order. Soldiers with slung weapons came to attention. Another command and they faced left, a third and they swung into step behind a black flag bearer, each company in a column of fours, each file twenty-two to twenty-five men—slightly less than three hundred men in the Liberation Army. Three thousand dollars American a day meant ten dollars a day per man, but I had no industry research or audit figures to tell me whether that was good, bad, or average for a Caribbean mercenary force.

The army marched around the margin of the area toward the trees, between which General Galindo, Major Gallegos, and the other officer stood at attention. It was my first experience reviewing an army.

The equipment was grouped around the flagpole; the three jeeps, and five olive-drab, two-and-a-half-ton trucks with canvas covers. Four of these looked considerably older than the one we had followed into the Hacienda Rodríguez, and I suspected they might not all be operative. There were also recoilless rifles, two big mortars, and many machine guns—newer models in front, older water-cooleds on tripods behind.

The companies came on, the strutting black at their head supporting the staff with its obliquely halved red-and-blue flag. The ranks dressed to the right as they passed the general. They looked tough enough, and they marched in step, but I was most struck by Galindo's obvious pride in them. He spoke in Spanish to the major, who translated: "The General Galindo asks what you think of this Army of the Liberation?"

"Very impressive," I said to the general's strained face. He smiled and bowed to Gallegos' translation. Cisneros stood beside Mickey, breaking matches between his fingers and scattering the bits on the ground

in a calculated offensiveness that Galindo ignored as he
went back into the office. This time Mickey did not
accompany us inside.

We seated ourselves, and an orderly appeared with a
tray of bottles: scotch, Coca-Cola, and beer, no ice. I
accepted a warm bottle of Carta Blanca. There was a
considerable silence. Then Gallegos cleared his throat
and said, "We will talk now." It was my turn.

I said, "The stockholders of the Sugar Company of
Santa Cruz are worried that President Flores means to
nationalize the sugar industry as he has already nation-
alized the railroad. I have been sent to ask General
Galindo about the plans of the Army of the Liberation."

Cisneros laughed again, continuing his destruction of
matches: He made it easy to dislike him. Galindo's
sleeves were rolled on his thin arms, and I noticed that
he wore two wristwatches, one facing in, one out. Time
was clearly important to Galindo, who was speaking
quietly to Gallegos.

"Señor Murdoch! Much money will be needed to
complete the training of the Army of the Liberation.
Once this army arrives in our beautiful Santa Cruz the
red Flores government falls like rotten fruit! But much
money is required for the Army of the Liberation to
come to our island that must be liberated from these
Communist serpents!" The major paused, the general
added something in Spanish, and Gallegos hastened to
say, "These serpents who will snatch away all of our
beautiful island to the great loss of American investors!"

Both looked at me intently, while Cisneros snorted
and stretched. "Señor Murdoch!" Gallegos continued.
"We must not let our beloved Republic become the
base for Communist Russia and Communist China in
this free American hemisphere like Cuba!"

I nodded. Cisneros watched me with his tawny, jeer-
ing eyes, snapping matches. I said to Gallegos, "I am

impressed with the Army of the Liberation, but it seems small for such important work."

Galindo held up two fingers in what might have been a V-for-victory sign, but Cisneros shattered the impact of the gesture by saying loudly, "Cigar!" He offered a leather case to each of us in turn, shrugged when there were no takers, lit one himself and exhaled powerful smoke. Galindo sat still holding up the two fingers patiently, with tired and defeated eyes.

Bowing in deference to Cisneros, Gallegos said, "The General Galindo says that two times this many men is enough. They are trained well. You have seen this."

"Certainly."

The general spoke, the major translated: "There are many men for this army. Many. Only money must come first."

There was a disturbance outside, and all at once the doorway was full of a kind of Laocoon struggle, a soldier and Mickey thrusting into the office a young man in cowboy boots, a blue yachting cap—Chuy, with his arms caught up behind him in a double hammerlock, protesting in shrill Spanish. The soldier cursed, Mickey's mouth was bent into an ugly grimace beneath his dark glasses, there was a confused rhythm of panting. The general and Gallegos leaped to their feet.

"Goddam spy!" Mickey cried.

Chuy's face was white with panic. He gasped something when he saw me. A smear of dirt blotched his cheek, the Saint Christopher glistened at his throat. Snarling through crooked teeth, Mickey jerked on his arm until he staggered onto tiptoe. "That's my chauffeur," I said.

"Tell these guys to take it easy, Tiger!" Chuy cried. "Tell these crazy—"

He stopped. Cisneros held a revolver propped on his knee, the barrel slanting up. "*Señor!*" Chuy whispered,

as the barrel tilted higher. There was a fantastic slow-
ness in the moment—time dropping into low gear—
disbelief, reluctance to believe. I jerked a hand out
toward Cisneros as the revolver crashed.

Chuy spun around, breaking loose from Mickey,
screaming in a continuum of the brutal echoing of the
shot. He fell against the desk and slid into a huddle on
the floor. His blue cap rolled with an eccentric motion
to stop against Gallegos' polished boots.

In the acrid, throbbing reverberation, the room
turned as though on a ratchet, one notch, another. A
little smoke penciled from the barrel of the revolver. I
knelt beside Chuy. The mole still twisted his face into
a half-smile. There seemed very little blood. I grasped
his arm and dropped it. Cisneros sat towering above me
with the barrel of the revolver protruding over a
checked trouser knee. His eyes were wild, excited, completely ruthless. Mickey in his tan silk suit stood behind
the Big Guy. He held an automatic in a hairless fist,
unaimed, gazing down at me with a kind of alert dis-
interest. There's bad men there, Chuy had said to me.
What now, Tiger?

Chuy's yachting cap lay against Gallegos' boots, re-
vealing a sweat-stained band. "Give me that," I said. I
placed it over Chuy's face, and rose. It was a long way
up.

Standing behind the desk, General Galindo had
turned as gray as stone. The major was smoothing a
hand over his gleaming hair.

"Your chauffeur was a spy of Paco Flores, Señor
Sugar Company," Cisneros said, stretching to slip his
revolver into his jacket pocket.

I stood looking from the defeated Galindo to the
nervous major, from the cool killer in the chair to
Mickey's impersonal dark glasses, from the soldier licking his lips in the doorway to the body on the floor

with the blue cap covering the face. More blood
showed now. I started out the door. My back crawled
as I passed Mickey. The soldier stepped out of my
way.

Outside the sun was blinding. There was no motion
in the compound. The flag of the Republic of Santa
Cruz drooped on its white pole. I stood with the gunshot still echoing in my ears and the sun's dazzle in my
eyes, and a sensation of the world turning faster than I
had ever known before. Mickey joined me.

"You want to go back now?"

I said I did. As the guards saluted our passage
through the gate I began to shake with relief. The red
eye of the two-way radio burned with a faint buzzing.
There was no sign of the grommeted Buick. "What'd
the Big Guy kill him for?" I finally managed, casually
enough.

"Can't take chances with spies, this kind of business," Mickey said. He lit a cigaret.

We had almost reached the hills before Cahula
when the radio came to life. "Murdoch," it said,
scratching and burbling; that was all. After a long time
it came again, Cisneros' voice: "Murdoch." Mickey
stared straight ahead at the road, as though he heard
nothing. The Toyota began climbing into the hills.

I got a ride to the Guadalajara airport with an elderly
couple from Oregon, who were sympathetic about my
having been stranded in Cahula. "You don't want to
ever trust these people down here," they said.

(5) THURSDAY

I ARRANGED to have my report on my day with the Army of the Liberation of the Republic of Santa Cruz delivered to the early Aeronaves flight, and by one in the morning was in my bed in the Mexico City Hilton, riding a drugged and head-aching turntable. I suspected chills and fever, the troubled bowels of the Aztecs' Curse, and I got out of bed to swallow *turista* pills. I also swallowed another Seconal, and hung over the washstand staring at my face in the mirror. It was just a face, still young, still a little sunburned, not so hardened as I had liked to think; the eyes looked bad. Drugs had not affected my conscience, which simply did not accept the murder of a Mexican chauffeur as unimportant, the murderer as unpunishable, and was not going to stand for inaction on my part while I waited to hear from Clipper Armstrong. Sometime in the dead bottom of early morning I telephoned a sleepy Herb Justin and told him about murder in Jalisco. The phone made an empty, blowing sound for a long moment after I had finished.

"I'll report this to our people and see what they think should be done," Herb said. "That émigré army is a pretty sensitive issue. There's a great deal of pressure on the government to expel it."

I lay in bed with the phone cradled to my ear and felt better. Herb said, "Rodolfo Cisneros is the bastard son of the old Protector, by the way."

I whistled at that information, and when I had hung up fell asleep like falling into a cellar.

The next afternoon I checked out of the Hilton and headed for San Angel.

Jenny was not in, but I located the proprietress of the Casa de la Fuente, Señora Pinal, a moustached grande dame, who condescended to show me her establishment. According to the señora, the Casa de la Fuente had in a past and nobler time belonged to a famous actress who had died for love. *Se murió de amor;* the phrase rolled lovingly from her lips.

Two apartments and a studio faced onto a delightful patio, two sides of which were a twelve-foot-high wall with plaster peeling in strips, and a crewcut of broken glass set into the top course. The patio was colorful and cool, with flowers, ferns, a pomegranate tree, and an enormous concrete-and-tile fountain. The *fuente* no longer flowed with water, but with orange geraniums which spilled from three levels. I was introduced to the green parrot, Pedro, in his elaborate tin cage beside the fountain. He regarded me with one round eye and then the other, opening his beak to show his fat gray worm of a tongue.

"Very fortunate for the señor," an apartment as well as the studio was available. The apartment was much larger, more expensive, and equipped with a maid, and Señora Pinal conned me into opting for it. There was a comfortable living room with a TV, a radio, and shelves of American paperbacks from previous occupants, a dining alcove with a glass-topped table, a pleasant bedroom and bath. In the kitchen the fat, dark maid, Lupe, presided over a zinc-covered table, an ancient

range, and a Sears Roebuck refrigerator of which the
señora was very proud.

She graciously consented to accept my check, and I
drove to the center of San Angel to lay in supplies.
When I returned, Lupe clucked over the cost of each
item as though she were auditing my expense account.
The Señora Pintura had come home, she said.

I presented myself at Jenny's door, which was a
barred gate with a solid panel with the ceramic letter
"B" centered in the grid. A young, pig-tailed maid answered my knock and showed me down a hallway to a
studio with high, north windows, where Jenny Gray sat
hunched on a barstool peering past her scarlet-tipped
palette knife at the painting she was working on. She
wore her stockbroker glasses and a khaki jump suit
smeared with paint around the thighs; her light-brown,
graying hair was pulled into a loose knot, her pale lips
were pursed. Her small, brown, triangular feet were
bare, one with toes whitely splayed on the rung of her
stool.

"Hello, Murdoch," she said, without enthusiasm.
"All moved in? Your sunburn's better."

"Come out to dinner with me."

"*Got* to work tonight," Jenny said. "I *must* get some
ideas on canvas." She seemed ill-at-ease. I had been
almost frantic to see her, as though she were a balm to
ease my queasy conscience, like Entero-Vioformo for the
intestinal tract; and now I felt a frustration out of all
proportion to a simple refusal of dinner.

"I really can't, Murdoch." She scoured her hands
with a cloth dipped in turpentine. She had a tilted nose
and a small, full-lipped mouth above a child's pointed
chin. It was a striking face even punished by the glasses
and the drawn-back hair, but it was her body in motion
that continually captured my eyes.

"Do you want some kind of rum thing to drink, Murdoch? Or just a glass of orange juice and a joint?"

"Fine," I said, though pot had never elevated me any higher than a sore throat and a headache. I watched Jenny bounce out to call to Pepita for *jugo de naranja*. Her glasses hung around her neck on an elastic band.

We sat on a couch before a stained table on which was a cardboard box filled with twisted tubes of paint. Four or five canvases were turned to the wall beneath the high windows. The one on the easel was composed of irregular rectangles of color, some dull, some of acrylic brightness.

Jenny lit a tightly rolled brown cigaret, drawing deep with the strained, unattractive expression of marijuana smokers. She passed the joint to me, I sucked air and smoke, we made desultory conversation until Pepita brought orange juice, in brown twisted glasses, and departed. "I sense a certain tenseness, Murdoch," Jenny said.

"I find myself thinking about you most of the time," I said. I watched a pinch of worry constrict her forehead as she took the cigaret from me. "I thought if you were feeling something similar, as consenting adults—"

"Well, if there ever was a consenting adult, I'm it," Jenny said rapidly. She held her clasped hands under her chin for a moment, turning pink. "Yes, of course we were reading each other clearly the other night. There *is* reciprocal interest. But."

"But?"

"The man I love is arriving tomorrow."

Of course John Doane Finch was arriving for the OAS. It was the reason I was in Mexico City now, and the reason I had moved out to San Angel. "Bad timing," I said, and managed to screw up something that used the same muscles as a grin.

"Very, *very* unfortunate. I'm sorry, Murdoch. You see—he's older."

My mind had a funnel shape. I sucked smoke into my lungs. "He's a statesman," Jenny continued. It was a very formal word, but of course the Great Liberal was a statesman. "A diplomat," she explained. "He's coming down here for a conference. He may be here a month."

"You've known him a long time?" I asked, looking at my fingers holding the roach. They tingled.

"More than four years," Jenny said. "I met him when I was with UNESCO in Paris. It's *very* important to me," she said anxiously, as though she had to make sure I understood. "He's the man I . . . *admire* more than anyone else in the world."

"I see," I said. Actually, I told myself, all was for the best. My record as a husband was spotty enough, and leverage with John Doane Finch, who might be hammering out American policy toward the expropriation dynamic of the Flores government, would not be best served through a consenting adultery with his mistress. What had seemed bad timing was very good luck. I pulled into my lungs one last draught of marijuana, which Eloise abhorred as leading to sexual irregularities, hard drugs, and tax-supported mental hospitals. Distantly there came the sound of a heavy vehicle climbing strenuously; it seemed to have a rubber kazoo for a tail pipe. Jenny explained that it was the second-class bus. I rose to go.

"If you don't mind I'll just watch you get back on your stool," I said. "I like to watch you in motion."

She turned scarlet, she dipped her head. "Why thank you, Murdoch," she said, and moved back to her stool.

In my own apartment, which had a ceramic "A" on

its gate—a white letter, not scarlet—I asked Lupe to
bring me a beer. Watching her fat bottom as she wad-
dled away, I knew that Jenny's marijuana was not going
to lead me to sexual irregularities with a tubby Indian
muchacha with warts on her fingers. I fantasied a trip
to the *centro* to engage a call girl, but one all curves
and slimness, sexy feet and lovely moves, might be difficult to locate. Chuy hovered on the fringes of my
mind, not quite accusingly, only *there—el amor y la
muerte*. I drank my beer and drove off to a restaurant on
Insurgentes where I sat alone and listened to a flamenco
guitarist.

The last bus came snarling and popping up the hill
just after eleven, and when the sound had died away I
put down my paperback, snapped off the light and
turned on my side. Now like pinups in a lonely barracks, color images of women spread through my mind;
the luxury of Eloise's tanned flesh as she sat on the
sand at Malibu with her face and breasts presented like
offerings to the sun; Eloise swinging a Kenneth Smith
custom wood with that weight shift from one buttock
to the other that was sheer visual delight. Less legitimate pictures arose, the imagined majesty of the Dark
Angel of Santa Cruz, all milk-chocolate flesh and crisp
white tennis dress on the court at Lomas de Chapultepec Saturday; and Jenny Gray in her bikini, with
that sweet descending line of fair hair. I started as
someone called my name.

In a panic of not knowing where I was or who had
found me, I heard the voice again. "*Murdoch!* Oh,
God!"

I blundered out of bed. The floor plan came to me,
but not the location of light switches. I made my way
down the dark hallway to the barred door, which was

bolted closed. Against the fretting a body was spread. When I opened the gate Jenny fell into my arms. "Oh, Murdoch, hold me! I'm having a bad trip!"

I held her cool shivering nakedness. Her breathing was ragged. I helped her back along the hall. Once she sucked in her breath when she scraped against the wall. "Sorry," I said.

"I'm having *such* a bad trip. Full of *death*. I keep seeing John dead. As though I'd killed him!"

I sat on the bed and held her on my lap. She sobbed into my neck, swallowing often. Her voice was thick. "*Whew*. This is what they mean."

"Do you want a doctor?"

"I just want you to hold me. *There*, now it's fading down. Down!" She sighed, over and over. In a near-normal voice she said, "I didn't really mean to do this. I was trying to get some ideas worked up before John came, and I took more than I——"

"Isn't there something you can take to stop it?"

"Have you got a tranquilizer, Murdoch? And some Kleenex? I'm all *soggy*."

She slipped off my lap and I went to get her a Thorazine and a box of tissue. When I turned on the light, she cried, "Oh, God! No *light!*" She huddled in the brightness, pink and palely glowing, with her arms over her breasts and her hands crushed to her eyes. I snapped off the light, gave her the capsule and water, and she blew her way through a number of tissues. "*Whew!*"

I was frightened, having had no experience with trips, bad or good. "Do you do this often?"

"Don't talk! *Cold!*" she whispered. She was shivering again, and I arranged her under the covers. "Why don't you *hold* me if you think about me so much," she said irritably. "Hold me so I won't come apart." She giggled as I got under the sheets with her. "Arms and legs and organs—parts of Jenny Gray spread all over the—all *over* the—"

She buried her face in my neck again. "All over some kind of terrible city *dump,* Murdoch!"

I held her until she stopped shaking. Now she was making a low sound, singing, I recognized a Billie Holiday lyric: "Man that loves me's comin' home to stay!" Then she said, "The iceman cometh home to stay. That's death again, isn't it? I'm all ice inside, Murdoch. Well, *fire* and ice. Ice versa? Or the ice next time? Oh, God, talk, talk, talk, *talk!* It's coming back!"

"Can I do anything?"

"Nobody can." Her martyr's voice immediately shaded into self-mockery. "Nobody knows the trouble I've seen. *Seen* trouble. Well, of course I am visually oriented, but—but—" She whispered, "I don't want to see *that!*"

"What do you see?"

Her face buried in my neck, her breath very warm, she said, "I see—I see John lying on some kind of pavement. A rough pavement, a very *strong* texture. I don't think there is any . . . blood. Just a twisted, ugly position of death. And I'm there with a very bright little nickel-plated revolver. I've . . . killed him. Given him the coup de grâce, that must be it. It's so *real!* Of course he has to die someday. Everybody. Who said it about his prophetical soul, was that Hamlet? But why do I have to feel this is prophetical? *Such* a bad trip. I've taken mescaline quite a few times. You *did* ask. I just take little ones when I'm working and no *vision* comes. But a prophecy is a vision!" She shook her head, disengaging, lying on her back beside me now. "Anyway, this time I took acid. Because John's coming. And he disapproves. And *it* disapproves because *he* disapproves? That's so complicated." She fell silent, sighing. "And you're in it! And you *don't* disapprove!" I had the impression she was beginning to surface again. "Maybe you're in it because I'm here," she said in a matter-of-fact voice.

I didn't like the wild swings of emotion. Her toes touched my leg. "Coming up or going back down?" I asked.

"Oh, definitely coming up," she said. She turned and pressed herself against me, differently this time. She drew away again. "My God, here I am in bed with you and you think I'm an acidhead. I'd better go home."

"Do you want another tranquilizer?"

"No thanks, neighbor." Contact and withdrawal again. "If you're going to be neighborly, be neighborly, I say," Jenny said, and giggled.

I smoothed a hand over her breast and the roused nipple, over her contracting belly, down the line of fine hairs. When I brushed her feathers her hand caught mine. "No!"

Silence, very heavy. She gripped my hand.

"It's what I came for," she said. "I thought when I was so frightened that a good balling was the only thing that would do. But now I can't. I'm *very* sorry."

I cleared my throat. "Timing again?" She gave me my hand back.

"May I have another Kleenex, please?"

With some masculine difficulty I got up to bring her more. "Perhaps some other time," I said, a good sport, as she sat up to blow her nose. But her attention had turned inward again.

"I had a vision and I didn't like it, that's all. Do you know how long I was out there at your gate, Murdoch? I shook the bars. I knelt in a little puddle of despair with my hair flowing into the tiles like an Art Nouveau nymph. I shook the bars and called your name." She was off again, talking faster and faster, with flights of punning and free association I couldn't follow. I abandoned the idea of another aggressive move.

At last she rose, holding a blanket around her, and paced up and down in the darkness. "Do you know there is a postbox just outside your window, Murdoch?" she asked. "You can reach out and mail your letters without even leaving the casa." And she said, "Please take me home, now."

"Is it all finished?"

"No, but I'm on the down side now. Murdoch, I'm sorry to have been such a *bitch*. But in the end I simply couldn't. With John coming."

"Please don't speak of it."

"Anyway, it's all your fault for coming over and saying you thought about me a lot, and wanted to watch me move. That was *very* titillating—as I'm sure it was meant to be. Take me home now, and see there aren't any . . . *goblins*. And I'll go to sleep with music on and come down to earth sweetly."

Clutching my hand, she led me outside and into the deep well of the patio, with stars overhead, the rough sandy texture of bricks underfoot, and cool leaves brushing past us. Walking my blanket-clad, acidhead neighbor home was very exciting in its bittersweet mix of sensuality and renunciation.

(6) FRIDAY

IN the morning I wakened to cockcrows repeated more and more distantly like ripples in a pond. Next came the rattle of cartwheels on the cobbled street outside my window, then a slap-slap, slap-slap identified as Lupe mopping, followed by the scraping of a rake on the old soft brick paths of the patio, and a single joyous squawk which must be the first greeting to the day of Pedro the parrot with his cage uncovered. There were sibilant whispers of the maids in the patio, and at eight o'clock Lupe came into the bedroom with a big blue glass of orange juice, her square face illuminated by what I was to find was her one smile of the day. "¡Buenos días, señor!"

The pleasant sounds continued during breakfast, which I ate at the glass-topped table in the dining alcove—soft calls of vendors outside the patio gate, the glass-and-metal tinkling of the milkman on his bike. Periodically there was the one disagreeable intrusion— the second-class bus climbing, shifting, gunning, backfiring. It had the quality of a personal affront.

When I opened the heavy shutters of my bedroom window, I saw just outside on the wall the postbox Jenny had mentioned, green with a yellow postman's horn painted on the side, close enough to reach. I thought I would write a letter to Eloise today.

I phoned Herb Justin's office to leave my new address and telephone number. Within half an hour the phone rang; it was Dr. Ibis. "Friend Murdoch! How are you liking San Angel? I live not far from you."

"It's very pleasant."

"Tomorrow you will go to the house of Senator Herrerro, eh? Perhaps today we will have men's doubles? I have already spoken to our friend Justin, who will bring Mister Sandy Brody from the embassy. We will play them for money, eh, and gain some pesos?" He laughed fatly. "I think you are a money player like me, friend Murdoch."

It seemed to be a demand of payment for the Herrerro introduction, but Ibis was right, I was a money player. The match was at four o'clock at Chapultepec. I was setting up my Olivetti to write Eloise when the phone rang again, the DCM's office had had a busy morning forwarding Murdoch calls. This one was from Clipper Armstrong at the María Isabel Hotel on Reforma, who wanted to see me immediately.

"Good to see you, fella!" the Clipper boomed, lurching out at me from the door of Suite D at the María Isabel. His big hand wrapped around mine, the other arm embraced me. He whacked me on the back, cupped my elbow. "Gee, it's good to see you, Tommy!" the sixty-year-old boy wonder rumbled, as he led me captive-by-the-elbow into a great expanse of white carpeting and zebra-striped furniture extending into a panorama of Mexico City so breathtaking it looked fake. The majestic snow peaks were visible if you were high enough above the smog. The TV was on—the

sound inaudible—on the sideboard were two bottles,
scotch and bourbon.

"Got a little sunburn there, didn't you?" Clipper
said. His face was pleasantly jowled, sun-lamp tanned,
his gaze distracting in that one eye was set at a different
slant than the other. I was not feeling at ease. I performed well for my boss, but never with him; in his
presence I seemed to have no traction.

"How about a highball to wet down the long, dusty
road, Tommy?"

I said that sounded like a good idea, and watched the
great man pass before the wall of windows, moving
with his heavy grace and athlete's pigeon-toed stride
across the skyline of Mexico City like Superman over
Metropolis, realms and islands as plates dropped from
his pockets, heading for the liquor and ice to play the
role of host, one of the many roles into which he threw
everything he had. He wore a camel-colored cashmere
cardigan and tan slacks, on his feet were size thirteen
shell cordovan wing tips polished into darkling mirrors.
His USC fullback's shoulders wove from side to side as
he stalked the bar—still broken-fielding with the TD
ball against Duke in the Rose Bowl almost forty years
ago now. His blond curly head was miraculously free of
gray.

After his two-touchdown apotheosis in the Rose
Bowl, the All-Time All-American had seized fortune at
the flood and married the heiress of the ruling family of
a major Hollywood studio—who now wasted her re-
maining days on earth in an upstairs bedroom of Bel
Air's Thornfield Hall, frantic with an inexpressible
misery. The USC Clipper had played a few movie roles,
moved into the production end of the industry, and
then began his first major phase buying up run-dry oil-
wells in the Long Beach–Signal Hill area with a partner—since returned to obscurity—who had developed a

secondary recovery system. After that he had put together Armstrong Savings and Loan, second largest in
the country, the Try Harder S & L, and now he was
majority stockholder in American Ventures, Inc., which
was in turn majority stockholder in more and more and
bigger and bigger undervalued and developable prop-
erties such as the Compañía Azucarera de Santa Cruz,
the Big Sugar.

"Before I forget it, Tommy," Clipper rumbled, rat-
tling ice in glasses. "I'm not getting any younger, and a
fellow's got to start making things over to the people he
loves. Otherwise the government just swallows it.
What I just did, I made over a hundred thousand of
those sugar-company shares to you and Ellie. It's a sort
of revocable trust for Ellie, actually."

I looked appropriately impressed for the glance from
the mismatched eyes, but with reserved enthusiasm.

"It's all done," he said, with a decisive jerk of his
jaw, intimating mortality, generosity, faith and trust.
"Of course, it's not worth a lot right now—but I'm
expecting there'll be one hell of a capital gain. Depend-
ing—" he said, and laughed his big, slow, "Uh! Uh!
Uh!" He splashed water from a carafe into a glass and
strode back across the Valley of the Anahuac to present
me with my highball.

"Thanks, Clipper."

The Old Trojan nodded gravely in acceptance of
gratitude. In his code the uses of hospitality were totally serious. It was a strange code, and I was continually surprised by new patterns and currents in it.
Grand, full of honor, and binding by a nod and a handshake in certain areas, it was very shabby in others. He
said, "Well, I was thinking about that Red Tower
thing you did such a helluva job on. Work your tail off
and sure you get satisfaction in a job well done, but
there's nothing like a stake in the operation, right,

Tommy? So if this screwed-up Compañía Azucarera can
get itself straightened out it's going to be a helluva
good deal for you and Ellie." He laughed again, his eyes
fixed on me calculatingly, maybe anxiously, certainly
humorlessly.

"Got your report on the Cahula caper," he said in a
different voice. "You missed the boat there, Tom."

I measured the veteran flutter of my nerves, and
braced for the wrench of fury to follow. "The boat
almost sank in Cahula," I said.

"Sit down, sit down, Tommy-boy!" Harpoon poised,
the Harpooner paused for a bit of hospitality to pro-
long the nerves' flutter and the churning of bile. I sat
down on zebra-stripes while he perched on a big otto-
man, frowning at me with a pout of his lower lip—the
man my wife loved above all others as the Wonder and
Glory of America. Usually I managed to keep my feelings toward him well repressed.

"How's Eloise?" I asked. Eloise was fine, fine, he said
with a little tic of annoyance. "How's Big Eloise?" I
asked. Eloise's mother was pretty bad. "Good trip
down, Clipper?" I asked.

"Wonderful scenery, wonderful," he said. "Yeah,
Freddy flew me down in the Lear. You really get some
wonderful scenery coming down here, don't you?" He
leaned forward. "I was disappointed in your report on
the Liberation Army, Tommy-boy. You let a tragic
thing like that shooting throw you. This has got to be a
tough league, fella!"

"It doesn't have to be that tough."

Holding his scotch between his knees, he blew out
his cheeks, and switched on his expression of disarming,
little-boy charm. "Tom, if this bird was a spy of that
Commie Flores'——"

"He wasn't."

"How the hell can you be so *sure?* How the hell can you always be so goddam sure a man *isn't?*"

This was a continuation of an old argument in which each of us was polarized, the very rational free-enter-priser and Troy-Boy became irrational, and maybe I did too. The Clipper viewed my middle-of-the-road Repub-licanism as the extreme Liberal Position, the fringe of sanity, to the left of me only bleeding-hearts, pinkos, fellow travelers, and the infinity of the Communist World Conspiracy. Politics was one area of his omni-science I felt compelled to challenge.

He leaned toward me again. "That fellow with the hair oil—Gallegos—came on in to the airport when we set down in Guadalajara. I didn't like to go behind your back, but I knew you had to be wrong about that Flores operative. Nothing made sense if he wasn't a Commie. It didn't make sense! Gallegos says he was a well-known Commie agent, no question about it."

"It's why I'm so valuable to you, Clipper. Everybody else tells you just what you want to hear."

We sat looking at each other. I drank. He drank.

"Something in you's just got to be soft on those babies," he said finally. "First you'll deny a man's a Commie when it's written all over him. Then when it's proved he is, you start excusing him for being one. I know you Liberals. Why don't you tell me how come you're so sure he wasn't a Commie?"

Because Chuy had spoken glowingly of the Mexican, noncommunist, revolution? Of cops falling from mo-torcycles and blowing their balls off with a cocked .45? Because of the expression on his dead face? It was a good question.

"Even if he was one—" I began, and stopped as he grinned.

"See? See how you are, Tommy?"

"I'll tell you how it makes sense he wasn't," I said. "He was killed because Cisneros and Galindo were having a power struggle, and Cisneros wanted to shock the sugar company out of supporting the émigré army. Cisneros has a chunk of the Santa Cruz treasury going for him and if Galindo doesn't get money soon Cisneros can take over the army. If we decide to fund Galindo then Cisneros can't play leader. If my chauffeur hadn't shown up—either because he was worried about me or just inquisitive about the Cruceños—I think Cisneros might have shot me."

Clipper looked pained. "You're not telling me anything I can believe, Tom! And what you're saying is you did exactly what this Cisneros wanted you to do. Left Galindo up a stump!"

"I left him where I found him. What's your hurry?"

"We can't afford to let that army get away."

"It's silly to put up three thousand American a day to keep it. The OAS or our own get-tough policy may back Flores down, and no armies necessary. The OAS starts next week, and I see Herrerro tomorrow."

"Herrerro's a pip-squeak." He continued to grumble, and it suddenly occurred to me that he liked the idea of an army, his own life-size set of tin soldiers.

"I'll tell you one thing," I said. "I'm not having anything to do with Cisneros."

The corners of his eyes tented quizzically in his meaty, clever face. "That doesn't sound exactly professional, Tommy," he said in a mild voice. "What if it turns out he's the only one that can make the thing go?"

I shook my head at Clipper Armstrong.

"What if it's proved to you that bird was a Commie and Cisneros shot him all copasetic?"

"I don't think you can murder even a Commie all copasetic."

"Did you think we were going to use that army to

chase Flores and nobody get killed, for Christ's sake? Tommy, I know you and me well enough to know if I tell you this Flores is a red, you'll swear up and down he's not. But you are not going to try and tell me he's on our side—America's side. So we are not on his side. If we can swing a change of government by sinking a few bucks in that army of Galindo's, it can be a goddam good thing for the Big Sugar, and for you and me and Ellie and your kids someday when you get Ellie off the pill." He took a deep breath, his eyes were as impersonal as gauges fixed on me. "And for that island, too," he went on. "A progressive, well-run company can be a really vital force in the economy of one of those backward goddam islands. Every time they nationalize it's a disaster for everybody. Look at sugar production in Cuba! Castro can't get a crop out!"

"Sending killers like Cisneros into Santa Cruz isn't going to help the economy except for the undertakers."

"The more you come down on that fellow, the more I may get to like him, Tommy," the Clipper said in a soft voice, and there we were again. Hectic circles of red had appeared on his cheeks, and his teeth showed prominently. The phone rang.

While Clipper answered it, I went to stand with my drink looking down on Mexico City's Golden Triangle smothered in smog. The embassy next door was not visible from this aspect. "Hey, Ellie!" my father-in-law said, for of course the phone call was from his daughter, my wife. ESP knew no international boundaries and friction between me and USC's most famous four-letter man had been disturbing her. Or perhaps it was not ESP at all but some manipulation of the Clipper's, who had arranged for Ellie to phone at a particular moment by a complex electronic system of signals. Paranoia seemed to be creeping in. "Hey, Tommy," the Clipper said. "Isn't that something? It's Ellie!"

I took the phone from him. "Darling!" she said in her husky voice with the catch in it. Maybe she was in the next room. "Is anything wrong?"

"No," I said. "Why?"

"Oh, I don't know." Now the Clipper was standing broad-shouldered before the wall of glass. "I'm so glad I caught you there with Daddy," Eloise said. "I've been so lonely for you. Are you sure everything's all right?"

"Why wouldn't it be?"

"It's just that Daddy didn't seem very pleased with your last report. He thought you'd written it in a hurry, or something. He's so proud of you when you're a go-getter, darling."

"Yes," I said. "Well, it might be the altitude."

"You sound so irritable. I've got marvelous news, though. Our Meander Hills membership has come through."

"Christ!" I said.

"Isn't that divine?"

"We already belong to two golf clubs, Ellie!"

"I thought you'd be glad! Why are you so *peppery*, darling?"

"A little matter of twelve thousand, that's all. Isn't it twelve thousand?" It was enough to support the Army of the Liberation for four days.

"Twelve thousand, five hundred dollars," Eloise said. Where others might give only the sum, she never failed to include the word "dollars." She liked the roll of it on her tongue, but there was more to it than that. Where I was fond of money, she adored dollars. She loved them as the key to all the beautiful things America had to give to her favorite children, those who worked hard, thought ahead, were the right color, and especially those hard-muscled, suntanned, romantic, free-enterprise heroes like Superdaddy—for which role I was a career trainee. Eloise loved the dollar, the making of it, the spending of it, the things it could buy and the anticipation of them, like courtship in bed, almost better than the ultimate beautiful things themselves. She might think that she loved me for other reasons, but basically it was because I earned the praise of her father as a go-getter, and lots of dollars. It was probable that I would not be able to earn enough dollars working for anyone else but her father.

"Well," I said, "that's good news about Meander Hills."

"I *knew* you'd be pleased. May I talk to Daddy again, now, darling?"

I surrendered the phone and went to sit on the edge of the zebra-striped couch, very carefully, as though any careless motion might light up the tilt sign. When my father-in-law had hung up we chatted about matters unrelated to the Compañía Azucarera de Santa Cruz. He thought Freddy would be flying him home in the Lear Jet sometime tomorrow. We parted amicably. Gripping my hand at the door, his other hand cupping my elbow, his mismatched eyes fixed on mine, my father-in-law said, "Tell you what, Tommy. You don't want us to go with Cisneros, you come up with a better route. Okay?"

When I went to the Hilton to see if I had any mail, a familiar figure was standing behind an empty chair in the lobby, a newspaper folded under the arm of his tan Italian silk suit, cigaret screwed into the corner of his mouth, dark glasses covering most of his pocked face. He looked like a caricature of himself. I walked over to him. "Well, hello, Mickey."

He regarded me through the dark lenses as though he'd never seen me before.

"The Big Guy come to town?" I asked.

He shifted his cigaret from one side of his mouth to

the other with a camel roll of his jaw. The lump
showed under his arm like a misplaced codpiece.

"Well, it's been nice chatting with you again,
Mickey," I said. There was a hydraulic sensation in my
knees as I went outside. I wondered if Mickey had
been looking for me. Driving out Reforma to Chapultepec for tennis, I made it a test of will not to look in
the rear view mirror.

As I stood on the base line feeding the ball to P. T.
Ibis' forehand, wafted over the Central Deportiva de
Chapultepec was an odor of overloaded sewers and
inefficiently consumed gasoline from the masses of
internal combustion engines charging up and down the
Reforma. Three boys were posed on the glass-sided
high-diving platform over the big pool. I was not
getting much concentration into my shots, but Ibis was
happily trying to flail the covers from the balls.

"Tell me, friend Murdoch, you like to win money?"

I said I didn't mind it.

"We will win money," he said, grunting as he
stretched for a wide shot. I was remembering his line
calls in our last match, and I decided to swallow my
Anglo-Saxon reticence about mentioning such matters.

"Just one thing, P.T.," I said. "You let me call the
lines."

He hit a Texas-leaguer into the top of the backstop.
"Then we will not win money! Always you give away
the benefit!"

"When I think there's been a bad call I'm apt to
drop the next point."

He stood glaring at me, mopping sweating cheeks.
He wore a handkerchief knotted around his forehead,
and sweat bands on both wrists. "You are saying you
are a loser, eh?"

"It's the way I was taught, P.T. It's not whether you win or lose, it's how you play the game."

"Do I not know how you have been taught!" he shouted. "Every day, every day, I see poor Americans dropping points because of guilts. Trying not to win because Superego hangs around neck like dead albatross." He made flapping, albatross motions. "I play to win! I play this game tennis for health, and is more health to win than to be loser. And more wealth!" He grinned big-toothily. Just then the embassy team appeared, Herb Justin and a taller, thin, crewcut stranger, not Sandy Brody. Both of them wore white warm-up jackets with red and blue stripes.

"Sorry to be late," Herb called. "Brass coming in for the big OAS do."

"But where is Mister Sandy Brody?" Ibis said in dismay.

Brody had been called back to Washington, Herb said, and introduced the replacement, Frank Timken, who had a firm handshake, jugged ears, and abnormally wide-apart hazel eyes that made him look like a worried shark. We settled on a hundred pesos a set, and Ibis was clearly very worried that Herb had brought in a ringer.

Ibis and I were off to a good lead before the embassy team, who played conventional American net-rushing tennis, discovered that they could pick off Ibis' big forehand at net. We managed to pull out the first set but slumped hopelessly in the second, for I was having concentration static from thoughts of Jenny and the arriving Brass, Clipper Armstrong and Eloise, Mickey and Cisneros, the pip-squeak Herrerro and the Dark Angel of Santa Cruz.

Ibis began to act exhausted, clutching his chest and muttering, tacking around the court with one shoulder higher than the other like a mother quail deflecting a hunter from her nest. He made bad calls, the first of which everyone ignored like a bad smell. The second I was able gracefully to overrule, which caused glares and more muttering. We lost the set 6-2 and took a break on the bench before the third set. Frank went to order *refrescos* while Ibis sulkily toweled sweaty flesh.

"Where will the Brass coming down for the OAS be staying?" I asked Herb, who stood beside the bench in his characteristic stance, hands in pockets and head inclined to one side. "San Angel?"

"No idea," he said, more than coolly. "Not my department."

"A big staff?" I asked.

"Very," Herb said. "The American posture in Latin America is to walk softly but carry a big staff."

Ibis didn't join our laughter, still nursing his resentments. I watched Frank Timken returning with his long-legged, scissoring stride, followed by a white-jacket bearing drinks on a tray.

"Well, here's to the only floating U.S. embassy," Frank said, when we had been served. He was referring to the embassy's foundations, which were a kind of boat floating in the mud of Lake Tenochtitlán. The North-American lampshade would never tilt like a Spanish-Colonial church.

"I will tell you Americans something it is important for you to know," Ibis said suddenly. He sat scowling with one fat sweating hand spread on a fat, sweating knee, the other holding his glass of Coca-Cola. "Do you Americans know United States has more laws than all other countries together?"

Herb said politely, "Is that so, P.T.?"

"I don't believe that," Frank Timken said in his harsh-timbered voice.

"Consider that I speak the truth, please," Ibis said, baring his teeth. "I tell you Americans United States of America has more laws than all the rest of world together. This includes Soviet Russia and Communist China, Spain and other fascist dictatorships, also Nepal. All. Do you not think it is bad for you Americans to have so many laws? So many rules. Soon how will you move at all?"

No one answered, and Ibis scowled with lessening severity. "Aren't you an American citizen, P.T.?" I asked.

"I am a citizen of the world!" he said. He jabbed a finger at me. "You will come to the bullfights with me on Sunday, my partner. This is something very against the law in United States."

Frank said unpleasantly, "You go to see the bull-fighters in their tight pants, huh, P.T.?" I thought he might be making a mistake to tangle with the old mother quail on that level, but Ibis regarded him with a pleased expression.

"Ah, it is a big world," he said. "One goes to bull-fights for many reasons, for there are many kinds of *afición*. You understand me, my-opponent-Mister-Timken? I ask you which is better—to go to bullfights to admire behinds of matadors in tight pants, or to admire animals bleeding slowly, slowly to death from sword in lungs?" He coughed and choked in illustration; it was not pretty. Frank's mouth was pursed with distaste, Herb watched with an eyebrow cocked.

"No answer, Mister Timken?" Ibis continued. "I tell you, then." He smiled from face to face. "It is better to go to see tight pants than to see agony and death, and it is better to admit one's interest. Otherwise come repressions for fat psychiatrists to deal with at great cost." He winked at me. Looking very pleased with himself, he rose, patting the bulge of his spare tire and gazing benignly down on Frank. I thought we would not have much trouble winning the third set.

We won it at love, and Ibis and I were richer by a hundred pesos. He was happy, and I was impressed with my partner, for in money tennis an ability to psych opponents is more valuable than a cannonball service. A date was made for a rematch, and I drove home to San Angel with a small physical euphoria melting like a popsicle in the sun.

There was a bouquet of mixed flowers on the dining table, and a sealed note which Lupe said had come from the Señora Pintura. I had to consult my pocket Spanish-English Dictionary over the message, "*me muero de vergüenza*": I die of shame. "*Sí*," Lupe said, an old one had come, and the Señora Pintura had gone away with him in a grand black car. A very important man, Pepita had told her; and could she be allowed to leave early this evening in order to go to the *cine* with Pepita? I let her go when she had ironed the store pleats out of a shirt and shorts for tennis tomorrow with the Dark Angel of Santa Cruz at the home of her father, the Senator, in Lomas de Chapultepec.

I was still awake when Jenny Gray and her statesman-lover came home that night—car doors, an engine retreating, scrape of shoes on bricks in the patio, a snatch of dialog, an intimate laugh. I lay in bed full of jealousy, and sexual tension. The latter was to be melodramatically alleviated soon, however.

(7) SATURDAY

HERRERRO'S house was an agglomeration of massive stucco and red-tile geometric shapes, with brown plaster frames around the windows and a stout central tower, the whole surrounded by a stone wall which was topped by an ivy-covered hurricane fence. Adjacent to the house were assorted angles of inner walls, steel beams and a fenced-in roof—a jai alai court. I had already seen a number of these monsters on the estates of Lomas de Chapultepec.

With my racket and zipper bag I approached a gate in the wall. A white-painted arrow pointed to a small white button, and as I pressed this I became aware of a shallowly curved dark glass eye watching me. Closed circuit television was much used at the gates of the Mexican rich.

"*Pase, señor,*" a mechanical voice said, and the gate sprang ajar. I entered a formal garden with hydrangeas in raised beds, and clipped cypresses. A comfortable old pepper tree seasoned the air, a lava-block path led toward the house, and on this appeared a flat-faced man in a black chauffeur's uniform, smiling, ducking his head, and making the Mexican gesture of welcome-it's-all-yours. Herrerro came out on a red concrete porch: "Hola, Señor Moordoak! Welcome to my house!" He grunted with the effort of stepping down to the path, and hurried toward me, wearing a black suit and a white silk shirt, with a red foulard scarf tucked in at the throat. His head was completely bald, freckled and liver-spotted, sloping flatly from the bony structure of his forehead. He clutched me in an *abrazo*.

He snapped his fingers and the chauffeur leaped to take my racket and bag. With his arm around me, he urged me toward the house. I was trying to think of him as a better man than Galindo to lead the counter-revolution, a better man than Cisneros; he might be the best of a bad lot, but he was a pip-squeak. "My daughter looks so much to the tennis," he was saying. "But I am so sorry, she cannot play, she has hurt herself, her leg—how do you call this last part?"

"Ankle?"

"Yes, yes, the ankle." He made a motion of twisting a cap from a jar.

"Then you and I will hit some," I said, trying to sound enthusiastic.

"Ah, no, no, no, no, it is impossible." Delicately the Senator tapped his chest, shook his head, flexed his eyebrows. "The doctor—" As we came up on the porch he called, "Aurelia!" in a singing, high-pitched cry I found chilling.

Immediately, as one who has been waiting in the wings, the Dark Angel appeared in a french door. She wore a white eyelet dress. Her smooth jet-shining hair was drawn back from tiny ears.

"Welcome to this house, sir." She had a very light voice. Again there was no offer to shake hands.

"It's nice to be here, Señorita Herrerro."

With an excessive number of gestures, Herrerro explained that his daughter was the Señora Velásquez. "She is married to a man name Velásquez who is dead." He beamed on us.

"Will you come in, sir?" the daughter said. She drew her father and me after her into what I thought at first must be a storeroom. There were many pieces of heavily varnished furniture, an abundance of tables: side-tables, marble-topped tables, high tables bearing vases. There were three sideboards along one wall, their progression broken by a glass-fronted cabinet filled with bric-a-brac. On either side of the french doors were tall Ali Baba jars painted in garish colors. From one of these protruded an ivory rod tipped with a bronze hand, from the other a profusion of peacock's feathers and plastic flowers. Over a far door was a boar's head with ferocious curved tusks, and a red-painted mouth like a clown's.

Sidling around the furniture, I joined the Señora Velásquez in a central clearing where a couch and easy chair fronted on a low table marked with tumbler-rings. Herrerro urged his daughter and me onto the couch, saying, "We will have Coca-Cola. You like Coca-Cola, Señor Moordoak?"

"Very much," I lied, and the Senator snapped his fingers like a gunshot. He shouted in Spanish. I glanced around at a glass lampshade, a ceramic black panther prowling the top of one of the sideboards. I met the Angel's amber eyes, which in the father were animal but in the daughter superhuman, and she smiled invisibly, a sensed relaxing of the severe lines of her mouth and nostrils. She said in her light voice, "My father have you here by falseness, sir."

"I beg your pardon?"

"I do not play tennis since a schoolgirl."

I supposed evidence that Herrerro was a liar was not even worth recording.

"I do not like to play tennis after so many year. You will not be sorry? We will talk. I talk English very bad. Do you speak *le français*, sir? I speak *le français* so much bet-tair." I made a foolhardy attempt, and quickly abandoned it, saying, "I haven't spoken *le français* since a schoolboy, Señora Velásquez." This pleased her so much I was rewarded with an actual smile.

A maid in starched black and white brought three glasses on a tray. Herrerro seated himself, rubbing his palms on his thighs, beaming. There was a pause of infinite duration while we refreshed ourselves with Coca-Cola.

Finally I said, "You have an impressive house, Señor Herrerro."

"Pardon, señor?" he said sharply.

"Very—" I made an all-encompassing gesture. "—big." Aurelia Velásquez leaned back on the couch, her glass held against her cheek as though to cool it. She smiled at me again.

Hunching forward in his chair, Herrerro said, "This house once belong to governor of state of Tamaulipas. A very rich man, also very bad. It is old now. Houses, people, all must grow old."

"But gracefully," I said, nodding to the ugly little man. I thought it a graceful compliment, but by the time I had dug myself out of the resulting misunderstanding I knew that it was going to be a long afternoon. I did not yet feel confident enough to inquire about Herrerro's position with the various émigré groups.

Aurelia said, "Do you like to come with me and see this very big house, sir? And gardens and playthings? This is time when my father like very much to see his telebision, and we will make a walk."

I said that would be nice, keeping it simple. The Senator apologized, the Dark Angel rose and led me from the room. Outside we walked along lava paths

where her heavy flower scent mingled with the spicy
redolence of the pepper tree. We wandered through
gardens, past the tennis court and the jai alai fronton. I
was shown the garages where I admired twin black
Cadillac limousines with white Mexico, D.F. Diplomático plates, and we encountered another liveried
chauffeur. Conversation was halting.

"What does your father do?" I asked.

"He do nothing. He is old." As we left the garages,
as though she had been pondering my question, she
said, "He go to watch polo in the parque, the tennis at
Deportiva, the *corridas* at Plaza Mexico, the—" She
jabbed her spread-fingered hands together.

"Cockfights?"

"Cokefeet," she said delightfully.

"Does your father ever think of returning to Santa
Cruz?"

"Ah, yes!"

"Does he have plans to return?"

"Yes, yes," she said, as we entered the house by way
of a hallway. "Always the plans. Someday I will return
to Santa Cruz, but my father—who know?" She
shrugged. A staircase swung upward and on the newel-
post was a life-sized carved wood maiden with a pot on
her shoulder and a bare lightbulb protruding from the
top of her head. She was not well-proportioned.
"Come," my guide said, taking my hand. "I show you
my room."

We mounted the steps that curved into the tower.
Her room contained a canopied bed with a snowy
counterpane and twisted mahogany posts. There were
white net draperies over three french doors that gave
onto a balcony and a view of treetops. A low table bore
a radio, record player, a disarray of records and magazines, a television set facing the bed.

"Do you like to make love with me?" Aurelia said. She released my hand to stand majestically before me, her amber eyes locked on mine.

"I am very hungry for love," she said. "If you like to?" She dipped her proud chin slightly.

"Very much," I said. I cleared my throat. "But your father?"

"He watch his telebision." She clasped her hands at her waist. "If you like me?"

I said again, politely, formally, "Very much."

"If you do not mind to play a little game which I like," Aurelia said.

"Anything," I said.

A record was spindled on the machine—drumming joined by strained voices chanting. The game was a teasing, slowly stripping, Caribbean mating dance performed to the increasing tempo of the drums, and Aurelia made it almost a ritual in her somber, heavy-fleshed, chocolate dignity, advancing and retreating, proffering and withdrawing, inviting and rejecting and reinviting, turning away to glance over a shoulder at me with a flared nostril, a white-rimmed eye, a flash of milky teeth that was totally erotic, while I, in my remnants of Anglo-Saxon self-consciousness, felt thin-blooded and pale-skinned, but enthusiastic. The ritual was cumulatively exciting in the extreme and just before the excitement peaked out, surrender came on the white counterpane beneath the white canopy, before the dead opalescent eye of her TV. But if the game had been played to stir her own deep fires, it had been unsuccessful, for she remained aloof and barely participant at the end.

I lay beside her dark lushness of heavy thighs and deep breasts, lulled by the airy movement of the net draperies in the breeze that cooled us. I was contemplating the possibility that she was a nymphomaniac, her pip-squeak father pimping up acceptable studs to keep his daughter from molesting the help, Ibis' engineering of the Murdoch-Herrerro doubles match a double convenience, and Aurelia's trips across the stones of Guadalupe atonement for an unassuageable tumescence. I was amotivational at the moment in regard to émigré inquiries. Aurelia put her hand on my chest in what was the first sign of any personal tenderness, and said, "Very white. Coffee and milk. You like coffee and milk, sir?"

"Very much, señora."

"Then we will have more *café con leche,*" the Dark Angel of Santa Cruz said. "My father like you so much." She rose, and I watched her inward-turned, indefinably tragic face as she dressed. In all this too highly seasoned sex game that was half overblown ritual and half whorehouse stunting, her grave dignity had never slipped.

We found Herrerro in the overcrowded room where he was sipping Coca-Cola. He rose and jiggled at us, apologizing for his TV addiction, friendly as a puppy and very attentive to his daughter as he ushered us into the dining room for an enormous, multiple-course, afternoon meal. Afterward there were little cups of black coffee and brandy, and, deadly sleepy, I propped my eyelids open and listened while the Senator talked about the beautiful young woman, his wife, mother of Aurelia, who had died so young, so beautiful; about happy years he had spent in Paris as ambassador for the Protector; about a race horse he had owned that he seemed to confuse with his wife, so beautiful, so fast, and dead so young—poisoned in Miami by American gamblers, so tragic. He eyed me cautiously: was I insulted that he would accuse Americans of horse-poisoning? I was not insulted, but the Armstrong anxiety signal of get-busy-you're-on-company-time was buzzing

in my head. I had done nothing to find out what plans
Herrerro had for returning to Santa Cruz. I was too
sleepy.

I was urged to come back, to come back soon, please
to come back on Tuesday. Tuesday was soon enough to
get down to cases.

Back at the Casa de la Fuente I sat with a highball
thinking about my last directive from the world's oldest
boy wonder. If I didn't want to go with Cisneros I was
to come up with a better route. Herrerro was seventy-
nine years old, if not senile at least silly, a trick-shot
artist and a liar, possibly a pimp. I sipped the sour mash
that was supposed to make reality palatable. It did not
make Rodolfo Cisneros palatable. On the other hand,
my feeling all along had been that the salvation of the
Compañía Azucarera de Santa Cruz lay in American
policy in action. The palatable solution would be American pressure against nationalization, or failing that,
American pressure to force out of office the expropria-
tion-committed Flores regime. In apartment B of the
Casa de la Fuente now resided the Brass who could
throw that pressure into gear. As though on my order, a
note produced itself, Jenny Gray via Pepita and Lupe
to me: "Come and have a drink with us."

Jenny met me at the barred gate with her hair done
up and her black-framed glasses on, so that her face was
at its most severe. But she wore a silk print dress that
clung to round breasts, narrow belly and round hips,
and showed round knees. "Come in and meet my
man," she said.

Jenny's man rose from a blue canvas sling chair, tall,
thin, stooped, considerably grayer than newspaper
photographs had indicated. He looked like a highly
civilized stork, and his face was full of the consciousness of honor. He seemed very much at home, with

half-frame glasses on his nose, his tie off, and cuffs turned back to reveal thin, veined wrists.

"How do you do, Mr. Murdoch."

"How do you do, sir." I shook a long-fingered, slack hand, and met cool eyes with intense dark pupils while Jenny fluttered about.

"Something rum, Murdoch? We're having rum and orange juice. I have bourbon, though."

Pepita appeared, big-eyed with importance in her pigtails and crisp uniform, and I asked for bourbon and water. Finch had been reading a soft-cover collection of modern Greek poetry in translation, and I was pleased that my country's diplomats were interested in such subjects. Finch sat down and gazed at me over his half-frames.

He might have been Jenny's father, inquiring into her acquaintances: "So you're a friend of Jenny's, Mr. Murdoch. And you're down here in Mexico on a little vacation?"

"Not exactly a vacation," I said. "And you're down here to straighten out the OAS?"

"That is not the way we usually speak of these affairs," he said mildly. He smiled at Jenny, who had perched on a footstool at his knee. Where Herrerro treated his daughter like a treasured mistress, this lover was like a doting father.

I asked about prospects of the conference, not pushing too hard, and Finch said there was some concern that the United States might be in for a painful time. "The OAS, it is felt, has been running our way since its inception. This may be the hour when the current begins to flow in other directions."

"Castro and Flores directions?"

Finch removed his glasses, folded and placed them in his pocket with professorial deliberateness. "These are matters of very complex relationships," he said. "There is ours with Fidel. And ours with the rest of the Latin American governments which fear Fidel, but admire his posture toward us. Flores, of course, is another equation."

Pepita brought my highball in a blue glass that made it appear very weak. It tasted weak. Jenny said, "John's *real* concern is *real* estate." I thought she would have continued if he had not glanced at her sharply.

"Jenny is referring to moral problems we have in regard to South American land ownership. If we could solve these problems we could act in much better conscience in other matters—and a very large piece of the world's land mass would have a chance to bloom. On the other hand, latifundia as it now exists is a rot that can destroy us all. Mexico, as you may be aware, is solving her real estate problem as we like to see it solved—with all deliberate speed, you might say. Fidel solved Cuba's immediately and violently. It seems to me quite clear by now, that if the problem is not solved by the one means, it will be solved by the other."

Jenny's glasses hung around her neck by their black elastic. She rose to kiss his forehead and sit on the arm of his chair. "Keep plugging," she said.

"One might wish it were the only persuasion it was one's duty to exercise," Finch said, with a smile plucking at the corner of his mouth. "However, it is comforting to know that you have faith in me, my dear."

"I think you're the wisest man in the world, *that's* all," Jenny said. This seemed a declaration of faith for my benefit; or maybe it was for her own. I did not think the Great Liberal was going to be as strongly set against nationalization as I had been hoping. *Murdoch*, Cisneros' voice whispered, out of the red eye of the two-way radio. Jenny was saying to Finch, "You're just a little square *some*times."

Finch's mouth tucked in again, differently this time.

"By the way, Mr. Murdoch, I'm very grateful to you for your part in last night's escapade."

Jenny looked for a moment as rebellious as a criticized teen-ager, then she wrinkled her nose and said airily, "When one is an artist, escapades are expected. And one does what is expected of one, doesn't one?"

"I'm afraid I cannot understand why you must ingest dangerous drugs merely because they are the current fad."

"I'm an artist! I hope you take that seriously, John. Because *I* take it seriously. An artist doesn't paint with his hand, he paints with his *eye*. And anything I can do to make my eye more penetrating, more all-seeing, or just *better*, I will do. Pot does it sometimes, and sometimes mescaline."

"My dear, you must be aware there is evidence that these drugs cause chromosomal rearrangements, leading to genetic disturbances."

Tight-lipped, Jenny retorted: "That's more than hypothetical in my case, isn't it?"

This was obviously a new installment in some long-term fight and hurt. They stared at each other. Then Jenny swung toward me. "Murdoch, I'm *sorry!* This is all because of the other night. I shouldn't have told."

I made deprecating gestures, while Finch smiled grayly. "You told because you are truthful, my dear. I cannot describe how refreshing it is for me to be with someone who is invariably and almost obdurately truthful." He turned toward me also, where I sat ducking behind a foolish smile. "Yes, I'm sorry too, Mr. Murdoch. But this matter worries me terribly, and my worry irritates Jenny as a threat to her independence—as you have seen. We have not been ashamed to bring up the matter before you because in a way you were a part of it."

The situation was even clearer: an older man ob-

sessed with a young and vital woman in a tangle of
fascination and disapproval. I didn't meet Jenny's eyes.
"You can depend on your friendly neighbor," I said.

"What if there had been no friendly neighbor? Or
no gentlemanly one?" And of course that was in it too,
those bright points of anxiety in Finch's eyes examining
the neighbor.

"Change of subject, *change* of subject," Jenny said.
In Finch's presence I was careful not to watch her as
she left the room to call Pepita to replenish the drinks.
She returned pink and smiling. "They are certainly
having some *stirring* riots at the university, John. In
your honor?"

"Apparently the Mexican authorities sense El
Chato's fine Cuban hand."

El Chato was Alfredo Villaneuve, Castro's one man
agitation-propaganda apparatus. "A devilishly clever fellow," Finch said. "Like the Scarlet Pimpernel. Whenever trouble arises that is to the Cuban interest, El
Chato gets the credit. I secretly admire the Cubans,
who do so many things with dash and color."

"Flores seems to be showing the same color," I said.

"There is certainly concern about the present Cruceño government," Finch said.

"What's our line going to be toward the Flores
regime?" I asked, encouraged by his reference to the
"present" Cruceño government, but Finch only smiled.

"What a charming apartment you have found, my
dear," he said to Jenny. They smiled at each other, they
looked at me; it was time to go. I took a long drink of
weak highball.

When I mentioned playing tennis with Herb Justin,
Finch said, "Oh, the DCM. Yes, I knew Justin in
Rome. In our work one continually runs across familiar
faces before different backdrops."

I drained my glass, thanked Jenny, shook hands with

Finch; as I left he adjusted his spectacles and picked up his book of poetry once more. Now it did not seem so fine that Jenny's lover was absorbed in modern Greek poetry, in their charming nest in the Casa de la Fuente. Jenny followed me out into the moonlit patio.

"He's very tired," she said in a low voice. "He's tired, and he seems so *sad*. They make him do things he doesn't believe in. It's just that there's no one *else* who can do them. I'm sorry we got into that silly fight," she said. "He is really *so* marvelous."

It was reassuring to be told that the Great Liberal sometimes did things he didn't believe in.

(8) SUNDAY

AS I was leaving for Polanco for Sunday brunch with the Justins, I encountered an embassy limousine maneuvering with difficulty in the cobbled alley. Finch appeared, a narrow black figure in Chesterfield and Homburg, carrying an attaché case. The Mexican driver let him in, and I trailed the limousine down the cobbles.

The limousine did not carry a flag, but as an ambassador Finch was entitled to one, Herb Justin said, over Bloody Marys. Finch was the mainstay troubleshooter for American policy, especially among nations with a liberal leaning. It was widely bruited, I must have heard it myself, that Finch and the President did not see eye to eye on many matters. There had been a scandal in Paris four or five years ago, when Finch had told friends at an intimate dinner that he was tired of pimping for U.S. policies he disagreed with, that he intended to retire and write his memoirs. His statements had been leaked, blown up by liberal columnists, the administration had been embarrassed, Finch had denied he was threatening to publish anti-administration journals, and the whole dustup had not settled for some time. Finch had a wife in Washington; there were grown children.

Yes, Herb said, there were riots at the university,

American domination of the OAS might be the cause, Cuban agitation was suspected. He did not know much more about the history of Santa Cruz under the Protector than I did, and nothing of Aurelia's dead husband. Had I met Finch yet? Had I enjoyed my visit with Senator Herrerro? When I said I had to leave for a bullfight date with Dr. Ibis, he said, "P.T. wants quite a pound of flesh for that tennis match, doesn't he?"

Ibis picked me up in his black Mercedes 230. He was in high spirits as he bombed Insurgentes through the passenger cars, taxis, busses, and limos headed for the Plaza Mexico. With his Teddy Roosevelt grin, straight-arming the steering wheel, the brim of his panama blown back, he sped along three feet behind the bumper of the car ahead. Stopped in a paralyzed crush, he said, "You are feeling better today, my friend Murdoch. I think you have achieved what is called an organismic balance."

"What's that, P.T.?"

Traffic began to move again, and one of the taxis decorated with a jagged toothy band, called a *cocodrilo*, slipped past him. He shouted *chinga-chingada* expletives after it, but his smile did not fade. He said, "We will take the simple case of a man sitting in Plaza Mexico on hot day. He sweats. Soon the organismic balance tips—dehydration." I braced myself on the panic handle as we screamed to a stop behind a packed-solid bus. Ibis continued: "Into the mind of this man come images of water, cool running streams, blue mountain lakes—so he buys a beer to restore organismic balance. Pleasure!"

With a screech and a roar he started around the bus in hero-driver style, jockeying, braking, accelerating, passing both the bus and the *cocodrilo*. Having accomplished this, he leaned back in his seat, nodding congratulations to himself. "Perhaps this man has two beers," he went on. "And soon the organismic balance is tipped other way. This time he must visit the *caballeros* to piss. Pleasure again! What is pleasure but restoration of the organismic balance, friend Murdoch! There is also of course the matter of organismic balance in secretions of the glands, and this is why I think you are so much happier today!" He leered at me; he laughed with fat heartiness.

"That's a very interesting theory."

He threaded the Mercedes at speed through a space that was certainly too narrow. "You know, my partner, your countrymen come to Mexico, they have driven expressways of Los Angeles, they think they must be finest drivers in the world. One passage along Insurgentes or Reforma at busy time and strong American men cry with terror."

In our *barrera* seats on the sunny side of the Plaza Mexico, we watched the enormous, steep-sided concrete bowl slowly filling and sipped beer to maintain the organismic balance. I asked Ibis about Senator Herrerro and the Protector.

"But he is a cousin, of course," he said in a superior tone. "I see like all Americans you know nothing of the affairs of neighbor countries."

"Educate me."

"I know politics and history of that terrible island because I know my Papa Freud. Also of course I read newspapers."

"What's Freud have to do with it?"

Sour *pasodobles* were heard, and the giant Coca-Cola bottle in the center of the ring began to move. Leaving wheel tracks in the sand, it made a tour before exiting, while Ibis clucked his disapproval. Horsemen paraded, the matadors and their troupes marched, the first bull stormed in, stout, black, and fast, resembling Ibis' little Mercedes. I felt the sickish excitement of adrenalin flowing. Ibis muttered that the bull was bad, very bad, and, when the picadors on their horses sidled into the ring, the animal charged only once. Having been spiked, he intelligently decided not to pursue the matter, and there was an ungraceful contretemps. Turning from the ring, Ibis said, "You must know what happened to the dictator, friend Murdoch."

"Murdered by his own henchmen."

He leaned toward the rail as the bull finally went for the horse again. One of the matadors took the bull away with what even I could recognize was an expert pass. "Ah, well done, very pretty!" Ibis cried, clapping. "See what a very handsome good-looking boy is this Jesús Obregón!" Then he said, "Now I will tell you what Sigmund said so long ago that fits this island exactly.

"Papa Sigmund said the very first original human group be*came* when one man dominated the rest. He was *father*, and all women belonged to him. He had pleasure of all women, other men had none.

"Santa Cruz Republic is such very pure case. Because the Protector had so many women—unthinkable! You have heard this? There were pimps with high titles in government, who only brought women to Palace. Each week. And the Protector selected so many and these he enjoyed, and the next week new ones came. Old, young, fat, black, everything—though younger and younger almost to babies as he became old. This was important thing in Santa Cruz, but of course you know *machismo* is very important to all Latin America men. The Protector had *supermachismo!*

"But you see, my partner, how it is classic Freudian situation. Of course the brothers and the cousins had many women. This thing of collecting women became so important because of *machismo* of the Protector, you see this? Because it became part of Protector's power. First it is result of power, but later it comes to appear prerequisite. These others had many women, it

would seem to us many too many, but you are familiar
with nature of man. If this one has just a little less than
that one whom he envies, it will seem to him he has
nothing at all. So—some of these make a conspiracy
and they kill the terrible old man.

"Then, as Papa Freud says, all the brothers form the
great oligarchy and rule together. They have all together become new father. But already we see the
father becomes all authority—laws, police, tax collector,
and so forth. But! We are not yet there in Santa Cruz,
I am beyond myself. Because the way in which oligarchy has made conspiracy and killed the Protector
is—they have promised freedom! But new father does
not allow freedom any more than old father. This is
not in nature of fathers. And in Santa Cruz this new
oligarchy father does not have great magic *machismo*
of old father, they are only little frightened men quar-
reling, and not one great, sure-of-himself, monster of a
man."

He stopped to watch the action. The matador, with
his red flag, faced the bull, and the stands were silent.
"Oh, these so-bad bulls," Ibis said. "If all are so bad
Plaza Mexico will riot like the university!"

The matador, who was bowlegged, did some ragged
sawing with the muleta and finally got action. He killed
badly, a bloody, maladroit, unbelievably lengthy, sweating, horrid business that left the Plaza Mexico with
only miserable relief that it was over.

The dead bull was dragged off by a team of mules, all
straining curved necks and bobbing plumes. The new
bull burst through the gate. This one clearly had more
machismo, and Ibis said, "Now we will watch this
stylish young man I admire so much, and perhaps this
man and this bull will show us something.

"So," he went on. "The sons have killed and de-
voured their father. You know Greek mythology, I

assume? But of course no oligarchy has ever maintained itself. Not in Thebes, not in Egypt or Rome or Santa Cruz. Never. One son must always prove himself the strongest. But does this strong son take the power, and the women and the money, in the name of freedom? No! He takes power in the name of the murdered father who is now holy!"

He was gesturing excitedly, to the amusement of our neighbors. The pic-ing of the second bull seemed to suit him. Jesús Obregón, the matador, placed his own banderillas, to applause and an off-key chorus from the band, which pleased Ibis even more. I was thinking about the Big Guy.

"Ah, this very fine young man!" Ibis said. "Do you find him handsome also, friend Murdoch? I will leave a note for him at matadors' syndicate."

"You do *that?*" I blurted.

"It is commonly done here. If one admires a man's performance with the bulls, it is improper to tell him so?"

"Oh, a fan letter."

"Not a fan letter! A small note only!" He glared at me through his dark glasses. "I suppose it would be against the law in your great repressed country to do such a small thing of appreciation." He turned to the action again. Obregón was dedicating the bull to someone on the shady side, holding up his Mickey-Mouse-eared hat.

Ibis leaned forward grimacing fiercely as his matador stalked into the ring with the muleta. The bull charged with an audible grunt, and there was music and applause in the Plaza Mexico. It was a good encounter, and Obregón received an ear for his pains. He took a circuit of the ring, holding up his hairy prize. Flowers were flung down on him, articles of clothing, winesacks, hats, a binocular case. Ibis sailed his Panama out, one

of Obregón's attendants flung it back into the stands
and it was passed down to us.

I prodded Ibis to continue. I thought his Freudian
history of Santa Cruz might not be entirely accurate,
but it had movement and suspense. "Then there was a
revolution against the oligarchy?"

"It is not yet finished," he said solemnly.

"We intervened."

"Certainly, the United States battleships came to
Santa Cruz. All the brothers and the generals of the
oligarchy have become afraid they will be murdered
and have run away. Every one of the brave assassinators
of the monster-father have run as fast as he could. But
not so fast as to leave any money behind in all the
island, you understand. So now the Republic is very
poor and must borrow money from the United States
and must do what United States says it must do or no
more money. They have had elections, they have a
president whom now United States does not like very
much. But it is not yet finished."

"What's going to happen?"

He gave me a bored look. "I cannot read the intes-
tines of birds, my friend. Who can know? There is
democracy, and to you Americans that may seem happy
ending. But perhaps more important to human soul is
that whole drama is acted out as Papa Freud tells us it
must be. What is more satisfying to soul, bloody Greek
tragedy or happy musical comedy from Broadway? No,
it is not finished on that very Greek tragedy island.
There is an émigré army training in Jalisco. You know
this, of course."

I knew this. "What's the matter with the Protector's
sons?"

"They hide in Spain and count stolen money. They
are not strong and bad, only bad."

"I understand there is an illegitimate son who's strong and bad."

"Ah! Perhaps he is answer."

"You think it has to be a bloody answer?"

He held up a hand for silence as the third bull arrived in the arena. His chin was tucked in, his blotchy face shining with sweat, his handkerchief knotted around his thick neck. "This is very bad bull," he announced.

It was a bad bull and it died badly, its destruction another miserable mess. What happened to a matador's career once he recognized the possibility that his trade was meaningless murder?

When Ibis returned me to the Casa de la Fuente, female Spanish voices rang through the patio, and Pedro sidled nervously on his perch. In my hallway were a sobbing Pepita and fat Lupe weeping and wringing her hands, while Señora Pinal berated them with a great deal of gesticulation. Also present was a strange girl in a white maid's dress. She wore green-tinted sunglasses on a thin, intelligent face.

"Ah, señor!" Señora Pinal cried. "What a bad thing we have here! This bad Lupe, she must go home for one month. To Cuautla! She sayez her papa is very sick. I think she goes to her *novio!*"

Lupe protested, Pepita sobbed gently. "*¡Gordita!*" the señora snarled at Lupe, who threw her apron over her head. The new maid smiled at me. She appeared more sophisticated than the two Fuente maids, both of whom were country girls.

"And nothing is sayed to you or me, señor!" Señora Pinal continued, waving a hand stiff-wristed to indicate Lupe and the newcomer. "This fat one only comes now and tells me she must go to Cuautla for one month. How does she know her papa is sick for one month

only? And she brings her *amiga* who will take her place
for this one month. How do I know this *amiga*? *¿Cómo
te llamas, muchacha?*" she asked suspiciously.

The girl's name was Gabriela something-I-didn't-
catch; she said to me, "I speak a little bit *Inglés*, señor." With this she smiled. One of her front teeth was
missing and the smile was droll and disarming.

"I think she'll be fine," I said to Señora Pinal.

She was instantly mollified. With a shrug that turned
all responsibility over to me, she said, "As you wish."
Daubing at her eyes with her apron, Lupe wouldn't
look at me. Pepita was crying because her friend was
leaving. Gabriela had assumed a solemn expression
again, her upper lip tightly shuttered as though to hide
the missing tooth, but I could diagnose stifled giggles
by the whitening of her nostrils.

The señora pushed the weeping maids out of the
hallway and departed, having reestablished control, and
I was left alone with my new *muchacha*. There ensued
one of those conversations in which each insists on the
other's language. Gabriela's English was stronger than
my Spanish. Her willpower was also strong. But there
was a merriness about her, with her gap-toothed grin,
that shook me out of the depression in which I had
come away from the bloody bullfights, the bloody
history of Santa Cruz, and Ibis' prophecy of a bloody
future with the Big Guy returning to that Greek
tragedy island in the name of his murdered father, the
Protector, who was now holy.

That evening Gabriela went off to the movies with
Pepita as if she considered Jenny's maid to be one of
her duties. Pepita was as captivated and admiring of
her as though poor fat Lupe were forgotten already.

(9) MONDAY

"WOULD you mind sending that rather ubiquitous girl of yours off on an errand?" John Finch said. "I have a private matter to discuss." I was just back from a lucrative money match at Chapultepec, and he had arrived for an evening drink. I went out to the kitchen where Gabriela was absorbed in a Mexican slick-paper magazine, and asked her to wash the Corvette. Before rejoining Finch I stood in the hallway making faces at the wall: I was sure he wanted to talk about Jenny.

But he said, "I have been asked to inquire if you will consider doing a job for your government."

I sat down. "What kind of job?"

"Of a covert nature." Finch passed a hand over his forehead. "I'm to urge you to do it. The thinking is, you see, that you will be overwhelmed by the fact that *I* have urged you."

"But what is it?"

"I have insisted that I be left in the dark about that. If you seem amenable, the matter will be fully explained. If not, it will end here."

He lounged, long legs crossed, lighting a cigaret and blowing a plume of smoke. Deep lines graven in his cheeks made him look like an overcivilized Lincoln.

When he inhaled these lines cut deeper, like claw-marks. I could feel an anxious torque in my own face.

"Tom, I think the general assumption in this matter of recruitment is that we all, at heart, consider our-selves a part of the great citizen army. And each of us will do what he can when called upon in the general welfare and common defense."

My mind pried gingerly under the corners of what might be expected of me. "What would *you* say?" I asked Finch.

"As you know, I do whatever I can."

"But not undercover. Is that what covert means?"

"Exactly. No, I've done no undercover work. My talents seem to lie in another direction." After a long moment he continued, casually, "I believe it has to do with a situation which our intelligence hopes to pene-trate, and into which you have an entrée."

Herrerro, then; all at once I had a glimpse behind the scenes where those busy stagehands Herb Justin, Sandy Brody, and Dr. Ibis were pulling ropes and arranging sets; the calculations and machinations that had produced that tennis match with Herrerro. The Mexican pro was probably the head of the Mexican secret service. Still, I seemed to be moving closer to the policy-making apparatus. "Am I supposed to pursue some course of action, or just spy?"

"As I say, I did not wish to know anything about the projected operation. I recognize that I am trying to dispose you toward buying a pig in a poke, but we must believe it is in a good cause."

"Who do I talk to about it?"

"You will work through a cutout. You will have contact with your case officer only through him."

"Tell them I may go along."

The recruiter nodded and said in a remote voice, "I hope you will find it interesting." He drained the scotch in his glass. "And I have also been asked to inquire if you will have dinner with Jenny and me tonight."

"I'll definitely go along with that."

A date had been invited for me. Her name was Pat Hepner, she had short blond hair and bubbled with an everybody-must-love-me self-confidence. She was shapely and tan, four years out of Michigan State, and she worked at the embassy. "Every day at three o'clock I take those sweet little lands-sakes tourists on the guided tour. See our diplomats hard at work!"

Finch seemed to find her highly entertaining, and Pat dominated the conversation, with her reactions to Mexican scenery, Mexican men, Mexican traffic, the architecture, smog, language, and bullfights. Jenny wore her black-framed glasses throughout dinner.

"How's Gabriela working out, Murdoch?" she asked me.

"She's fine. I like that grin. Lupe wasn't strong in that department."

"She has captured Pepita's heart," Jenny said.

Holding out her wineglass for Finch to refill, straight-backed and brightly smiling, Pat asked, "Who are these people?"

"I'm afraid they are talking about their maids, my dear," Finch said, and Jenny glared at him.

It seemed to be expected that I would drive Pat home. Outside in the patio, with a little wind rustling in the pomegranate tree, she said in her bright voice, "Oh, it's such a pretty place! Are you going to ask me in for a nightcap, Tommy?"

I asked her in for a nightcap, and brought out the brandy and glasses. I was intrigued by her blond, blue-eyed, fresh-skinned, long-legged Americanness, as though I was already an old Mexico expatriate with

yellow eyeballs. Pat Hepner reminded me of home and
Eloise.

She crossed one golden leg over the other and kicked
it up and down to work her heel loose from the heel of
her white pump. "Now, Tommy," she said briskly.
"I'm to tell you what you need to know about what you
may be doing for us."

I sat down hard. "You're the cutout."

"If you decide you want to back out of this at any
time, there is no one involved but you and me. Okay?"

"Brief me."

"We are interested in the émigré movements that
exist in opposition to the government of President
Flores of the Santa Cruz Republic. It would be very
helpful to have someone placed who could keep us
aware of what is going on. We don't like to be surprised. Now, Tommy, your American Ventures connec-
tion—the sugar company—is a perfect cover."

I felt complimented.

"We are interested in the Dark Angel as well as her
father. She may be more important than he is. We
want to know all we can about their activities, attitudes, their friends—have you met many people there?"

"No one."

"What have you learned about the émigré movements?"

"Nothing yet." She raised an eyebrow and I said
defensively, "I've only been there once."

She steepled her fingers together and I felt a familiar
pressure, one that Eloise also generated when she was
unhappy, displeased, or disappointed. Somebody had
better do something about it.

"Why don't you tell me just what you want me to
do?" I asked.

"We want you to maintain your present penetration
of the Herrerro household. It would be helpful if you

could build a relationship with Aurelia Velásquez in which she confided in you everything that was going on."

"Going on specifically in what direction?"

"Specifically we are interested in any efforts that may be made to combine the various émigré movements. They have been separate and hostile to each other, and we think pressure is being brought to join them. Watch for meetings, and so forth. The name of the Protector is still very potent in the Republic, you know, and we would look for any concerted attempt to form a single counterrevolutionary force to take advantage of the Protector's name. Is that clear?"

I nodded, to Pat, and to Ibis' prognostications. She asked when I would be going to the Herrerro house again. "On Tuesday," I said.

"There is no need for *us* to be secretive in the slightest. We are only a couple of expatriate Americans dating." She produced a semi-official giggle. "Come and take me out to dinner on Tuesday night." She had me memorize phone numbers, hers at the embassy and at home, and an emergency number. "Now, about remuneration."

"I don't want your gold."

"But—"

"Conflict of interest. I work for American Ventures, as you are aware."

She looked worried. "Well, we'll talk about this next time. Now, there's one other thing, Tommy. You'll have to find another apartment. The coincidence that you are here in the same place as Mr. Finch is *not* good. I'll be looking around for you."

To an already intricate edifice of manipulation was added the strong possibility that John Doane Finch wanted to be rid of the friendly neighbor. I had entered the arena of suspicions. "I like it here," I said.

"But you can't expect us to ask them to move!"

I was feeling both resentful and ashamed of myself. "No, but you can't *order* me to, can you?"

Pat shrugged. She rose, combed fingers through the back of her short, blond hair, and with a jerk of her head shook it loose. She wore a strand of pearls at her throat, and the line of her collarbone was young and vulnerable. Part of my resentment was due to the fact that she reminded me so much of Mrs. Thomas Murdoch.

Suddenly she smiled. "Well, *that's* over. You can take me home now and we'll see how you perform on Tuesday."

(10) TUESDAY, I

JENNY appeared around noon, in her jump suit. She wore an orange scarf tied over her hair, and her face had a colorless, peasant look. "Tennis game today, Murdoch?"

"Not today."

"You like to win at games?" she asked belligerently.

"I like to win at everything. Nice party last night, Jenny."

"Speaking of which," she said, but didn't go on. She plumped herself down on the couch and folded her arms over her breasts. I asked if she would like something to drink.

"That was my idea."

I called to Gabriela, who was beating something in the kitchen with great vigor, and she came bounding into the living room looking expectant in her green-tinted glasses. Jenny wanted sherry, which caused a communications problem. Finally I got it myself while Gabriela struck herself on the forehead: "Ah! *Jerez!*" She brought me a gin and orange juice and retired. Jenny looked depressed and shook her head when I asked if she were working well.

"What's your image of me these days, Murdoch?"

"All pink and white and beautiful on my bed, crying for help one minute and making puns the next."

"Would it wreck my image if I sat here in my dirty overalls and poured my heart out?"

"Enhance it, probably."

"I'd rather Gabriela wasn't listening," she said, lowering her voice. "Inconvenient that she speaks English so well. I had to speak to Pepita about her spending so much time *among* us." She turned her face from side to side under my eyes. "John's aged so terribly this last six months," she said. "But of course being in Washington—and his wife's been a *harpy*. And he's been ill." She stopped; she looked miserable.

Everything grows old, Anastasio Herrerro had said. I examined my feelings, which verged on smugness, and didn't like them. Jenny said, "But he's gotten so—jealous."

"No cause."

"He is, though. You the most. But any and all. I guess I talk too much, but I've been married twice and I've gone to bed with *quite* a lot of men and enjoyed it thoroughly. I think it can be a fairly casual, pleasurable business. The trouble is I've *said* so to John. At the embassy party the night he arrived some great stud made a pass at me. I was amused and told John about it, but *he* wasn't. It upset him terribly. And telling him about my trip and flying over here *was* a mistake, as you saw." She looked down at her hands in her lap. "He's changed. Now he's afraid."

"Afraid of what?"

"I think he's afraid of everything."

She sighed and said, "You know, when we were together in New York I could actually feel I was influencing things. Like a Pompadour, or Maintenon—the great sexy ladies who had good minds and could swing some leverage in the world. He always said I was his *conscience*. That I kept him on the *truth*, and wouldn't let him take the *easy* way. But all that's gone now."

I was beginning to feel little electric charges when certain subjects came up, like the peaks of a polygraph. "He's worrying about the OAS?" I said.

"Oh, they've painted the Aleman statue at the university red again, and you see '*¡Cuba, sí! Yanqui, no!*' chalked up everywhere. Things like that depress him.

"But I don't blame them!" she said. "Our Latin American policy is so *stupid!* Our whole foreign policy is only anti-communist, *negative*. Our Latin American policy is only anti-Castro, John is down here just to be sure the OAS makes a lot of joint statements against Cuba, Castro, and Communism. Maybe slap Flores' hands with some sanctions against Santa Cruz. But that's *all*. He's not to rock the boat about latifundia or any of the other things he really *believes* in. *Used* to believe," she said. "Just—get Castro. And of course it's not going to go smoothly. You know Mexico *never* has gone all the way with us on Cuba. There's still the daily Cubana Airlines flight, and some trade—to remind us we can't tell *every*one *every*thing they have to do. Maybe he can get a joint statement against Castro, but he can't get both that and sanctions against Flores, too— Oh, I don't know *anything!*"

Tears shone on her cheeks. I felt a base urge to prod her into telling me more about those sanctions against Flores, and a stronger urge to restraint. Jenny burst out, "But I do know more about *us* than I used to. We *really* put the pressure on down here when they don't act the way we want them to. Oh, we don't send gunboats and *Marines* much any more, we just send the little gray economics people. And they snip-snip at the money until we get what we want. When Cuba didn't please us we snipped away at the sugar quota,

96 A GAME FOR EAGLES

but Castro thumbed his nose and Russia bought the sugar.

"Castro said he'd give fair value when he expropriated," she went on. "The big American corporations that owned just everything in Cuba had always set their own appraisals for taxes, and they were such cheaters, of course they'd set them ridiculously low. And that's what Castro said he'd give them.

"Now Flores has done the same thing in Santa Cruz. He took over the railroad, which was in *such* a rotten mess, and now he's threatening the sugar industry. And the corporations are furious because he'll only pay the amount of those low tax appraisals. Well, I think it's *really* funny. But John doesn't. He says I'm being simplistic."

She had drawn her knees up and she huddled as though she were cold, everything in her face slanting downward with unhappiness. "I told him if he was just down here to do rotten, *threat*ening things he can't believe in, he should go home. But he says he thinks he can do some good.

"He thinks he has—credits. Because he is who he is. He thinks he has these credits to use, like *trumps*. When something's really important, of *world* importance, then he can put his credits together to accomplish *some* . . . *good* . . . *thing!*"

She sat looking at me with her hot, damp, honest eyes that were like another set of the ubiquitous mirrors of Mexico City. She said, "But he can't see that his *foreign* credits are going to just slip *away* if he does rotten errand-boy *blackmail* for the administration! And then he won't have any credits with the President either, because he doesn't get those for what he's done, only for what he can still do. And . . . and Murdoch, suddenly he'll just be a helpless old man!"

"I suppose it's a gamble worth taking, Jenny," I said.

I didn't know why I felt the need to defend Finch from her truth-seeing artist's eye. She shook her head at me.

"You know, I wanted so much to have his *child*," she said. "But he says he won't give any hostages. To the future, you see—so he mustn't believe there will be any future. I didn't want a hostage, I wanted a *child!*"

I rose to stand by her, and pat her shoulder awkwardly. As her confidant, I was learning things about her and Finch it might be a disadvantage to know. She gripped my hand against her wet cheek. "Oh, *shit!*" she whispered. "I feel so helpless. My self-confidence is *all* gone. Do you still think about me moving around sometimes, Murdoch?"

I said I did.

"If I can just think about you thinking about me moving around—then maybe I'll have better form."

"More self-confidence."

"Yes, like when this Rodolfo made a pass at me."

"Rodolfo who?"

"I forget his last name. A great playboy type, all shoulders and no hips, a little moustache and a hell of an appraising eye. Described in *some* detail what he could do for me." She gave a little laugh. "It was *gross*, but fun."

I was feeling some empathy with John Finch.

"What I *really* came for," Jenny said abruptly. "Murdoch—that girl Pat. I don't want to be nosy, but it's an area where I have a little wisdom. They do good, *necessary* things, of course they do. But don't get involved in something where you have to hold your nose, thinking that after *that* you'll be doing some *good* thing. I mean—think about not doing the *first* thing. Oh, I'm not saying it very well."

"Well enough," I said.

"I'd better go home now." She rose, and we faced

each other. She smiled, but the smile faded and crystals
of tears beaded her lashes. I brushed them away with a
hooked forefinger, and she smiled wanly.

I walked out with her. From the kitchen came
potent cooking smells, chili and onions and tomatoes.
Gabriela was leaning on the zinc-topped table, grinning
broadly at us. "*¡Buenas tardes, señora!*"

"*Oh, buenas tardes, Gabriela,*" Jenny said.

"The lunch is served, señor!" Gabriela said a little
later. She had decorated the glass table with a bouquet
of flowers very prettily displayed in an earthenware
bowl. Centrally located with this were yellow paper
napkins in a water glass, and a thin green bottle of
potent-looking *salsa*. Ahead of me was another long and
heavy mid-afternoon meal at Herrerro's, but I didn't
want to disappoint Gabriela in her first big effort.

She was not wearing her uniform, but a freshly
pressed and pleated tan dress with an apron, and
pearls in her ears. She stood watching me as I sat down,
her nostrils quivering and her upper lip under tension.

I knew it was very bad precedent when I said, "Will
you join me, señorita?"

"*¡Sí!*" said Gabriela, whose willpower had again
proved itself. Her apron disappeared and she brought
another place setting. She had a very clear pale skin
with only a soft hint of tan to it. Apparently she never
removed the green-tinted glasses.

We sipped pallid soup. "Good soup?" she asked.

"Very good."

"Not very good," she said, with a toss of her chin.
"Do you wish beer, señor?"

"Please."

She sailed out with the empty soup bowls. She did
everything with dash, as though she constantly must
make a game of her occupation. She brought back two

dark brown bottles of beer, then plates of rice. I noticed that she didn't feed herself in the usual head-down Mexican fashion. Whenever she caught me looking at her she grinned as though we had some joke together.

"Tell me something," I said.

The grin disappeared, a worry line marred her forehead. "¿Sí?"

"How did you lose that tooth?"

She leaned forward, took her arm back and swung it with the motion of a smack on the mouth.

"Who?"

"Police."

"What did you do?"

She shrugged grandly. "But nothing! In *Estados Unidos* you must do something for police to hit?"

"Usually."

"In *Estados Unidos* you like police," she said, nodding; and when I felt a need to protest this, she interrupted: "You like this rice, señor?"

"It's very good."

"I get better, eh? Next course, *varooom!*" She repeated the gesture of a blow on the mouth, and took the rice plates out.

She returned with chops smothered in tomato sauce and sprinkled with a finely chopped, unidentifiable green. "Varooom!" she said. She watched me cut the meat, spear a bite, and take it to my mouth. "It's good?" she demanded.

I nodded, chewing.

"Not too bravo?"

I shook my head, chewing. Her fingers drummed on the table. Finally she sighed and said, "Very tough, eh?"

"It's very tasty," I said, as she began to saw at her

own chop. "Where were you when the police hit you?"
I asked.

She raised both palms, and then in rapid sequence
pressed the left to her breast while leaving the right
upraised, as though on oath. "Not at the university,"
she said.

"Writing '¡Cuba, sí!' on a wall?"

"Promise, no."

I ate the tough chop and drank the good Mexican
beer. I was enjoying her company. She volunteered the
information that she went to college. This answered
certain questions about her sophistication, but raised
others. "What college?" I asked.

She typed, punched the buttons and pulled the lever
of an adding machine, scribbled on a stenographer's
pad. "And English."

"But why are you working as a maid?"

"No more money. So I must be a maid for a little
while. It is better than other things. Another beer,
señor?"

She brought it to me resting on her palm as though
her hand was a tray, guiding the tray with speed and
great skill between the crowded tables of the café.
"You have a wife, señor?" she asked, seating herself
with a flourish, and leaning her elbows on the glass
tabletop.

"Yes."

"Where?"

"In California. Los Angeles."

"And child?"

"No," I said, "no hostages."

"Your wife is there, but you are here," Gabriela said,
and added, "The Señora Gray is a divorced woman."

"But I am not a divorced man."

"The Señora Pintura is in love with you. *El alma se
ve en los ojos.*"

I frowned severely at her.

"She is not in love with that old man," Gabriela said.

"You are very romantic."

"I will tell the señor something. I am not romantic since I am a little girl with ribbons in my hair." She measured the height with a crooked finger.

"And now you are in college."

"Now I am in life."

I asked if she had a *novio*. Yes, she had a *novio*. He worked for the government.

"And when will you get married?"

"I think we do not get married," Gabriela said. "I think we will only be *novios*. This way when people ask if I have *novio*, I say yes. People ask if he has *novia*, he says yes. Now I bring *postre*."

Dessert was jello with bits of fruit in it, slumped in a glass dish. This time Gabriela didn't ask if I liked it, but said, "I make very good coffee." Over coffee I asked what she and Pepita gossiped about all day in the patio.

"About the Señor Güero."

"Who's the Señor Güero?"

"You, señor." She touched her hair. "It means the color of the hair. The Señor Güero, and his rich lady in Lomas de Chapultepec. The Señora Pintura and the very old man. Lupe, Señora Pinal. Everything."

I was shaken by her knowledge of the lady in Lomas, where I was due soon. I looked at my watch. Gabriela was watching me with an eyebrow raised, lips slightly parted. She was pretty, older than I had thought, and she had a will like a hand on the nape of my neck.

I put my napkin down beside my coffee cup. "A very good lunch, Gabriela," I said.

"Thank you, señor." She rose and gathered up the dishes, and I left for Lomas de Chapultepec and my post in the great citizen army.

(11) TUESDAY, II

A SMOGGY afternoon in Lomas de Chapultepec, the valley of Mexico drowned in gaseous muck and no shining mountains even imaginable, in the tower room a repetition and a progression, with the ritual considerably embellished and hints that a Puritan reluctance was beginning to operate in Thomas Murdoch. Yet my coffee-colored angel preserved a kind of innocence and her glance over her bare shoulder retained its transfixing power. Maybe my reluctance to proceed, chapter by chapter, toward the advanced exercises at the back of the book, was because the game had been changed. I was no longer able to concentrate on pleasure within a kind of adolescents' wet dream, because I should be gaining Aurelia's confidence as a working spy.

We became Aurelia and Tomás in a shy little ceremony, resting flank to flank on the white counterpane. Aurelia's hand lay on my chest in somnolent affection, but it was time to punch the time clock.

"Do you miss Santa Cruz, Aurelia?"

"Miss?" She smoothed the hairs on my chest, first with the palm, then the back of her hand. "What is miss?"

"You said you hoped to go back to Santa Cruz."

"Ah! Yes, I miss. The province of Los Pinos I miss very much. So much," she said. "But perhaps it is better there is no hope to go back."

"Why?" I asked, but she rose.

"Come, Tomás. My papá is finish his telebision."

I lay watching her great breasts and powerful thighs. Her flesh was as fine as dark toffee as she stepped into white underthings, turning away from me with the melting, light-eyed, coyly regal over-the-shoulder glance that pleased me more than the wilder shores of love. "Come, Tomás," she said.

At dinner Herrerro was embarrassingly attentive, crooning as he offered her tidbits from the serving dishes, and candies and portions of ice cream from his own plate, indulgences I considered unwise in view of Aurelia's heft, although he was clearly proud of the amount of daughter he had.

"Aurelia says she misses Santa Cruz very much, Señor Herrerro."

The Senator turned his body like a puppet in his chair. "Of course Aurelia miss our *finca* in Los Pinos. My daughter is very much love in the Republic, señor. She is name an angel because she is so good!"

"When do you think you will go back?" I said, itching with self-consciousness.

He lifted his arms in the air and held them there to illustrate his suspension. "Ah, who know! Politics!"

"You don't like this government?"

His toad's face broke into a merry smile. "It do not like me, señor!"

"You know President Flores?"

"Yes, yes!"

Aurelia glanced up with a flash of her honey-colored eyes. "Santa Cruz is very small, Tomás. Señor Flores

come to Los Pinos when I am little girl and put me on
his knee and play with me."

Herrerro blew his breath out through his lips. "Paco
Flores is a worm that eats of dead peoples!"

"Señor Flores is a man I like very much in Los Pinos,
Papá," Aurelia said with a lift of her chin. Her father
gazed upon her angrily.

"How can you like this man that is *enemigo* to your
papá?"

"For my papá I will not like him. For this reason
only." They stared at each other for a brief, intense
moment, and I got the polygraphic electrical peaks
again.

Herrerro turned back to me, all smiles. "And maybe
Paco *el gusano* will not be *presidente* much longer,
Señor Moordoak."

"Why is that, Senator Herrerro?"

He laid a finger impishly alongside his nose. "Because, señor, this *gusano*, this worm that eats meats of
dead peoples—" Squinting at me, grinning, he traced a
line with his forefinger on the tablecloth. "—this worm
has little red line in his back that I have known long
ago, but now government of the United States also
begin to see."

Aurelia watched him stiffly as he sat with his back
pressed to the back of his chair, his hands fisted on its
arms. "And so I think Paco *el gusano* will not be for
very long *presidente*," Herrerro said. He hopped up to
bring a box of Cuban cigars to the table. He lit mine.
Aurelia plucked a mint from the cut-glass bowl—a
pleasing contrast of white disc and dark fingers.

"How do the people of Santa Cruz feel about
Flores?" I asked.

"They have vote for him," Aurelia said, and popped
the mint into her mouth.

"People of Santa Cruz are very wise," the Senator

said. "All people who have live near United States become wise. *El Protector* has said—" He pondered. " '—when he lives near to eagles, it is wise to be friend to eagles.' "

Aurelia spoke rapidly in Spanish. I recognized the words, *águilas, enemigos,* and *amigos,* and I thought she was saying that eagles did something to both enemies and friends. Herrerro scowled at her.

"We must speak *Inglés* for our friend, Aurelia."

"Pardon," Aurelia said, without looking at me. "It was not of importance." After a moment she said, "*El Protector* was very good friend to United States." Another pause and she added, "And United States was very good friend to *El Protector.*"

Rings of smoke mingled above the table. Herrerro sat in his ducal chair, impish and smug, and Aurelia nibbled another mint with teeth as white as what they bit on.

"So perhaps we go back to the *finca* in Los Pinos one day very soon, my daughter," Senator Herrerro said, making talons of his fingers. "Carried in the hands of eagles."

Slowly suffusing her face came the total sadness that lay always visible within her, but now so filling her stoic features that without comprehension I felt tears of empathy scrape at my own eyes. Aurelia sat racked by her private anguish for an eternity of a moment, her pale eyes staring at nothing; and then she said, "*Con permiso, Papá y Tomás.*" She swept out of the room.

"My daughter love her island so much," Herrerro said nervously.

"How did her husband die?" I asked.

He stirred in his chair, he licked his lips, squinted, made revolving motions with his hands. "He has been traitor in army of Santa Cruz," he said finally. "He has

died for this." His gestures now expressed that this had
been sad for Aurelia, but was otherwise of no importance.

"Do you know Rodolfo Cisneros, Señor Herrerro?"

He squinted his goat's eyes against the cigar smoke.
"But of course."

"I met Cisneros and Galindo in Jalisco."

He closed his eyes, he nodded slowly. "Yes, yes," he
said. "Rodolfo is with Galindo in Jalisco."

"No, he is here in Mexico City."

Herrerro blew smoke, watching it as though it held
answers, nodding. "So. Rodolfo is here."

"I must tell you that I am interested in the Compañía Azucarera de Santa Cruz," I said, "My father-in-
law is C. E. Armstrong."

"Father-in-law" shut off whatever flow of communication there had been, and by the time I had explained,
Herrerro had gone into hiding behind a smoke screen
of semi-comprehension. I was never sure if he understood who I or C. E. Armstrong was, or that American
Ventures had acquired the sugar company. I went
through it carefully, but Herrerro gave no sign of knowing what I was talking about. He was in a total funk,
and pathetically relieved when I got up to leave. I went
to report to Pat Hepner.

She lived near the embassy in a *condominio*, a stack
of glass-fronted shoeboxes with white walls and black
trim, and a fourth floor view of the Reforma with
traffic raging and smog hanging in tatters between the
black glass buildings. We sat facing each other in chairs
like red-upholstered marshmallows. When I started to
speak she touched a finger to her lips and made a circu-
lar motion encompassing the room.

"Do you like my apartment?" she asked.

"It's very nice."

"The third floor apartment is for rent, furnished. Would you like to look at it?"

I didn't want to look at it. Pat said, "I really think you'd be happier here than way out in San Angel, Tommy." She wore a pleated tweed skirt and a white blouse, her mouth was iced with pale lipstick. She fluffed at the back of her hair with both hands. "Where are you taking me for a drink? There's a nice little bar across the street."

Either her manner or our relationship aroused such an antipathy in me that I was irrationally prejudiced against the little bar across the street. "Fine," I said, and we rode down to the lobby in the tiny elevator, most of which was occupied by the fat magenta-uniformed operator. We crossed the street at a run, almost wiped out by a VW that raced honking around the corner. When we reached safety, I said, "Were you trying to tell me your apartment is bugged?"

"It's always best to be careful. You know, Tommy, you are being urged very strongly to move out of that funny place in San Angel. Aren't there any other apartments out there?"

"None," I said, holding open a heavy glass door. Above our heads an enormous neon sign buzzed like a hive. Beyond the glass door was total darkness, white shapes moving like ghostly fish in a tank. These proved to be waiters in white jackets, one of whom took our orders with that snotty obsequiousness that comes from having received too many tourist tips. *Pasodobles* played faintly, my eyes began to accustom themselves to the dark. Pat leaned on the table, smiling at me in an over-cocktails manner.

"And what did you learn today, Tommy?"

I told her what I had learned today. She prodded me with questions about the dinner-table conversation. "I had the impression he was in a flap," I said. "That he either had to consult someone, or get a better grip on himself."

"Impressions can be useful sometimes," Pat said, with no implication that this had been one of the times. She produced a white tube of a cigaret, and I lit it for her. The match flame was a startling violation of the darkness. "What were you able to learn alone with the daughter?"

When I said it was difficult to be alone with the daughter, she stared in disbelief, and the sensation of manipulation overcame me again. I said I would ask Aurelia to the bullfights on Sunday, and Pat frowned, drew on her cigaret, and sipped her Margarita. She was not pleased, I had not performed well enough.

"Herrerro seems sure we want Flores out of Santa Cruz," I said. "Has our policy been established on that?"

"I have no idea." A middle-aged tourist couple wandered in, the man in a Harry Truman sport shirt, the woman in slacks, and Pat frowned at them in disapproval.

I asked if a name existed for what I was.

"A stringer."

I laughed out loud, first at the connotations of the word, then at Pat's response to my laughter. I asked if there were a stringer attached to General Galindo.

"I wouldn't know."

"What about Rodolfo Cisneros?"

"That's not for you to ask me, or for me to ask anyone else," Pat said primly. She transferred her cigaret from the ashtray to her lips.

"I feel a credibility gap," I said. "Does Senator Herrerro know more about what we are up to than I do? If the United States is going to back an anti-Flores coup shouldn't I be told?"

"I'll ask about that," Pat said. She finished her drink. "Is that all? Can I go now?"

"But aren't you going to take me out to dinner? That's our cover, you know. That we're just a couple of ordinary Americans dating."

I had forgotten how expensive it was to entertain long-legged blond American girls for an evening on the town, a major item for the expense account. I drove home to San Angel very late, blasting 427 horses out an empty Insurgentes. I wound at speed up the winding lane to the Casa de la Fuente, the exhaust making a lovely, rocketing sound between the walls.

Headlights sprang at me and I tramped on the brakes; a chrome-gleaming grill topped by the Mercedes' trisected circle, a big limousine not a sports model. The blinding headlights gave no sign of retreating, so I backed into a driveway before a garage door.

The headlights followed me closely, blocking me. The blurred figure of a man appeared; I got out to face the dark shape across two hoods, a red wink on one of his hands: Mickey. Now I could make out that the Mercedes was empty.

"Did the Big Guy send you?" I asked, trying to grasp some initiative.

The ring winked, a match was struck, the sharp-featured, pockmarked face illuminated for a moment. I leaned against the Corvette's fender as Mickey flipped away his match in a tiny flaming arc. "I came on my own, Murdoch. We're both Americans, after all."

I was not touched by his sentiment.

"You're still messing in it," Mickey said. "You didn't learn anything up at the ranch."

"What was I supposed to learn?"

"He is one goddam hard motherfucker to get in the way of."

Hardmouthed rejoinders seemed called for, but none came to mind.

"You're getting in his way," Mickey went on. "I thought I ought to wise you up—you're getting in the way of something that just don't stop." He slapped his hand down on the hood, not hard. The small thunder was an effective bit of dramatization.

Mickey said, "There's only one guy that's ever going to do this thing everybody wants. If the sugar company wants a piece of Santa Cruz after the dust settles, you'd better get in touch with the Big Guy. I'll tell you something, Murdoch. He's too fucking proud to come talk to you."

"It's mutual," I said.

"It's what?"

"Would you mind getting this load of kraut sheet metal out of my way?"

"I'm trying to tell you something for your own good, for Christ's sake!"

I slapped my hand down on my hood harder than he had on his master's. "Get out of my way!"

"Very tough, Murdoch," he said, but he retreated into the limousine. The engine roared, the headlights snapped off into reddish afterglow, the parking lights came on as he backed away. As I eased the Corvette past him, he called to me, "So long, wise guy." We had seen the same movies in our youth.

(12) THURSDAY

I AWOKE late and set up the Olivetti and rattled off a report for Clipper Armstrong. American Ventures' man in Mexico City was also a U.S. agent now, but just a little his own man, too. I told the Clipper what I thought he ought to know, enclosed a note to Eloise, slipped the papers into a manila envelope, stuck on a strip of airmail stamps, and leaned from my window to post the envelope in the mailbox on the wall outside.

A scuffling of shoeleather on the patio bricks, a rattle at my gate and a voice called: "Hola, my partner Murdoch—here is Ibis!"

He entered, preceded by an outstretched hand, and followed by Gabriela, who looked doubtful. Ibis' red face wore a rubbery smile. "I have walked from my house to ride to tennis with you, my friend. My little car visits a mechanic."

I asked Gabriela to bring two beers. Hands on hips, Ibis surveyed the room. "I have been here before. Last year a patient of mine resides here, an American woman, very sick. She is sick inside a sick society, what can be done? And the artist Madame Gray lives in this place, does she not? A lovely lady and much talent, one understands."

He sat down with his hands spread on his knees, and

Gabriela returned with the beer. "Ah, you have pretty *muchacha*," he said. The thick lenses of his spectacles caught sunlight in distorted glints as he leaned forward to receive his glass. "This one fits much nicer in the bed than ugly Indian of my patient."

"I stay in my own bed, señor," Gabriela said.

"And speaks English well," Ibis said. "Ha! Ha!"

Gabriela brought me my beer. She wouldn't look at me, color burning in her cheeks.

"She has very pretty boy's figure, my friend," Ibis said, reestablishing his foot in his mouth.

Gabriela left the room. In the hallway, behind Ibis' back, she turned to flourish a fist.

"I am sorry," Ibis said. "It seems there was too much momentum to stop gracefully."

"Watch out for knives when you pass the kitchen."

"Ha! Ha! Very well, I blundered. Usually I am very good with women." He sipped beer, swiped at his upper lip, and made a business of polishing and adjusting his glasses. Finally he said, "We will play well today, friend Murdoch? Another defeat for the forces of the American embassy and an increase to our bank accounts? Tell me, what do you feel is the most important ingredient in this game tennis?"

"Faith," I said.

He stared at me with his big, square teeth wreathed by fat lips. It pleased me to have shocked him; usually it was the other way around. "You think *faith*? But how in tennis?"

"In everything."

"You think this?"

"I'm impressed by the Mexican faith in the Virgin and the revolution. The trouble with the rest of the world is lack of faith. We need a new America to sail off to, leaving the tired, cynical, old world—"

"You are making jokes with Doctor Ibis." He waggled a reproving finger. "My friend, faith is no good because faith is future and life is present. And revolutions are only opium of the people."

He laughed heartily at his cleverness in having retrieved the advantage. "No faith in nations, friend Murdoch. No."

"You reject my America?"

He looked suddenly serious. "No, my friend, I have not rejected your America. She has rejected me. When I was twenty-seven years of age—half my life ago—your country accepted me. America took me in with great hospitality, and I am grateful. But your America has changed—as you recognize when you joke that you wish to find a new one. America is now too powerful and too frightened, too impatient to have her way in everything. The America we have loved no longer exists, my friend."

"So you have no country and no faith," I said.

"Faith in one thing," Ibis said, and slapped a fat hand to his chest. "In this only! You know that society tries very hard to make all men the same. It is better for collective society that way, it is easier. Yet it is essential we have faith in man, the individual. Insist upon the individual! Absolutely, a man must be governed by reverence for these differences; that is the only thing that is holy. I tell you when we have at last a government of individuals, not selfish but wise!—then we will have lawfulness without laws. Which is freedom!"

I raised my beer in a toast to his words.

Driving into Mexico City in the Corvette, he was inclined to patronize my car and my driving, but he did finger the chrome and leather cockpit goodies around him, saying grudgingly, "They do these things not badly in Detroit." Then he asked, "And where is your pretty *muchacha* from, friend Murdoch?"

I didn't know; "Maybe from Cuautla."

"You think Cuautla? I would have said Tampico." The brim of his hat was flattened back by the wind of our passage, and he had put on his sunglasses. The Sears Roebuck complex on the right seemed to throw him into an anti-American mood again. "Too big. Too powerful," he muttered. "You know, my friend, the normal manner in which nations deal with one another is called diplomacy. One wishes something from another, it gives up something in exchange. A very wealthy nation gives up only money. You have seen this in your America? But the too-powerful nation becomes impatient when it cannot buy. Then it begins to threaten. Then comes force. To rationalize the use of force there is always the danger of communists."

"What rationalization do communists use?"

"For communists there is the rationalization of the danger of revisionists," Ibis said, and laughed inordinately. Then he said, "You are a good, loyal American, friend Murdoch."

"With faith, a conscience, and a country."

"These are difficult times, yes," Ibis said. "Do you know that it has been said one is loyal to one's country because it represents all the good things to eat one had in one's boyhood? In Vienna were many, many good things to eat in my boyhood, yet it was not difficult for me to give up my country. If I had not I would have died in Buchenwald."

Smog smarted in my eyes as I gunned away from a stop signal. I was suddenly, desperately homesick for my country, my California, my Los Angeles, for the hamburgers and milk shakes, Cokes and tamales and pizzas of my youth. Perhaps it had not been as sophisticated a menu as the Viennese, but the mnemonics were potent. And I was homesick for my wife, for her hand on my leg as we drove out to the beach on a spring day with the jacarandas in flower and minor smog. At the beach everyone was young, golden and beautiful, as my wife and I, America and Americans, were golden and beautiful; as America was my country, right or wrong. But she had to be right, didn't she? In the other countries the people were small and dark and poor, always in trouble and always demanding.

I turned out Reforma past the monument to Cuhua-temoc, whose feet the conquistadores had burned using force in their impatience, and drove on out to the tennis courts at Chapultepec. Frank and Herb were already there.

Frank warmed up with Ibis while I waited for Herb, who was prone to blisters, to adjust his several layers of socks. I said, "Aurelia's husband was executed as a traitor in the army, according to Herrerro."

"He was involved in what's called 'the colonels' plot' against the Protector," Herb said. "They were all murdered when it failed. Valásquez had been a good loyal *Protectorista* until that ill-advised venture. They were tortured horribly."

"Miserable goddam place," I said.

It was not to be a day of defeat for the forces of the American embassy. Frank Timken was all over the court on his long legs, giving Ibis a hard time, and me, too, for my concentration was off. Frank was overbearing, with his thin-lipped grin, and Ibis a very bad loser—worse and worse as the rout worsened and I overruled his line calls. Once he said to me, "I tell you something, my partner, what you have is no faith."

Fatso was still sulking when we had showered and dressed, and went out to the parking lot. Angled over the steering wheel was a sheet of paper, a note signed "Pat"—"Can we talk? I'll be walking around the block."

I put Ibis, offended and frigid, into a taxi, and circled

the block. When I saw her walking toward me, I let
the Corvette lug, not hurrying to meet her, because in
her pale blue sweater and skirt she looked like the
fondly remembered southern California girls of my fit
of homesickness this morning, like Eloise ten years and
fifteen pounds ago. It amused me that this was the
shape of duty summoning me to my country's welfare
and defense.

She waved in classic style as I approached. When she
got in she kissed me on the cheek. She put her hands to
her hair as I accelerated. I was proud to have her beside
me, with the natives staring at the Corvette and her
blond beauty as we passed them. Hands to her hair and
her breasts brought into prominence, she said, "It's so
much fun being blond down here," which gave my
pleasure in seeing her its first setback. "Let's go sit in
the park and talk," she said.

Parked near a lake, in dappled shade, she said,
"About your request for more briefing. Negative."

"Negative?"

"Negative."

My response to my case officer, as it came through
our cutout, was also negative.

"Tell me something, Pat. Does our C.O. sit in a kind
of web with little threads like you reaching out to a
great many baffled stringers like me? And each of us
knows only a little , while he knows all?"

"Something like that," Pat said, producing a cigaret
for me to light for her. "Now, Tommy: are you able to
commit the Compañía Azucarera to support Senator
Herrerro to coordinate the émigré movements against
Flores—if *we* will also agree to support him?"

"I think so."

"Then listen carefully. You are to go to Herrerro and
tell him that if he will undertake to bring together
under his leadership all the movements in opposition to

the present regime—that he will have very important support."

"But unspecified support?"

"The sugar company to be specified, anything else only implied."

"But just between you and me—*we* are committing ourselves to backing a movement against Flores?"

"Tommy, you must listen carefully. All you can promise Herrerro is *very* important support if he will bring the movements together. He will also have support as a future presidential candidate, but we commit ourselves to nothing more than that. Actually we are committing ourselves to helping the sugar company help Herrerro."

"And he has to make his own deals with Galindo, and—"

"Galindo no longer enters the equation."

"Why not?"

She paused a moment. "Well, he's dead."

A heaviness beat behind my eyes. Something that just don't stop, Mickey had said of the Big Guy. But U.S. policy was now committed to the support of Herrerro. It was what I had wanted, wasn't it? I had won, hadn't I? But what had seemed a perfectly legitimate piece of self-interest on the part of American Ventures did not seem so legitimate on the part of the United States of America.

And Pat said, "Now, about Rodolfo Cisneros. He is illegitimate, but his mother was a Cruceño woman of quite good family and we think an effort will be made to prove that just before he died the Protector intended to introduce legislation to make the boy his heir. We think there is a possibility Cisneros might be used as a figurehead for a combined movement against Flores. On the basis that he was the favorite son. Do you feel you can take this matter up with Herrerro?"

"No," I said. I sat watching her fingers fiddling with the hem of her skirt, where it lay half-covering the tender golden flesh of the inside of her knee. I was having the sensation of a carefully constructed edifice, just finished, with its cupola on and flag flying, collapsing into splinters before my eyes. I found I was a little short of breath. "Pat," I said. "I just have to get this one thing straight. Isn't it against the rules for OAS member nations to try to overthrow the governments of other member nations? Isn't that what they're trying to get Castro for?"

"Tommy, all we know is that this particular operation is trying to bring all the émigré movements under one leader. Then we can penetrate the movement and even control it. So if it does succeed we will have a better chance of friendly relations with the Republic. Et cetera. Or we might be setting Herrerro up just to knock him down for the PR splash of supporting a man with a more liberal record later on. I don't have any idea of the whole picture. It's not our place to make policies."

Think about not doing the first thing, Jenny had said. Pat asked when I would be seeing Herrerro. "On Sunday. I'll be going there on Sunday."

"Now, Tommy, you are to talk to the daughter alone. She is very important. Find out what she knows about the movements, what her attitudes are. We know she is very loyal to her father, but she also has a very strong anti-*Protectorista* record. We want to know what we can expect of her."

"I'll see her on Sunday," I said. I was in a hurry now to phone Clipper Armstrong on the green phone, and as soon as I had let Pat off at the embassy I had the call put through by the Hilton's English-speaking operator.

"Armstrong here," the Clipper's voice said. "Tommy-boy!" he said with warmth. "Sock it to me."

"There's a report in the mail, but this has just popped." Before I had finished telling him what had popped, I heard his big, admiring chuckle. He said something in an aside and Ellie's voice came on, familiar and beloved, soft with the soft rasp to it like an instant echo.

"Tommy, I miss you so! Are you doing just wonderful things?"

And the Clipper chimed in: "I knew you'd manage to work it out the way you wanted it. That's very cute getting Uncle to carry the ball for you. Herrerro's your baby, huh?"

"Yes," I said. There was a curious double silence from Bel Air whenever there was a pause, an intensification of dead air. I said, "Can I speak for American Ventures and the Compañía Azucarera?"

"You might be speaking for Ferrocarriles de Santa Cruz, too," Clipper said. "There's a group out from New York trying to peddle the railroad. They may get to me." I took the receiver from my ear so the sound of his laughter wouldn't fill my head.

"Galindo's dead," I said.

"I heard that. I got a call from that hairoil major. Turned over in his jeep, something like that. Here, I'll get off the wire and let you kids talk."

"You haven't found any Mexican girls down there you like better than me, have you, darling?" Eloise said.

"I've been thinking about you in your white golfcart."

"I haven't played golf in days!"

"I've been thinking about your bottom when you swing one of those new woods. I'm missing you."

"Well, that's good, isn't it? We're missing you, too, Tommy. I—"

"That's the trouble with this language," I said. "You can't tell singular from plural in the second person. I've been missing you singular and in bed, too."

"Oh, *Tommy!*" she said, but she was pleased. She was pleased because the Clipper was pleased, and so I was gratified. It seemed a simple mechanism. Clipper came on again.

"You want some of that Ferrocarriles stock, Tommy? I think I can get it for about three cents a share."

"I don't think so," I said. I felt suddenly and strongly that I wanted nothing to do with Ferrocarriles de Santa Cruz. There was the double buzzing silence, the double pressure of Clipper Armstrong offended. "I seem to be building a portfolio of country club memberships," I said, and heard myself laughing phonily.

(13) SUNDAY

I WAS viewed by the dark lens, the mechanical voice said, "*Pase, señor,*" inside the wall a breeze riffled the feathers of the pepper tree. Herrerro came down off the porch, grunting with the height of the step. His face was wreathed in concentric monkey grins, and my heart did not leap up to see him—leader of the émigré groups, strongman, presidential candidate.

"Come in, come in, Señor Moordoak! Aurelia is here! *Aurelia!*" he called in the piping, singing tone, and she appeared on the porch all in white, color of purity. Her father guided me to her, a hand patting me encouragingly.

When the three of us stood together, I said, "Senator Herrerro, I have an important message for you."

His clownishness vanished. His mouth stiffened, his yellow eyes bulged and stared like a Pekinese. "And what is this message, señor?"

Aurelia stood rigidly by with her hands clasped at her waist as I said, "That you will have very important support if you will bring the Cruceño exiles together into one movement."

"And what support is that, señor, that is so important?"

"The Compañía Azucarera. But other support also."

He stared at me. He seemed to swell, for a moment

he looked almost a man. He also looked terrified. He laid a finger alongside his nose and said, "How can one refuse the support of eagles?"

"*No! Papá, no!*" Aurelia cried in a voice that rasped on my nerves like fingernails on a blackboard.

"*¿Porqué no?*" he said to her. "I am the right man, Aurelia! I have been chosen well, señor!" he said to me. The Dark Angel looked as though she would faint.

"So," Herrerro said. "What must I do to say yes I will do this thing?"

"I will give your answer. That you can bring the émigré groups together under your leadership."

He executed a dancing step of delight. "Yes! You will say that Anastasio Herrerro is the man who can do this! These many peoples—I know them well! All! I have known them always! You do not come here to dinner today, then, señor? You return with my answer?"

I exhibited two red, white, and green bullfight tickets. "I hope Aurelia will come with me to the Plaza Mexico this afternoon."

Aurelia stood stunned, tugging a handkerchief between her hands. She shook her head once, dumbly, as Herrerro said, "But of course! Aurelia will come with you to the bulls." He patted her arm. "You will go with our good friend, eh, my daughter?"

The Dark Angel said she would get ready, excused herself, and disappeared inside. Herrerro clutched my arm. "It is so strong emotion that we go back to our home," he said. "Come! We drink a *copa* to the end of Paco *el gusano!*" He led me through the maze of furniture to a sideboard, where he poured heavy slugs of Fundador. He shouted, "To the Republic!"

After an interminable time, Aurelia reappeared in a long white tiered skirt, a fine white rebozo covering her shoulders, a white rose in her hair. Her face was lifeless. Herrerro ushered us out. I was feeling an ashamed relief at this respite from the tower duty.

A lobster dinner at El Conquistador was a hideously expensive flop, with my Angel as stolid and silent as the wooden nymph with the lightbulb on her head. I labored an idiot monologue on the way to the bullring.

I had heard the admiring whistling when a beautiful woman made her way down through the stands of the enormous Plaza Mexico. Often it was a blonde who set it off; as Pat Hepner had said, it was fun being a blonde down here. I had heard the storm of whistles sitting in the sun with Ibis when the expensive beauties entered on the other side of the ring. Now, on the shady side with the Dark Angel of Santa Cruz, I was in the eye of the hurricane. The whistling was deafening as we descended the steep steps, Aurelia ahead of me. At first I was horrified, then I was proud watching her in her pride, her head coming higher, her back stiffening. Once she looked back over her shoulder in the melting glance I was not to see today in the tower, and there was a tinge of rose in her cheek. We sat ringside on pillows a vendor scampered to provide, not far from one of the television cameras.

When the whistling had subsided, I said, "You made quite an entrance."

"Pardon?"

I had to think to rephrase it. "You are very popular here in Plaza Mexico."

"Yes."

"Do you like it?"

"It is compliment. Sometimes they make this for me in Santa Cruz."

"You are very beautiful," I said.

She thanked me.

When I took my foot off the throttle the conversation died. Vendors approached with offerings, and Aurelia accepted a Coke and some peanuts. We watched the great bowl in multitudinous motion as it filled.

The first bull was killed immediately in front of us. The sword thrust was through the lung, and blood streamed from the bull's black muzzle and blew in bubbles when he panted. Soon gay braid and bright pantaloons were stained as the matador's assistants turned the bull with their capes, turned him and turned him in the effort to make the embedded sword sever something vital, so the suffering animal would die. And the suffering matador brought his arm down, time and again, in the signal, the command, the prayer to death. But the bull lived, and panted blood, and scarlet blood streamed across his flanks and down his legs.

At last the animal lay down with legs tucked beneath him and head raised, in a heart-wrenching, sleep-now position, while the daggerman slipped around behind him and drove home the knife that cut the spinal cord and turned him in one spasm into dead meat.

Aurelia had turned to face me. She had put on sunglasses. In a steady voice, she said, "It is like Santa Cruz with the Protector."

I apologized for a bad start to the day. The dead animal was hooked to a team of mules and dragged away. Peons flung shovelfuls of sand from a wheelbarrow. Aurelia remained staring at me.

"Do you know they have kill my 'usband like this? Only for pleasure. They have kill him a long time like this, for their pleasure. After it I do not want to hear, but I have hear."

"Do you want me to take you away?"

"If you will take me away from this place I will be glad. Surely man is not meant by God to have pleasure in death."

The whistling when we had come in was a zephyr compared to the catcalls and shouted comments as we fled the bullring. In light traffic I drove Aurelia to San Angel, and up the curving lane to the Casa de la Fuente while she silently daubed at her eyes with a wadded handkerchief.

Two honks in the alley, an impatient wait, and Gabriela swung open the garage door. A twist of the wheel and the Corvette was inside. Aurelia leaned on my arm like a faint Victorian lady as I guided her across the patio, where Pedro preened on his bar and Pepita peered out from the shadows of the pomegranate tree. I told Gabriela to borrow a couple of Cokes. Now, I knew, Aurelia Velásquez was going to tell me about her husband, her father, the Cruceño émigré groups, and all that Pat Hepner wanted to know.

I seated her on the couch and she wiped away her tears and regained her self-possession. Now she tended to be coy, as though it was extremely daring that she was alone with a man in his apartment. Gabriela speedily reappeared with Cokes in tall glasses.

"Señorita, Coca-Cola," she said, presenting one glass to Aurelia. "And Cuba Libre for the señor." It was not a drink I liked.

"I'm sorry about the bullfight," I said, when Gabriela had gone. "Why didn't you say you didn't like them?"

"My papá want me to go with you." Her superhuman amber eyes gazed into mine. "Why do United States do this, Tomás? Compañía Azucarera I understand, but United States—why?"

As soon as I began to explain the importance of the émigré groups combining, she closed her eyes and shook her head. It was not what she had meant, and I had known it was not.

"Santa Cruz is democracy now," she said. "Is it not what United States has wanted? It is said United States has made the movement to kill *El Protector* so Santa

Cruz can be democracy like United States. Why it do this now?"

I said, "It has only been decided that your father will have support if he will bring the émigrés together to—" It rang as false in my ears as it must to Aurelia's, who wasn't listening anyway, something in her face blunted and inattentive as though from generations of listening to hairsplittings and lies.

"Tell me, Tomás, do people of United States not know of *El Protector*? The—how do you say—the second president of United States has come to Santa Cruz and there is photograph in newspaper of *abrazo* of these two men. I tell you, Tomás, people of United States should kill this second president for this terrible thing he does, this *abrazo*. Do people of United States not know *El Protector* is truly monster, this man who have young son kill men for pleasure? This monster has for himself one school of very young girls. This convent school, he thinks this very funny, these little girls in—" She fumbled for words, making motions of head scarves, veils; nuns, I thought. But she said, "*Comunión.* Little girls in *comunión* dresses to do him pleasure. How do your second president *abrazar* such a man? And Tomás, how will now your country send other monsters to my island to kill and kill and kill, like *El Protector* again, and the little, little girls in *comunión* dresses!"

I brushed at the sweat on my forehead. "But that's all past. Your father is to try to take power by—"

"Rodolfo Cisneros will take the power!" she cried. "There is Papá, and Galindo with his *soldados*, and Jorge Vian, but they do no matter. Rodolfo will take the power!" Her head swayed from side to side, she made a sound of anguish. "I do not know *Inglés* to speak so much," she whispered. "But this can not be!"

"But Flores is a red," I said.

She shook her head wearily. "It is why the United

States does this? They will have the red of so much
blood and not the red of *comunistas?* For Rodolfo
Cisneros will be *el máximo líder* and there will be much
blood. Rodolfo is favorite son of *El Protector* and *El
Protector* makes him play to kill men as men kill bulls.
Rodolfo kills and *El Protector* watch and laugh to see
this young boy kill men."

She was talking about her husband, and her eyes
were the eyes of an El Greco saint turned toward
heaven. "*Por favor, Madre de Dios, no!*" she crooned.
"Tomás, you must go to these ones of the *embajada
norteamericana* and tell them very strong that Paco
Flores is not red, and that *Protectoristas* must not go
back to Santa Cruz. Never! Never! Never!

"And your sugar will taste of blood, Tomás," she
said. Her body began to rock with her grief and her
protest. "No, no, no, no, no, no, no, my papá!" Finally
she rose and said it was time for me to take her back to
Lomas.

In the patio we encountered Jenny, and I made introductions but Aurelia was haughty and cold. In front
of Herrerro's house were a number of black limousines
like resting beetles, Cadillacs, Continentals, an Impe-
rial, a Mercedes. When Aurelia had disappeared
through the gate, I sucked in a deep breath as though I
had just come up from a long time underwater, and I
spun my wheels getting started back to San Angel. This
time Gabriela didn't open the garage when I honked.

"That's the most beautiful woman in the hemisphere, Murdoch," Jenny said, when she answered my
knock at her gate. "Is there any way I could get her to
pose for me?"

I said I had to see Finch, and she led me inside. He
rose from his chair and she padded out of the room on
her small bare feet.

"I need advice," I said.

"Sit down, please, Tom," he said, regarding me mildly over his half-frame glasses. I had come to him for advice because he had recruited me, and working for my country was different from working for Clipper Armstrong.

"I know you don't want to know anything more about the operation I was recruited for than is absolutely necessary," I said. "So I'll speak in general terms. It appears to me that I am helping to set up an invasion. To replace a democratically elected regime with a right-wing dictatorship. I realize that I am seeing only a small piece of the action," I said. "And that I may have a mistaken view for that reason."

Finch removed his glasses and spun them in an arc around one earpiece. "I think you can accept the statement that what you see from your particular position may not be the course our policy is following at all. Intelligence must plan far ahead in order to be in the right place at the right time. In other words, if a movement is starting and will not come to fruition for several years, we must act immediately. Later on, if the penetration comes to be of vital importance, it may be too late to effect it. Consequently there is a constant flurry of placing people in situations where probably nothing will ensue. Do you follow me?"

I nodded, and he continued in his dry, professorial voice, tapping his glasses on his wrist from time to time to emphasize a point. "Now in a situation such as you describe, I suspect that the major decisions are a long way off."

"Who makes the final decisions?"

"They are made at a very high level."

"How high?"

"High enough to be outside intelligence, as is proper." There was a heavy pause, he sighed and said,

"In the end it all depends on whether or not one believes our government is acting in our best interests."

"What if it comes at you that that might not be the case?"

Finch looked at me with his tired eyes. He said in a tired, gentle voice, "An abyss exists, tens of thousands of feet deep. To explore it, one must make up his mind to explore it all the way. I confess that such a prospect is too much for me. Perhaps all one can do is one's own small part, and hope for the best."

"Have faith, you mean."

"I suppose that is exactly what I mean," said John Doane Finch.

When I returned to my apartment there was still no sign of Gabriela. I poured a heavy jolt of bourbon and wandered around the apartment grumbling about the servants. I had the schizophrenic sensation of watching Tom Murdoch pace the room with a drink in his hand, occupying his mind by fuming over an A.W.O.L. maid instead of coming to grips with an issue of blood and tragedy, right and wrong; who could fool himself so easily, and, when he couldn't, ran to John Doane Finch for reassurance, but could not face honest Jenny Gray.

On the dining table I found a folded sheet of paper with my name on it, a note from Ibis:

I have seen you and this most beautiful black angel at Plaza Mexico. I whistled very hard! But you have left too soon, my friend. I come to your house to tell you that you have missed most beautiful brave bulls of the season, even if first one is slaughtered so badly. Your black woman has weak stomach? I take liberty to leave note for you here as I cannot find your pretty muchacha from Cuautla. Ibis.

I found Pepita doing laundry. Someone had come for Gabriela, and she had gone away with him. Yes, a man. No, she did not think he was Gabriela's *novio;* just a man. She hadn't actually seen Gabriela go away with this man, but she had not seen her since. Languidly, Pepita took the tightly wrung garments from her galvanized pail and hung them on the clothesline.

I had my second drink in hand when the phone rang and it was Pat Hepner. "Hello, Tommy. What kind of an answer do you have for me?"

"He says he can do it," I said, and a date was made to meet in the embassy cafeteria in the morning for a chat.

That night I dreamed I was trapped on a platform hanging over an abyss thousands of feet deep which I had no wish to explore. I protested that I only wanted to be part of the busy and thoughtless flux of life I could see on either bank, but I remained marooned and embarrassingly prominent and visible. I longed to be with the others in their anonymity where my opinions didn't show and didn't matter anyway because there was nothing I could do about them, and where, if a man wore certain clothes and his hair a certain length and drove a certain kind of car, it was obvious that he lived a certain kind of life, and the police would never bother him.

But I was hassled and badgered into court by men who didn't seem to have any detail to them. The judge was Eloise, and I babbled piteously that I was working as hard as I could, fingers to the bone, nose to the grindstone, ass off, for hearth and home, wife and future, the Rams and the Dodgers, Trojans and Bruins, but I could see it wasn't enough, her face was merciless. Her voice boomed with the familiar catch to it like something blurred in the printing, roaring like a whirlwind in the great, packed hall, my sentence. I couldn't comprehend what the sentence was, and I woke up sweating.

(14) MONDAY, I

ON the lower level of the embassy I walked past rooms where Mexicans in worn clean clothing and hats in hand waited for work permits or visas, and passed along a glass-walled corridor that looked onto a central patio and pool. Pat was waiting alone at a formica table in the cafeteria, with shining hair and bare brown arms. I was glad to see her; patriotism was not merely the good things you had eaten in your youth, but the golden girls you had dated.

"Good morning, Tommy! I'll get your coffee. Cream and sugar?"

"Black, please," I said, and sat watching her tacking between the empty tables toward the coffeepot brooding on its cherry-red warmer. When she returned, smiling, with my coffee, we sat with our heads together.

"Your maid's been picked up," she said.

"*What?*"

She leaned back to disengage herself as two crewcut men in dark suits entered, each with a hand in a coat pocket, the first holding the door for the second. "Hello, Pat."

She presented gleaming teeth. "Hello, Hal! Hello, Don!"

They sat at a table across the room. Pat turned back to me. "*Who* picked her up?" I said.

"The police. She's a Cuban spy. Do you see why we wanted you to move away from Mr. Finch?"

"She was planted as my maid to spy on Finch?"

"Well, I would assume so, wouldn't you?"

Too many items had clicked into focus for me not to assume so. I asked how they had known Gabriela was a spy, and Pat said, "We've had a report from the Mexican Security Police. She is Gabriela Bazán." When this brought no response, she added, "She's the wife of El Chato Villaneuve."

"The *wife!*"

"Oh, probably common-law wife, I don't suppose those people bother to get married really. And from what we understand there would be no point in El Chato marrying anyway." She colored, her face took on an expression that was half-smug and half-embarrassed; it seemed to me that the clutch of my mind must be slipping.

"I don't know what the hell you're talking about, Pat."

"He's not really a *man*, I mean. The SIM tortured so many of that first bunch of Castroites they captured at the Moncada Barracks."

"What's the SIM?"

"They were Batista's secret police," Pat said, sighing at my ignorance.

I did not like to think of the police with Gabriela, who might be a spy and the wife of a spy, but was as real as salt or sunlight. She had asked if the police in my country needed a reason for hitting you, and she had brought me a Cuba Libre.

"I've been penetrated," I said.

"It was because of the possibility of something like

this that we asked you to find another apartment," Pat
said. She sipped her coffee. "But of course the *Seguridad* was very glad to get hold of her. They're sure she
and El Chato are behind the riots at the university.
They are very expert at manipulating student groups.
Everyone would love to catch *him*."

"Will they put her in prison, or deport her?"

"I have no idea," Pat said, pursing her lips with disapproval. "I'm sure you see the necessity for moving
now," she said.

"Negative," I said. "But I'll let you find me a safe
new maid."

"We are not an employment agency, Tommy."

"I talked with the daughter of Herrerro as per your
instructions. She says the *Protectoristas* are bloody
monsters. The United States will be supporting murderers and rapists-of-little-girls, and the sugar will taste
of blood."

"So she is fanatically anti-*Protectorista*," Pat said.
"How did Herrerro act?" I sat for a considerable interrogation on what Herrerro had said, until Pat was
satisfied she had it word for word. Then the question-
ing about my afternoon with the Dark Angel began.
On this I was more vague, Pat less satisfied. When we
left the cafeteria we walked along the glass-walled corridor together, two expatriate Americans on a casual
coffee date. Pat stopped at the bottom of the stairs,
where double glass doors opened on the patio. Visible
were the patient lines of Mexican peasants waiting out
the red tape.

"Do you know why we have to keep these doors
locked?"

I didn't know.

"Once one of the men waiting to apply for the
bracero program brought his wife along, and *she*

brought her laundry. Before anyone noticed, she'd done her washing in the pool and spread it out in the patio to dry. Isn't that fan*tas*tic?"

I mashed my features into a grin of appreciation. "How many get in?" I nodded toward the waiting lines of men.

"I think it runs about ten percent. We're very strict."

Back at the Casa de la Fuente, I opened the garage door and parked the Corvette. Crossing the patio, I caught sight of Pepita's lorn, pig-tailed figure carrying a bucket. In the kitchen Gabriela's copy of *Vanidades* still lay on the zinc-topped table. I dropped it into the trash.

The phone rang. When I answered it, the wire seemed empty, and premonitory feathers brushed the back of my neck. "Tomás?" It was Aurelia's voice. "Tomás, you must come to help."

"What's the matter?"

"Please," she said. "I am so glad if you will come, Tomás."

I braked to a halt in the shade of the tall fence. The gate hung inches ajar. Inside, the deep shade of the trees made complex patterns on the lava walks and the flowerbeds. I ran up onto the red concrete porch and jerked to a stop with a hand braced against a corner of the wall. Half in the sun, on the concrete, lay a shape covered with newspapers that had been thickly spread to hide all but one black-shod foot.

"*Aurelia!*" I called, and immediately she appeared, tall in a black dress.

"My papá is dead," she said, indicating the newspaper-covered form that seemed too small to be a man. The single black shoe was polished to a high gloss.

When I asked how he had died she made a gun of her hand. When I asked who had shot him she shook her head from side to side. "Please do not ask me this, Tomás." She stood gazing at me calmly while the wind whispered in the treetops. "You will please tell me what I must do," she said. "Julio is no good to do anything."

I saw behind her the big, flat-faced chauffeur with arms folded over his liveried chest. He gave me a bow of greeting. Flies circled and crawled under an edge of newspaper covering the body of Senator Herrerro, who had not succeeded in combining the Cruceño émigré groups.

"I'll call the Americans first," I told Aurelia. The telephone was in an alcove beneath the tower stairs. I dialed the embassy number; Miss Hepner was out to lunch. I identified myself to the colorless male voice that answered the emergency number, explained the situation, and asked for help. When I returned to the porch, Aurelia was alone, reclining in a lounge chair, head back and arms stretched along the chair's arms, nostrils flaring as she breathed.

I sat beside her. The spice of the pepper tree grew stronger than her flower perfume as the breeze rippled and turned the leaves of the trees. Across the porch, before another chair, a little pile of torn-apart paper matches was scattered. I sat looking at them and counting the dead: Chuy, Galindo, Herrerro.

"Did Cisneros kill him, Aurelia?"

"Please, Tomás."

"But Cisneros was here."

"Yes, Tomás."

The chauffeur reappeared with a Coca-Cola for her. Dark, fat drops of liquid spilled down her dress as she brought the glass to her lips. The wind whispered in the trees and one of the newspapers became airborne, and collapsed on the lee side of Herrerro's body.

"*Ay!*" Aurelia whispered.

We sat watching the corners of the newspapers rip-
pling and flicking. Another sheet moved, slid a few
inches and stopped, finally progressed to join the first.
A third sheet began to go.

"Julio!" Aurelia breathed.

The chauffeur, treading as though in deep sand, went
to replace the sheets of newsprint. As soon as he had
retreated they blew off again. In successive gusts of
wind others were blown scraping across the porch to
plaster themselves against the side of the house. A
black-sleeved arm was exposed.

Most of Herrerro's side was uncovered when I heard
brisk footsteps on the lava path. Two tall men wearing
hats and sunglasses appeared. The first, a Mexican,
jumped up on the porch and thrust aside the newspapers that still covered Herrerro's face. The other was
Frank Timken.

Frank nodded to me bruskly, nodded to Aurelia. I
did not feel a need for introductions. It came as no
surprise to realize that Frank was my case officer.

Aurelia said, "Please, I go in, Tomás." I helped her
up. The chauffeur, who had been sitting in an attitude
of despair just inside, jerked to his feet as we passed
him. Aurelia collapsed on the settee.

The Mexican entered with Frank a step behind, the
two of them simultaneously removing hats and glasses.
The Mexican had a thin, small-moustached face with a
deep line bisecting the forehead, as though it could be
halved like a peach. He ignored me.

I was unable to follow the interrogation, but Frank
seemed perfectly at home in Spanish, and from time to
time made queries or comments to the Mexican, whom
he addressed as *"Capitán."* I had the impression Frank
both deferred to him and patronized him.

Each question to the chauffeur rattled him like a
knife thrown at his head. Aurelia's responses came after

long pauses, as though she were thinking carefully, or inattentive in her grief, and each time I felt that the Captain, in his impatience, was on the verge of speaking to her sharply. But finally she would answer, usually in monosyllables, though several times she repeated the words, *"amigo de Santa Cruz."* I heard the name "Rodolfo Cisneros"; she was reciting a list of names, which Frank jotted down in a small brown notebook.

There was some back and forth about people named Maria and Zozo, Aurelia shaking her head while the chauffeur seemed affirmative. Finally I understood that the Captain was asking Aurelia about relatives and friends, and she was saying, *"No hay,"* no relatives, *"No hay,"* no friends. She had no one to go to, sitting slumped on the couch but proud-headed, nostrils flaring. I couldn't understand why she was protecting Cisneros.

When the Captain desisted to light a cigaret, I beckoned Frank out into the hall with me. Standing beneath the wooden nymph, I told him that Aurelia could come to the Casa de la Fuente if she had no place else to go. The studio apartment was still empty.

Frank frowned at me with his anxious shark's eyes, brushing a hand over his crewcut. He wore a dark suit with a vest. "That might not be a bad idea, Murdoch."

"Who are Maria and Zozo?"

"That's the maid and the other chauffeur, they're missing. Pat told you about that Cuban *muchacha* of yours? What we think happened, we think Chato got onto what was going on over here through Bazán at your place. I see Bazán and Chato in this, and I think Rafael does too."

It seemed incredibly far-fetched. "I thought they had Gabriela Bazán in custody," I said.

"That's right."

"How is she supposed to have done this if she was in jail?"

"I don't mean she pulled the trigger," Frank said. "Probably that was Zozo. That's not my problem. It's the big machinery that counts here."

I thought I would not bring up the matter of Cisneros until I'd had a chance to talk to Aurelia. I asked what she had meant by *"amigo de Santa Cruz."*

"All she'll say is it was a friend of Santa Cruz that shot him."

Capitán Rafael Leal of the Federal Security Police strode out into the hall and shook my hand with a grip like a pipe wrench. The Captain agreed it would be a good idea if I removed Aurelia to San Angel, I arranged it with the Dark Angel, and we were gone. Driving down Reforma toward the park she began to cry, a lonely, rusty sound. I put an arm around her and she leaned against me, sobbing. I made one stop, to pick up a case of Coca-Cola; I hoped that Jenny would be at home.

She was. At first she overplayed the role of sympathetic neighbor, and Aurelia retreated into hauteur, but presently each of them relaxed. Jenny was determined to get Aurelia's mind off her sorrow, and the friendship was sealed when Jenny asked if she could sketch Aurelia. Then a strong strain of vanity appeared in the Dark Angel of Santa Cruz, and there was a great deal of hairbrushing and primping before the mirror, while Jenny went for her sketchpad. "I like very much your *amiga*, Tomás," Aurelia said.

"She likes you."

She continued to brush her hair, presenting one profile to the mirror and then the other. "They are so *estúpidos*," she whispered. "So many questions of Zozo and Maria. Are they *comunistas*? Who they see when they not at work? They think they are *comunistas* and have kill my papá and run away. Zozo and Maria run away because they are frighten because my papá is kill. Tomás, why do always, always, *norteamericanos* live inside a box with a hole and all that can be seen through this hole is *comunistas?* You also, Tomás."

"What else did they want to know?" I asked.

"Who has come to meeting of El Tres de Julio Movement. Do you know what means El Tres de Julio for Republic of Santa Cruz? It is day the Protector is *asesinado.*"

Ibis had said the son would conquer not in the name of freedom but in the name of the murdered tyrant who was now holy, and Pat had said the movement might capitalize on the magic of the Protector's name. "What about Rodolfo Cisneros?" I said.

"Ah, my papá and Rodolfo have big *abrazo!*" she said in a bitter voice. "*Camaradas!* They fight together! ¡A *la lucha!* They will return *camaradas* to Santa Cruz *en gran triunfo!* Yes! There is very big *abrazo* between my papá and Rodolfo."

I remembered her anger when she had spoken of the *abrazo* of the Vice President of the United States and the Protector—"people of the United States should kill this man!" And she had said with scorn that North Americans lived in a box with a hole in it, and all they could see through the hole were communists. All I had been seeing through the hole in my box was Rodolfo Cisneros.

"Did you kill your father, Aurelia?" I said.

Her eyes met mine in the mirror, white-rimmed. Her eyes slid aside, and I turned to see Jenny just inside the room, sketch pad in her hand.

"Police do not know this, Tomás," Aurelia said.

"No."

"And so you know this also," Aurelia said to Jenny. "Please, do not speak to police."

Jenny shook her head silently, hugging her pad to her breast.

"For maybe I am not finish yet," Aurelia said.

I retreated and sat down, and Jenny seated herself at the table, arranging her pad and charcoal with finicking care. Aurelia turned from the mirror to face us. "You are my friends," she said. "It is very hard to have no one for *confianza*."

My mind had not moved ahead much. I blurted: "And so now you must go to the Basilica of Guadalupe on your knees."

Aurelia hissed like a frightened cat: "What is this?" When I explained that I had seen her there before I had met her, she cried, "You do not understand! Not for this, Tomás."

Jenny was sketching with swift strokes of her stick of charcoal. Her face was stiff with shock. Aurelia took a step toward me. "The *Virgen* of Guadalupe, she see and understand all!" She raised her hands to cup her dark face. "Tomás, it is terrible day when you tell my papá United States and the Compañía will help him go back to Santa Cruz and kill Paco Flores."

Jenny's eyes flashed up at me. I protested, but Aurelia cut me off with a slashing movement of her hand.

"To kill!" she said fiercely. "To kill and kill! Do not deny! So the *Virgen* of Guadalupe understand why Aurelia Velásquez must do this. All things I have done for my papá! All he ask that I do; all! But this my country ask. The Republic!"

I sat impaled on Aurelia's *Do not deny!* "Was your father so bad?" I asked. "I thought—he wasn't."

"Yes, bad, Tomás." She seated herself on the couch, in profile to Jenny. She said, "*Norteamericanos* can not know how it has been in Santa Cruz with the Protector. In province of Los Pinos where is our *finca*, it must be that no *pobrecita* girl is marry until my papá make

love to her first. I do not see this, but I am told. And
many many killing. I do not see, but I know. I am told
these thing and I do not wish to believe, but I must
believe. Can you understand, *norteamericanos*, how
one can know these bad thing and also love her papá?"
I watched Jenny nod jerkily.

"Can you understand another thing?" Aurelia continued. "How it can not be that my papá go home to
Santa Cruz? Can you understand that I love my papá
but I must kill him?"

Jenny sketched. She had put on her stockbroker
glasses.

Calmly, Aurelia said, "Do you think United States
will now help Rodolfo to be *el máximo líder* of El Tres
de Julio Movement, Tomás?"

I thought so. "No," I said.

Jenny broke the tension by showing her sketch to
Aurelia and me. She was not satisfied with it. She had
not got Aurelia right, though each detail in itself was
true—the nostril, eye, and delicate ear. She had in-
cluded me, and those few swift lines revealed more
than I liked to see. Jenny wanted to try again, and this
time I posed Aurelia in the flared-nostril glance over
her shoulder.

"Yes, I see," Jenny said, bending to her pad. The
second sketch was better by far, Jenny said she would
go to spray it, and asked Aurelia if she would like something to eat. Aurelia admitted she was hungry.

When Jenny had gone, she said, "Tomás, I think we
do not make love again."

"No."

"You think I must go to Guadalupe because I kill
my papá. Maybe you think I go to Guadalupe because
we make love together, both married peoples."

I said nothing, and she shook her head at me. "Not
for this," she said. "I have kill my papá for the Repub-

lic, but I have also make love with you for my papá.
Nothing is for me."

"For your father," I said, and cleared my throat. The
meaning of the tower games began to present itself.

"He is old. He is nothing left. You understand he
can only look?"

"At his television program." I got to my feet, but I
didn't know what to do, so I sat down again.

"It is like the telebision at the gate, Tomás. Do not
be angry. It is a thing I do for my papá because he is
my papá."

I nodded.

"Do you have no pleasure, Tomás?"

"Very much," I said. I fluffed up a grin.

This appeared to gratify her, and though there was a
temptation to ask how extensive her television career
had been, it seemed inconsequential compared with
the knowledge that she had murdered her father.

As soon as Jenny returned with a tray for Aurelia, I
excused myself. I walked to the San Angel Inn, with its
flowers and parrots in a patio like a larger and more
kempt relation of the Casa de la Fuente, and called the
emergency number from a telephone booth. I insisted
that I must speak to Frank Timken immediately. I was
told to call back in fifteen minutes.

I went to the bar, drank a Carta Blanca, and then
phoned again. Frank said in a disagreeable voice, "The
arrangement is that we communicate through Pat."

"There's a decision you have to make. Herrerro was
murdered by his daughter."

In the pause that followed, I wondered if I would
have run to call Frank quite so rapidly if I had not
learned of my comedian's role in the television series. I
supposed I would have from duty, and to keep Frank
Timken, as my superior and my country's agent, from
making a ridiculous box-and-peephole error.

"She tell you that?" Frank said in a disapproving voice.

I related in detail what Aurelia had said. "This finishes your El Chato and Gabriela Bazán theory," I said. "But I don't see why this information has to go any further. In fact, I damned well don't want to see Aurelia Velásquez arrested."

Silence on the wire. I had a sense of an IBM whirring, tiny fingers probing for tiny holes in cards: in a proliferation of complexity all must be computerized, and orders accepted on faith from the machine.

"Call me back after a while, will you, Murdoch?" Frank said.

I had another Carta Blanca, salted and limed, and called again. Frank was not available. Think about not doing the first thing, Jenny Gray had said; I thought about those few harsh strokes by which she had established me in the background of her sketch of Aurelia. I had had several beers and it was growing dark in the patio of the San Angel Inn when Frank became available again. "Okay, Murdoch."

"Okay, what?"

"Affirmative on your request."

I groped for something gracious to say in response to this. Frank added, "As far as can be seen for the present, that is."

"You do mean affirmative you won't pass this along to the Mexican police?"

"I mean nothing is going to be done with your information."

"Whose decision?" I asked. "Yours?" He did not answer, and I began to see widening implications. "So the Mexicans will proceed on the assumption that Herrerro's death was a Commie plot?"

"For Christ's sake, Murdoch! You got what you wanted and now you're crabbing!"

"I'm not crabbing." I mugged idiot gratitude at the mouthpiece of the telephone. It occurred to me that I might be through with them now. But there was still the Dark Angel of Santa Cruz in my care.

I walked home along the curving, cobbled lane in the dark. A tiny red flame trembled above my head, a votive candle set in a red glass before a shrine built into the wall. Around each curve I found myself expecting to meet the Mercedes limousine with Mickey at the wheel, as though at the same moment that I had recognized that Cisneros was the only possible strongman now, the only one who was ever going to do this thing that everybody wanted—he had recognized that I was the only one who might get in his way.

In the patio of the Casa de la Fuente a few smoky orange lights glowed, and the bulb over the door of the studio was lighted. My own apartment was empty, so Jenny had Aurelia settled for the night. I made myself a highball, turned the radio on to Mexican *rocanroleros*, and snapped if off again. Chuy hovered on the corners of my mind like something indigestible eaten for lunch; remember me? I nursed my drink and waited for Jenny Gray.

Finally I heard the whisper of her bare feet on the tiles. She sat down beside me on the arm of the couch. "She's asleep. I gave her a pill."

"Where's Finch?"

"He's stayed in for a meeting. I suppose you've heard about Gabriela?"

I'd heard.

"Did you tell them about Aurelia?"

I'd told them. I looked at the curve of her thigh in her bleached denim pantleg, on the arm of the couch beside me. Her small paint-stained hand rested lightly on it. "I thought I had to," I said. "Do you think I had to?"

"I don't know," Jenny said. Her hand closed into a fist, like a small animal curling up against danger. "What are they going to do, Murdoch?"

"Nothing."

We sat there, close but not touching. I watched her hand relax to lie palm open, palm up, on her leg. She said, "I wonder if our saran-wrapped lives could still get caught up in great emotions. Like patricide. Like tyrannicide for the Republic. We've come a long way from those great simplicities, I'm afraid."

"Maybe we're caught up in one right now."

The noisy, peremptory climb of the second-class bus became audible, snarling louder, then fading. The phone rang.

"Tommy-boy!" Clipper Armstrong said in my ear. I had had a superstition I was going to encounter Mickey and the Big Guy again, but here came the Clipper, like Mr. Outside when you were set for Mr. Inside. I asked where he was.

"Right downtown here, having a few drinks at this place called Bar Jorgenson, something like that." There was comradely laughter in the background. His voice sank to a highly audible whisper. "Some good-looking broads hanging around here. How about coming down?"

"Can't make it," I said.

There was a prickling silence. "Got something going there, huh?" the Clipper said. "Well, I'll see you tomorrow, then. Same hotel, same suite." I felt an anxiety like a pressure in my head that I had offended him, and the immediate reaction of irritation at my anxiety. I gauged the exact decibel of the clatter of his hanging up.

I tried to cheer myself by looking at the blunt tips of Jenny's breasts pressed against the man's shirt she wore, and she crossed her arms self-consciously. I didn't have anything going here.

"People like you and me don't *do* anything," she said. "Maybe we don't know how. Things are *perpe*-trated that we disagree with violently, but we don't *do* anything. Complain, but don't make *waves*."

"Maybe there's never any clearcut thing to do."

"Being a liberal involves an infinite capacity for making rationalizations," Jenny said.

"I wonder if I could do something if things ever did come clear," she went on. "I have *dreams* of doing things. Great, swooping things. Unfortunately they are always quite abstract."

"Isn't being an artist enough?" I had always considered surfing and skiing, tennis and golf, eating and drinking and screwing and making money, enough, but I could see how you might begin to think it wasn't, if you let yourself go.

"I suspect that of being another handy rationalization," Jenny said. She began to walk up and down, head bent forward and her hands tucked into her hip pockets. She looked like a graying teen-ager. "The trouble with art is the separation," she said. "Everything seen through a window, or in a mirror. The immediacy is what's necessary—some rationalization-smashing, clearcut—action!"

"Like Aurelia."

"Maybe violence is necessary and the clearness comes after it." Her voice took on an excited edge. "I've read that adrenalin, the *ash* of adrenalin—so the clarity *does* come after—the ash of adrenalin has an effect like ergot, which is what lysergic acid comes from. And things come clear sometimes with LSD. Oh, do they not!"

I heard the small squeak of my barred gate opening. Jenny muttered, "Oh, hell!" We both looked toward the hallway for Finch to appear, but there was no sound of footsteps. I went to turn on the light.

Pressed into the corner of the wall just inside the door stood a dirty, tattered figure, the kind of gypsyish beggar encountered on the streets of Mexico City with a dirty child in tow, desperately poor but generating more resentment than sympathy in her reproach and arrogant demand, the abrasive human equivalent of the popping of the second-class bus climbing the hill into San Angel. Roughly I asked what she wanted.

She pulled the rebozo from her head; Gabriela gazed back at me from a battered face, a swollen cheek, blackened eye. The rims of her ears protruded from greasy hair, there was no gap-toothed smile. She leaned in the corner with her arms folded on her breast.

"Are you hurt?" I asked.

"Yes, the police have hurt me very much," she said. She caught sight of Jenny behind me. "I did not know where else to go, Yankees!"

"Your face!" Jenny said.

"The face is nothing." She moved forward in a strut that failed. She snatched her arm away from me, and managed to move into the living room under her own power. She collapsed onto the couch.

Gazing up at me with her good eye and her bruised one, she said, "You did not know I was with the police, Señor Murdoch?" Her English was less heavily accented, now there was no need to maintain her cover. It came to me for the first time that there was another side to this operation, *the* other side, the enemy like a photographic negative.

"Yes, I knew where you were, Señorita Bazán."

Her eyes turned to Jenny. "You have told the police to come, señora?"

"Not I," Jenny said. "But my *God*, Gabriela, you handled yourself so badly!"

"So badly!" Gabriela scowled.

"And your *novio* who works for the government?" I asked.

"Please tell me if I am safe here for a little while," Gabriela said. "They have let me go so they can follow me to Chato, but I think they have lost me."

"You're safe here for a little while," I said. This time I would not run to report to Frank Timken.

"I am tired and hurt so much, Yankees," she said in a roughening voice. "Is there a doctor who will come to help me and will say nothing?"

"What have they done?" Jenny demanded, sitting on the couch beside her.

Gabriela unbuttoned her stained muslin blouse, tearing the edges finally away to bare small breasts. Around each nipple were dark craters, burns, many on one, not so many on the other. "They have put their cigarets out on me."

"*Bastards!*" Jenny hissed.

As I started for the phone Gabriela covered her breasts and leaned back on the couch. She said, "Your countryman was there, señor and señora."

I dialed Ibis' number. He answered on the third ring, he said he would come. Jenny's eyes were round with shock. "What countryman?" I asked Gabriela.

"I did not see him. But he was around—behind—" She made an arc with her hand. Her eyelids were bunched with fatigue. "He came with the *teniente*. The *teniente* came three times to see if I have . . . told where is Chato. No. Then he makes a face—" She frowned theatrically: "—wuff, wuff, wuff. And then he goes around and I can hear him talking to someone who knows Spanish well, but not as well as—" She stopped, and shrugged, and said, "I know."

Jenny said, "Did the *teniente* do things to you?"

"No, señora. The *teniente* is told what is wanted,

and he then tells the others. The *teniente* does not say, 'Hurt this girl with cigarets and big litro bottles!' He only says, 'You must find out from this girl where is El Chato.' No, they are only men who have a job. Only one is a truly bad man, and on this one I have left a mark so I will know him again." She made a savage, ugly biting motion, like a snake striking. Immediately she touched her cheek and said, "He has left his mark so he will know me, also."

(15) MONDAY, II

IN the semi-darkness of the dining alcove, sipping brandy and sometimes pressing the cool glass to my forehead, I watched the dramatic grouping in the aureole of the lamp. The girl spy lay on the couch in a peach-colored nightgown of Jenny's, her breasts given a squarish contour by the gauze pads on her wounded nipples, and on her face a partly worried, partly dreamy expression from the injection given her by Ibis, who stood over her with his thick glasses glinting in the light, shirtsleeves rolled back on his fat arms.

"You no longer have pain, my little Cubana?"

"No, very nice now." Smiling, she brushed a hand in front of her face as though at a cobweb.

"Is she going to sleep now?" Jenny asked, seated round-shouldered at the foot of the couch with her arms hugged over her own breasts.

Gabriela shook her head. Her lashes made soft lines on her cheeks. When I thought of her torturers I was filled with fantasies of confrontation and revenge. I tipped more brandy into my glass.

"She will not sleep because she has will of iron," Ibis said indulgently.

"Sí," Gabriela said.

"It is will of iron or she reveals her secrets to police. I

think you must understand these places they have hurt, little one. That women have so much higher tolerance for pain is infuriating to *macho* men. But there has been no imagination here."

Enunciating clearly, Gabriela said, "It is not hard to have a will of iron when one has nothing to tell."

She didn't know where El Chato was; I nodded to myself.

"So there was no way to make them stop," Jenny said in a stifled voice.

"Only to make them kill me," Gabriela said dreamily. "But I do not wish to die. And they do not wish very much to hurt me. In prison after the attack on the Moncada Barracks there was much torture, and they have brought to María-Antonia Portocarrero the eye of her brother. If she will not tell them what they wish to know they will bring her the other eye. That was very bad, because the thing they demanded of her did not exist at all."

"They didn't wish to hurt you, but they managed," Jenny said.

"But there is a switch that turns off so the pain can be supported. And then the men must become a little crazy to do what they hate to do. One can feel sorry for them."

"You are a little Christian revolutionary," Ibis said, smiling down at her.

"Yes, I would shoot these men with least possible pain," Gabriela said. "But yes, to be a Christian is best, Doctor. Never to hate. Because to hate must show and this gives these men relief. So I have made only one mistake this time. I have bitten a sadist very hard, and this gives him good reason to be very hard with me. Still, it is nice to see him shout with pain. But one must never try to be brave. When women beg and cry it is very difficult for men."

Laughing, Ibis sat down in the easy chair and crossed his plump legs. "This one is very comical, is she not, friend Murdoch?"

"This one is very experienced in torture," Gabriela said. "Two by Batista, and one by United States of America."

"So you claim," I said, for she was speaking to me.

"Should I not say what I believe because it troubles you, señor? It would be more polite for your guest not to mention this, perhaps."

"Anyone for brandy?" I asked.

I was pouring glasses for Jenny and Ibis when I heard a car outside, and voices. There was a swift torque of tension in the room.

"Maybe it's John," Jenny said.

The car engine continued to run as a door slammed. We waited. Ibis lit a cigar, eyebrows arched over the enlarged eyes behind his glasses.

"Hey! Tommy!" a voice called, and it was not Finch nor the Federal Security Police nor Frank Timken, not Mickey nor the Big Guy nor El Chato Villaneuve. It was Clipper Armstrong. "Hey!" he shouted. "Am I in the right *place?* Hey, *Tommy!*"

"It's all right," I said. I went out into the patio where headlights were visible through the gate. The tall figure of my father-in-law loomed unsteadily against the light.

"Tommy, *boy!*" he had started again, when I said, "Right here, Clipper."

"I was afraid I'd come to the wrong place. Come deal with the goddam cabbie, will you? He doesn't speak one word of English."

I paid off the taxi and sent it away. Clipper was breathing heavily. "Really bombed out, Tommy," he said. "I don't know what went wrong, I was giving this really cute chilipepper the blitz when all of a sudden— Christ!" I took the sexy sexagenarian by the arm to lead him inside. "What the hell you got going on here, a *party?*"

I introduced my father-in-law. "Hi, Doc," the Clipper said. "'Lo, miss," he said to Jenny. Hands were shaken; Ibis stood at heel-clicking attention. Clipper lurched from one to the other, great-shouldered in a beautifully tailored cashmere jacket and a shirt with a high soft collar. His curly hair needed combing, there was lipstick on one cheek.

"And this is Miss Bazán," I said. "She's a communist spy."

Clipper leaned over to shake hands, almost going all the way over. "Hi, babe. Going to bed already, huh?"

"How do you do, señor."

"Well, it's one of those goddam nights," Clipper said to her. He got a fix on me with his mismatched eyes. "I'm hell for barging in on people when they're going to bed," he said.

"Mr. Armstrong is a very famous man!" Ibis said, still standing stiffly erect.

I watched with disbelief the train of expressions crossing Clipper's face: pleasure, coyness, pride, humility. "Thirty-nine years ago," he said. "Would you believe thirty-nine *years?*"

He said to Jenny's uncomprehending expression, "You're too young to remember. The Rose Bowl—Duke had us down nine points going into the third quarter. But we went seventy yards in ten plays. Benny missed the kick."

Ibis watched him, mouth drooping open. Gabriela said, "¿*Futbol?*"

"Football, yeah," Clipper said with a flickering scowl. He raised his hands to set his helmet on straight, bull-dog-jawed. "Froze the ball," he said. "But we got it. Two minutes to go. We had to move." He tapped his chest, he crooked his arm to cradle a ball. "Made five, made four. Made the first down." He hunched, now he carried the ball against his chest. He swayed, he showed his teeth. "*Yaaaaah!*" he cried. "Off tackle slant! Benny took out that end! *Bam!* Ran over that second string All-American Bill-Dick Weber! Safety man coming up! Gunderson. Hundred and seventy-eight pounds! Fast! Sprinter! Gunderson! *Hoooonk!*" He shot out a mighty straight-arm and Ibis clutched for the lampshade.

Clipper was running for the goal line and the winning touchdown, not moving but his shoulders shifting with his speed and deception. He was over. He threw the ball into the air.

"Marvelous!" Jenny whispered.

Grinning, panting a little, the Clipper scratched his head and said, "That was a great day for ol' SC, let me tell you. Great day for Clipper Armstrong! Thirty-nine years ago, can you believe it?"

"Ah, you are sports hero!" Ibis said.

Clipper frowned in confusion; what else? I had seen these implosions of old fame before, most notably at the reception after the Armstrong-Murdoch nuptials.

"All-American fullback two years running," he said. "Four letter man my last year at SC." Jenny was gazing at him with slightly glassy eyes. Gabriela seemed to be dozing again.

"But you are also very famous entrepreneur," Ibis said. "Industrialist, banker—"

"Say, what're we drinking here, Tommy," the Trojan Clipper interrupted, pushing a big hand through his curls. He laughed the big, slow "Uh! Uh! Uh!

"Not that I really need one," he said. "I'd just like to join the party." I poured him a brandy. "Thank you kindly, kindly." Turning to Gabriela on the couch, he said, "Say, you're pretty cute, miss. What's Tommy putting me on about you being a Commie spy? How about letting the Clipper in on the joke?"

Gabriela looked up at him helplessly.

"What a delicious moment this is!" Ibis said, rubbing his fat hands together. "There is famous encounter at the Battle of Alma when Russian High Command and British High Command meet face to face, in great embarrassment for both. And here we have member of the dominant apparatus of the left meeting with member of the dominant apparatus of the right—and what are they? Cute girl—and sports hero!"

Clipper gave me a confused glance, and Gabriela protested: "I am not a member of a dominant apparatus! You talk nonsense."

"Ha!" Ibis said. "What is revolution but one side of wheel going down, other coming up? And the side of wheel that is up must do all it can to see that wheel revolves no more. Now the people of Fidel Castro are the dominating apparatus, and repress as they were formerly repressed. Is it not true, my little *socialista?*"

I had the sensation that I was watching ad-lib theatricals staged for Clipper Armstrong's benefit. Gabriela was spitting with indignation.

"It is nonsense, fat doctor! In Cuba the people will rule! We who have made the revolution with Fidel, almost all have been bourgeois. University students. And we . . . *we* . . . have helped Fidel to give the revolution to the people of Cuba! All of it! To all!"

"Say!" Clipper remarked, but did not go on. He looked pleased and interested. Ibis was grinning broadly.

And a new voice said, "This seems to be where the party is." It was Finch; I saw Jenny's guilty start. He stood in the doorway, a tall thin figure in black, with his emaciated gray face like a beardless Uncle Sam. Finch in black tie, Chesterfield and Homburg like a cartoon statesman. Jenny hurried over to take his arm. "Come and see who's come home," she said.

I made introductions, but Finch seemed to know everyone already. "Well, well, Armstrong," he said to Clipper. "Good to see you again," he said to Ibis. "Doctor Ibis, is it? This *is* like old times." Ibis had clicked his heels to attention again; Finch did not offer to shake hands. "Hello, Gabriela," Finch said.

"You have sent the police for me, Señor Finch?"

He set his Homburg on the table as though it were very fragile. "Not personally."

Clipper pulled me into the dining alcove. His breath was an alcoholic affront. "Tommy, what the *hell?*"

I explained the situation as briefly as I could, while Clipper looked unable to absorb what I was saying. It amused me to consider producing my beautiful black patricide from across the patio, just for the effect.

Ibis was rubbing his hands together and saying, "Of course, Mr. Finch, as the German Clausewitz has said of war, torture may be also the continuation of diplomacy by other means."

Finch assumed a bleak smile. Clipper shook my arm: "I don't get that! What's *that* mean?"

I didn't answer as Finch said, "I'm very sorry that Señorita Bazán has been harmed, but I'm sure she has always been aware that she would be dealt with severely if apprehended."

Clipper sat down abruptly on one of the dining chairs.

Jenny said, "She says there was an American there, John."

"My dear, I feel as though I have been summoned to some bar of judgment, when in actuality I only looked in to see if you were here. I freely admit that I warned the authorities that the maid in the adjoining apartment was more than she seemed. This I would have been foolish not to do. I was then informed that the maid had been taken into custody, and had proved to be Señorita Bazán, a Cuban national and accomplice of Villaneuve's. I am shocked, of course, to learn that Gabriela has been tortured, but I do not believe for one moment there was an American involved. In the first place, it was not our business. In the second, that is not the way we conduct our business."

Gabriela said, "Pardon me, señor, but it is exactly the way you conduct your business. Your lackeys conduct your dirty business for you always."

Finch gazed down at her—with compassion, I thought. Harsh lines bit into his cheeks. Clipper was watching as though he had a very hot ball game on the tube.

"There have been too many photographs in news-papers, señor," Gabriela went on. "Of gooks—that word which is the worst word you have in your lan-guage. Photographs that all of us gooks who live to the south of you have seen—the American adviser looks on as anti-communist gooks torture communist gooks."

"You claim this American was looking on and advis-ing? I do not believe you, señorita. You are merely trying to make capital for these good-hearted, gullible people."

Clipper sat up straight with a chuckle. His team had got a hit.

I watched Gabriela shrug her light-bathed features. Wearily, Finch said to her, "We would like to be your friends, señorita."

"It is too dangerous to be your friends," Gabriela said. If Clipper recognized it as a hit for the other team, he did not show it. I tipped up my brandy glass to finish the last drops.

Finch said, "My dear, we are not against socialism per se. We have come to accept that in many ways and in many countries it may be a solution. But you must see that the kind of forcible and violent expropriation Fidel has engaged in can only hurt Cuba. I am not speaking of any holy rights of private property, I am talking about the simple fact of money. Anything which reduces the confidence of investors discourages investment. Without investment, a country will lie stagnant, and the necessary economic basis for social progress is denied. Can Fidel alleviate poverty in Cuba without American investment? You know he cannot, Señorita Bazán!"

"They've got to listen when you give it to them straight, Finch," Clipper said.

I noticed that Finch and Gabriela, while appearing to ignore this, assumed curiously similar expressions. To Finch, Gabriela said, "Perhaps you are right. But you can not know what it is to be Cuban. I have been to college in Florida for one year, and I never found one American student who had heard of the Platt Amendment."

Finch said smoothly, "The Platt Amendment was an interventionist asininity that gave us the right to interfere in Cuban affairs almost whenever we saw fit. It was repealed before you were born, señorita."

"To intervene whenever there was danger to property rights," Gabriela said loudly. She had learned English very well during her year in college in Florida. "It exists still in the minds of Americans, the Platt Amendment which protected American property. Do you know how much of all that had value in Cuba was owned by Americans and American corporations? About forty percent of the sugar production, fifty percent of the railroads, all of the cattle ranches, with the British all the petroleum industry, ninety percent of the electricity—for which Cubans paid the highest rates in the world. This is what Americans do not know—how much American corporations own in the Caribbean, and in South America. Also in Canada and Europe. But now no more in Cuba, no more in China, which you would like to make war against. Eh, Señor Capitalist?" she said to Clipper Armstrong.

Clipper held up his hands as though she were throwing something at him, laughing, clowning it up: "Hey, wait a minute, put down that machine gun! Hey, help, I'm being expropriated!"

Ibis seemed to think him very funny. Finch continued to ignore him, Jenny looked depressed, Gabriela exhausted. I leaned a hip against the table and explored my empty brandy glass with my tongue.

Gabriela said, "Fidel has given Cuba back to Cubans, *señores y señora.*"

"To Communism," Finch said, shaking his head. "I must believe in freedom, Gabriela."

"And I also!" she cried. "And to us Communism is freedom—from you!"

Clipper Armstrong got unsteadily to his feet, tall, broad-shouldered, with the star quality of gathering every eye. I watched him with a total absence of curiosity as he raised the little glass in his hand. "I guess we can all drink to freedom, señors and señoritas," he said. All dutifully drank except Gabriela and me. She had no glass, and I no brandy.

"I am very interested in my own freedom," Gabriela said. "What will you do now, Señor Finch? Do you speak again to the authorities?"

"I will not see those authorities until tomorrow afternoon," he said, and rose and plucked up his hat. "I am very tired, my dear," he said to Jenny. "Do you mind if we say good night?"

She took his arm again, her face inclined away so that I couldn't see it clearly. There were good nights and handshakes. I remembered Finch saying that he

kept running into the same faces before different backdrops. When I accompanied him and Jenny to the
door, he said quietly, "See that she gets out of here in
the morning, Tom. For her own safety."

"Right," I said. Back in the living room the Toast-
master was pouring himself more brandy, and Ibis was
saying to Gabriela in a jovial voice, "Tell me, little
Cubana, one has heard these stories of Villaneuve—
that the police of Batista have ruined him for women.
Is this true?" He picked up his bag.

"What is it to you?" Gabriela said with worn com-
bativeness.

"Hey, everybody's *going!*" Clipper said. "Hey, Doc,
the night's young—how about you and me and
Tommy—"

"Include me out," I said.

Clipper winked at Ibis. "He's married. Married my
daughter. She may be beautiful, Tommy-boy, but she's
putting on the pounds. You know how to keep these
girls slim? Keep 'em on their toes!" He laughed at his
joke. He and Ibis seemed to have a reciprocal trade
agreement of joke appreciation. I wished they would
leave.

"Thanks for coming," I said to Ibis.

"It is a pleasure for me to be at beating heart of
world events."

Clipper thought that was a howl. Ibis said, "Come,
Mr. Armstrong, we will go to celebrate the youth of the
night in the *centro*. I have my little car, if you will
permit me."

"Include me in," Clipper said. "Good night, señorita," he said to Gabriela. "If all the Commies were as
cute as you we'd give 'em the old world."

"Thank you," she said, with her eyes firmly closed. I
walked with Clipper to the door, following Ibis; I said
I'd see him tomorrow.

He nodded. "I guess it's back to the old drawing board on that management problem," he said. His eyes were as sober and wise as original sin. The harpoon struck its mark, and he winked and slapped me on the arm. "Cute little piece you've got there," he whispered. "Hey, wait up, Doc!" he called. "I get lost in that jungle out there." They left the Casa de la Fuente noisily.

I moved heavy-footed back inside to sit beside Gabriela. "Is there some kind of airlift for getting you out of Mexico? Finch says you'd better go tomorrow morning."

"Tomorrow," she said. "Now I am so tired. Tomorrow I can use your bath, maybe, and I will be— varoom!"

I leaned over to kiss her bruised cheek. She placed her hand there. "But what is this?"

"It is the kiss of a brother."

"Ha! It is the kiss of a good American Capitalist boy for an evil Communist, and now you must do what I demand or I will tell the FBI." She made a violent motion with her fist. "And they will send you to Alaska forever!"

"It might be a blessing," I said.

"Will you do a thing for your sister, Señor Thomas Murdoch?"

"Maybe."

"Take a message for me. Maybe tomorrow is not soon enough."

"So there was something you could have told them."

"It would have been no good to them. There are many"—she made motions—"between." Cutouts.

"Where do I go?"

"To the Plaza Garibaldi, the plaza of the mariachis. If you will bring paper and pencil, please."

I brought them to her, she sat up, and, wetting the

tip of the pencil, began to draw. "I think Mr. Finch
keeps his promise," she said. "But the father of your
wife—he tries to seem stupid when he is not." She
folded the paper and handed it to me. On the exposed
surface was a figure that looked like a llama, though
perhaps it was a dog, with the figures 27/7 in a box
drawn in the belly.

"For a mariachi leader named Marcelo el Gordo, in
Plaza Garibaldi," said Gabriela Bazán.

I left the Corvette in the guarded parking lot in front
of Bellas Artes. It was after midnight, I was no longer
tight, but I was in an irresponsible mood. From working for American Ventures on the Big Sugar project
there had seemed no conflict of interest in taking on a
hitch of covert operation for the government. In fact,
the two jobs had seemed to complement one another.
Now it would be not much more of a step to become a
double agent. If I turned over Gabriela's note to Frank
Timken, I could run my score to a triple. Then be-
traying Frank to El Chato would be a kind of undercover equivalent of four major sports letters your senior
year at USC. I was not looking forward to seeing the
Gross National Product tomorrow. Was the prospect
of an unpleasant session with the boss the basis of all
defection?

I boarded a second-class bus for the plaza of the
mariachis, to deliver Gabriela Bazán's note, which I
had scrupulously left unopened, to a band leader
named Fat Marcel.

My first view of the Plaza Garibaldi was a taxi
surrounded by laughing musicians. I got off the bus and
walked around the struggling mariachis and the tourists
they had snared. The plaza was not so well lighted as
the avenue, but more groups were visible in their

charro costumes, with florid designs in silver embroi-
dered on hat crowns and pant legs. On the façade of a
bar an enormous cowboy in static amber and flashing
blue neon twirled a neon rope, and here and there were
piles of instruments, the broad carapaces of guitars like
boat bottoms. Mariachis were playing at intervals
around the square, for tourists, for parties of Mexicans,
some apparently for their own amusement. I was approached to finance a song. "*¿'Guadalajara,' señor?
'¿Cielito Lindo?'* "

"*Busco Marcelo el Gordo,*" I said confidently, having practiced it on the drive from San Angel.

"Over there, señor."

I passed on around the square (" *¿'Cielito Lindo,'
señor? '¿Guadalajara?'* ") and approached a cluster of
big-hatted musicians. Marcelo had a beefy intelligent
face illuminated by pulsing blue neon. He held a violin.

"Marcelo?"

He bowed. Dark faces watched me from the shadows
of hat brims, light spun in a cornet's rosy throat.

" *'Cielito Lindo,' por favor,*" I said. Instantly I was
surrounded by smiles. Mariachis crowded close around
me and began loudly to play. I assumed an embarrassed
expression for a trio of Americans who strolled past
grinning at my captivity. The music ceased, the dark
faces drew back, I handed Marcelo Gabriela's note and
a bill. "*Muchas gracias, señor,*" he said, and I walked
on feeling much relieved.

Cooking smells reminded me that I was hungry as
well as tired. A corrugated steel roof sheltered scores of
tiny kitchens, each surrounded by a counter, each with
charcoal burning beneath pots on grates. I ordered
posole, and a man in straw hat, on which aluminum
paint had been sprayed, dished up an enameled plate of
very hot corn soup covered with a salad of shredded

cabbage and radishes. I finished it with a burning mouth and went outside once more, into the tangled strains of music of the Plaza Garibaldi.

A cracking trumpet was playing a familiar song that was neither "Guadalajara" nor "Cielito Lindo." There was a crowd gathered beneath the neon cowboy, and flickering blue was reflected on grinning faces as Clipper Armstrong, tall as the fancy hat-crowns around him, raised the trumpet from his lips and pumped it up and down like a dumbbell above his head. He sang hoarsely, "Fight on, for old SC . . ."

There were roars of approval. He blew the trumpet again, not so badly, the old horn-tooter out on a toot. Beside him I had a glimpse of Ibis' face, all red and yellow, with blue-gleaming glasses and a grin full of exploding teeth. He was singing the USC fight song along with the Clipper.

"Fight on, fight on, to *vic*tory!" they sang. The trumpet blared again.

I was almost out of the Plaza Garibaldi when I was aware of a presence at my elbow. "What do you want, señor?"

My shadowy face was doubly reflected in mirror glasses worn by a small man, neatly dressed, beneath a narrow-brimmed hat. He had a pockmarked face as taut and lumpy as clenched knuckles. It came to me that this was El Chato Villaneuve.

"Do you want a little girl, señor? A little girl only eleven years old? Like this, señor?" He held up a thumb and forefinger pressed tightly together.

"In a communion dress?" I asked. I had my free associations mixed.

"Anything the señor wishes," the little man said. As happened so often in Mexico, a country of mirrors, my face gazed back from what I looked upon.

"I wish nothing," I said, lengthening my stride to

leave him behind. When I glanced back he had halted, only a Plaza Garibaldi pimp and not El Chato at all.

I took a taxi back to the Bellas Artes. There was a crucifix set into the speedometer dial where no needle operated. The driver inquired if I wanted a girl. I told him I already had too many girls. The señor was very lucky, he said. Driving the Corvette back to San Angel everything seemed gray and dull with weariness. To-morrow I saw the Clipper, hung over from singing the USC Fight Song with Dr. P. T. Ibis in the Plaza Garibaldi, and he would or he wouldn't insist on a management programming for the El Tres de Julio Movement which would or would not be acceptable to me. I could stand on principle, or I could give in gracefully as I suspected it was my nature to do. What did it matter?

Would Jenny Gray claim that cynicism was the ultimate rationalization? Everything tonight had seemed a fraud, Gabriela and Finch, Ibis and the Clipper, Frank Timken and the *teniente* and the wrecking crew, and the little man I had taken for El Chato, as though all humanity were only cutouts and stringers in some grand-scale, theatrical conspiracy, on the farthest periphery of which I bungled and stumbled.

(16) TUESDAY, I

I WAS awakened first by the early round of cockcrows, again, disagreeably, by the second-class bus, finally by a metallic squall from the patio. This last was Pedro-the-parrot's pleasure at greeting the day with the cover removed from his cage. What sound would he make if the cage itself vanished, one of terror? I listened to Juan-the-yardboy whistling and raking. The phone rang. I waited to see if my returned maid was going to answer it.

"Señor Murdoch!"

I put on my robe and went out into the living room where the couch was empty, Gabriela nowhere in sight. Empty brandy glasses and overloaded ashtrays recalled last night's discussion group.

Pat Hepner said in my ear, "I thought I'd better phone in case you had any stray females there." She giggled. "I'm coming out to see you."

I arranged instead to meet her in the embassy cafeteria again, and when I hung up had a moment of confusion as though Pat had been in the room all the time. A slim blonde in a dark blue suit leaned in the doorway. But the bruised swollen cheek was visible, it was Gabriela in a wig, wearing nylons and needle-heeled black pumps that made her look leggy and tall.

She had quite a lot of the blond tan college beauty Pat Hepner cultivated. When she grinned there was another shaky moment; the missing tooth had been replaced. She was a very smooth object, and I whistled.

"You like me, huh?"

"I'll bet you knock them dead in Havana."

She raised an arm, snapped her fingers, and twirled into the room. "Who is this lady who telephones so early? The wife?"

"Just another blonde," I said. "How do you feel?"

"I hurt," she said with a jerk of her chin. "But the morale is up. Now I vanish."

I said I would take her into the *centro*.

"Yes, if you will take me into the *centro* in the beautiful auto. Perhaps I can borrow a hat I have seen the Señora Pintura wear; for this—" She indicated her cheek. "Then it will only be noticed that Señor Murdoch has another lady. Come, we must hurry before Pepita arrives and there are too many questions."

She went to make breakfast. She had been a tornado in the bathroom, having abandoned her role as my maid. The former bourgeois University of Havana student must have once had servants to clean up after her. After breakfast I went to call on the painter-lady.

Jenny appeared in her working jump suit, looking tired, dark slashes like paint smudges beneath her eyes. Her pilot light seemed to have gone out.

"Bad night?" I asked.

"I've been thinking that with just the tiniest twitch in the ordering of the world, you and I might be the ones being tortured, Murdoch. This morning I've been trying and *trying* to find some way to paint that awareness of . . . horror. And, oh, the beastliness of just going along doing the usual things when so much evil exists. But I can't, I feel *all* dried up." Finch was still asleep, she said, and went to get the hat for

Gabriela. Even without her pilot light she was a day-making sight going away in her jump suit.

Pedro kept an eye on me when I knocked on the door of the studio apartment. "Come!" Aurelia called.

She was still in bed, a dark jewel in a white setting of sheets, blankets, white nightgown and peignoir. It seemed a pathetic admission of her morale being down that she had let me in while still in dishabille, and I felt it necessary to be very formal. "Have you slept well, Aurelia?"

"Very nice, thank you, Tomás." Her chin trembled.

"I must go into the center on business but I'll return as soon as possible. Jenny Gray will bring your breakfast."

"It is not necessary you think too much of me. Perhaps it is not good to have me here."

"It is very good to have you here."

"Tomás, I have thought—" She clenched her two hands together beneath her chin. "Perhaps I will write Paco Flores to see if it is welcome I go home to Santa Cruz. Now that my papá is dead. I think there is money to come to me now. I do not know how I can get this money, but there is a friend to my papá who know. There is money in Zurich and Miami and perhaps if I give this money back to the Republic. There is much good I can do there, Tomás."

"We will talk of this when I come back," I said. Jenny brought breakfast on a painted tin tray, and I returned to my own apartment, where Gabriela tried on Jenny's hat in front of the mirror.

"Come, we must go now," she said.

Starting out, we brushed together, she swung slightly toward me, I put my arms around her in an *abrazo*. Then I kissed her. She looked up at me unsmiling. "What a man for women," she said.

"Good-by, Gabriela Bazán."

"Thank you, Thomas Murdoch."

We went on out and she opened the garage door for me one last time, and, when I had backed the Corvette out, closed it behind me one last time. She climbed in and I started down the close-walled, curving alley. She was less nervous than I about peering in the rearview mirror.

When I had joined the Insurgentes traffic, I said, "Last night after I'd delivered your message a man came up to me I thought might be El Chato. A little man with a pockmarked face."

"Chato is big. Not so tall as you, but big." She made gestures with her shoulders. "No marks on the face."

"And you love him very much?"

"Like a brother," Gabriela said. After a pause she said, "Yes, I love him very much. Do you know why? For I will tell you what the fat doctor has said of him is true. He is not for women. But he is for his fellow men, and he has very much to give to his country and to all of Latin America. And he gives all he has to give."

We rode in silence until she said in a cool voice, "And you. You have much to give to women, that is clear. But perhaps it is not enough."

My face prickled with heat. "And you," I said. "You have a great deal to give as a vestal virgin, and that is fine for the state. But what about your own self?"

I braked for a changing light. On a corner kiosk, clothespinned over the bright shingling of magazines, were the morning papers, headlines leaping out in the disorder of incomplete comprehension: ASESINADO EN LOMAS PISTOLERO MUERTE CRUCEÑO POLITICO SANGRE EN CHAPULTEPEC.

As I accelerated with the green light, Gabriela said, "Perhaps you should give yourself a vestal virgin to your country, Thomas Murdoch. Perhaps if you of the good hearts in your country would give yourselves then the

United States would not be the Negro-hating, gook-killing, money-loving Imperialist devil it is!"

She had spoken with machine-gun speed, she looked angry and unhappy, and unhappier when I didn't answer. When I braked to a stop for a light, she kissed me on the cheek with a hard push of her lips, opened her door and swung her legs out. "¡Adiós, amigo!" she said, and fled through the halted cars. She waved to me from the curb as I drove on.

Our own vestal virgin was sitting in the empty cafeteria with a cup before her when I showed up ten minutes late.

"I'm a little jealous," she said, when she had brought me coffee. "Even if she is so dark."

"Perhaps you confuse jealousy with prejudice," I said.

She looked hurt. I apologized for being late, which seemed to help. I asked what the papers were saying about the murder.

"Just that Herrerro was a wealthy Cruceño. Servants are missing, and there is a suspicion of theft. I guess there is a regular formula they follow so people won't know too much."

She sipped the remains of her coffee, loosened the heel of her shoe in the usual manner, and focused her eyes on a point above my right eyebrow. Time for business.

"What have you found out from Aurelia Velásquez, Tommy?"

I sampled the pressure to answer like a good agent, savored the simultaneous resistance that was apt to flow into antagonism and smart-aleckry, and realized, with last night's new complications, the necessity for maintaining each little fund of information in separate bank accounts.

"This morning she said she was thinking of returning

to Santa Cruz. Turning back the money her father
stole, if she can get hold of it. If Flores will have her
back." Immediately I regretted having told Pat this.
She looked worried, too.

"But isn't she interested in the movement?"

I stared at her. "In what?"

"In the El Tres de Julio Movement," Pat said.

"Not interested in the movement, no," I managed.
"Definitely not," I said. "A negative interest only. No,
Aurelia Velásquez is not interested in the El Tres de
Julio Movement, the name having been selected to
commemorate the assassination of that bloody old bas-
tard the Protector, who had her husband slaughtered.
She definitely did not want her father going back to
Santa Cruz with the movement. She felt so strongly
about it that she shot him."

Pat was frowning at my sarcasm. She said firmly,
"You are to persuade her to support Rodolfo Cisneros."

"My God!" I said. I could not believe this fantastic
obtuseness. "Pat, the point is that she hates Cisneros!"

"Oh, hates," Pat said. "She doesn't have to sleep
with him."

"So we have decided to support Cisneros for strongman," I said. I could accept such logic from Clipper
Armstrong, for there was no room for sentiment in
business. But I had plenty of sentiment about my
country.

"You must realize there is no one else, Tommy."

"He's a murderer."

"So is Aurelia Velásquez."

Once again there was the kind of tantalizing, irrele-
vant logic operating, as though the only possible argu-
ments lay in peripheral matters. Finch had said that the
major decisions were a long way off, but the decision
had been made to support Cisneros as leader of the

El Tres de Julio. I found myself shivering with a kind of nausea; maybe I had the *turistas* of the soul.

I said, "So once we conspired to have the Protector murdered to bring the blessings of democracy to that island. And now we're conspiring to send the son back as dictator. Democracy is much too risky. Right, Pat?" Speaking rapidly so my mind only skimmed the surface of what I was saying, like the wolf in the cartoon running in air before he realizes he is over the abyss, I rushed on: "And the answer is no, I will not try to persuade Aurelia to support Cisneros. I advise you not to have anyone else do it, either—she might kill him. She's a strong girl. She could probably strangle a couple of smallish agents at one time. Pat, can't you understand that that fun-loving boy tortured and killed her husband?"

She looked as though she might burst into tears. "But Tommy—I'm sure it just doesn't matter so much to these people. No, *not* because she's a Negress! I mean at these *levels*. Tommy, the Protector *did* intend to have legislation passed so Cisneros was declared legitimate and heir apparent. There is a document—"

"The fact that that bastard is or isn't a bastard is not the point!"

"He and Aurelia are the point!" Having silenced me, she continued, in control once more; businesslike and officious once more. "There will be a public meeting. A big PR thing. It is very important that she come and do—you know, the things they do. *Abrazos* and all that. She simply has to do it, and you have to persuade her, Tommy. After all, she did murder her father and we are withholding that information from the Mexican police at your request."

"Christ!" I said.

"Now, will you do this today, so we can complete the

plans for the El Tres de Julio Movement rally? You understand that the dramatic moment will be the announcement that the Protector intended to name Cisneros his true, spiritual son. And that Aurelia Velásquez embraces him as the—"

"I want to talk to Frank Timken."

"He's not here now."

"I can't talk to you any more. Where is he?"

"Maybe if you called the other number after twelve," Pat said.

From Suite D in the Maria Isabel Hotel, high above the U.S. Embassy, vistas opened, a comprehensive view of the valley of Mexico was possible from here, mountains showed, snow-capped and majestic—all it took was money. Clipper Armstrong was going through his elaborate routine of bringing me a highball I didn't want.

"Say, I enjoyed your friend the Doc," he called from the sideboard. He strode back across the landscape in his burnished, handmade, wingtipped brogues, to hand me a dark tan potion.

He stood over me as I sipped. "How do you like that scotch?"

It tasted very expensive. "That's *straight* scotch," he said. "I'm in love with the stuff. Pure smoke, isn't it, Tommy? Like drinking liquid L.A. air!"

"It tastes like money," I said.

He laughed his big, free, "Uh! Uh! Uh!" but the mismatched eyes were fixed on me coldly.

"Maybe we ought to take up this management situation," I said.

He nodded, drank, brushed a hand through his curls, and raised an eyebrow at me. "Okay, shoot."

"You remember the hamburg mix for the Red

Towers—how much chuck, how much plate, how much soybean meal? Minimum cost and maximum taste; we even had it programmed for a computer. But it came out pretty much the way we knew it was going to."

"Sure it did."

"I'm trying to tell you how I feel. What if the computer had come up with ground glass as the best adulterant for the minimax?"

He sat looking at me with his front teeth showing up to the gum in what was technically still a smile. I wondered why I was going through these motions. "You're talking," he said. "But saying what?"

"I'm talking about Rodolfo Cisneros."

"And saying?"

I shook my head; negative. Smiling still, he said, "Stick around a half an hour. Mr. Ground Glass is coming up and we'll see if we can't iron out our differences."

I shook my head again. "Once you begin exploring these things it's hard to know where to stop. I've bumped into some logical conclusions that just won't seem to iron out."

"Like?"

"We have no right to go into Santa Cruz and overthrow a legitimate government."

"You know what?" he said. "You can get people to really go for ground glass if the promotion is right. You have a group singing spots on radio and TV—'Ground glass is good for you, baybee!' Catchy tune, maybe a sex angle. They'd even vote for it."

"If you rigged it."

"These gooks *like* their elections rigged. It's part of the fun." His smile vanished, and he leaned closer. "I'll tell you how *I* feel now. An old-timey, fourth-of-July-type feeling. A revolution's got a right to happen."

"It doesn't have a right to happen just for your profit."

"I thought you might be having this kind of constipation when you said you didn't want any of that railroad stock. Flores is a Commie, Tommy."

"Maybe he isn't," I said. "Maybe it's only handy to think so."

He shrugged his big shoulders. "The needle gets stuck there every time, doesn't it? Okay, you're relieved from duty, Tommy. Time to go home."

I wet my mouth with the smoke-tasting, full-bodied, wide-track straight scotch whiskey and said, "No, I don't think it's time to go home yet."

"Ellie thinks you're having an affair down here." His big laugh banged on tender nerves. He shook a finger at me with heavy-handed lightsomeness. "Cute little Commie babes out of beard-and-cigar heaven aren't really in the line of duty, Tommy-boy." I looked away from him, out to the valley of Mexico where the great, permanent snow peaks were fading into obscurity, as he said, "Don't ever kid yourself Ellie doesn't have you by the nuts if she wants to go for a divorce."

It was not one of the things I kidded myself about.

"Tommy, it's your business and I wouldn't want to know anything about it," he said, tactful as a nuclear strike. "But Ellie really got the goods on you, some piece of ass or other—infrared photos, affidavits, the whole gig."

I cleared my throat. "You're talking," I said. "But saying what?"

"Just you'd better get home and convince Ellie you still love her."

I got up, and Clipper rose too, looking genuinely concerned. "Aren't you going to finish that scotch, Tommy?" I wondered if he would put it in a doggie bag for me.

He came heavy-footed after me as I started for the door. "Why not stay and we'll talk things over with Cisneros?" he said. "That's not so bad a guy."

"Yeah, he is."

"Tommy, it's got to be tough when you're in the bigs."

I turned to face him. "It's too tough for me. It might even get too tough for you."

"I don't think so," he said, squaring his shoulders. "I'm kind of enjoying the hell out of this international crap. Well, when I call Ellie tonight I'll tell her you're on your way home, huh? We'll get something going for you back in L.A., don't worry about that." He put a hand on my shoulder and squeezed. "Okay?"

"I've got other commitments," I said, and went on out the door. Commitment was an exaggeration. I only had the shaky beginnings of a conviction that whatever Clipper Armstrong wanted ought to be opposed by someone. I hurried along the thick-carpeted hallway to the elevator, hoping I wasn't going to run into the Big Guy and Mickey on my way.

I strolled along Reforma counting over Clipper's threats. In a divorce settlement arranged by the kind of divorce lawyer Eloise could afford, the alimony would reduce me to peonage unless I made the kind of money I could only make working for Clipper Armstrong. I thought of idealism and practicality, of necessities and luxuries, of my very pleasant life that I would find it difficult to change. I was not the retrenching kind. A taxi almost ran me down as I crossed an intersection, honking furiously and shrieking to a stop inches from me, still clamoring. I stood looking at the driver through the windshield until the honking ceased.

At twelve o'clock sharp I dropped a *veinte* piece into the slot in a phone booth and dialled the emergency number. Frank Timken came on immediately. "I have to see you," I said.

"A little tennis, Tommy?" he said heartily. "What about right now and I'll take a long lunch hour?"

I sat on the bench looking at the neat geometry of white lines on the reddish clay courts, waiting for Frank and sorting through all the lies, half-truths, cover-ups and impostures I was involved in. The overloaded sewer smell was very distinct today. On the teletype of my mind was the repeated message that the best thing to do was go home to Los Angeles, tail between my legs and licking the hand that fed me, home to convince Eloise I still loved her, home in the Corvette with my expense account still operative, to whatever assignment Clipper would find for me. I did not like the international crap.

Frank arrived with his long-legged, scissoring walk, full of nauseating male good-fellowship. We rallied, making all the appropriate remarks and calls, as though our cover were being probed through high-powered binoculars and listening devices by all the *Fidelista*, Sov and Chicom agents in the hemisphere.

When we began to play I double-faulted, missed putaways, netted volleys, overhit my forehand and elbowed my backhand while Frank covered the net like an iron curtain and powdered anything I did manage to hit over. He won the set six–four.

"Do we have to do two of these?" I complained. "I've got to talk to you."

We moved over to the bench to sit down, and he armed into his warm-up jacket. "Pat said you were pretty upset," he said.

"There's a very acute girl."

"In fact she said you were pretty obnoxious." He fixed me with a severe glance of his wide-apart hazel eyes. There was a beaded line of sweat across his fore-head at the hairline, a fleck of crusted blood under his nose from a shaving cut. He had big, hairless hands with deeply graven knuckles. "You have to accept the fact that a lot of material is going to remain classified as far as you're concerned, Tommy. As long as you refuse to sign the security pledge."

It was another piece of logical irrelevance, but this time I did not fall into it by protesting that I had only refused their gold. Frank continued in an earnest, confidential tone: "I know I don't have to say any of this to you, Tommy, but let's talk about it anyway. You know the world is pretty much divided in two by what's called the cold war. Or what *we* think of as the secret war. Sometimes the war hots up here and there, but if we do our job right it's never going to get really hot. And most of the time it's so secret a war people hardly know it's going on at all. You know this?"

I nodded.

"You know that the other side has been damned clever at using—misusing!—all our good old words. You'd think they'd invented the word 'revolution.' When we had the only revolution that ever made anybody free. We've got to face the fact that they've had tremendous PR in this. They've tried to make 'freedom' their word. 'Freedom fighters' are Commies now. And 'national liberation' and 'imperialism.' What about *our* war of National Liberation? We broke out of the British Empire and they're calling *us* imperialists!

"You know what a hell of a life-and-death struggle we're in. They've taken over our words, our slogans— these goddam arch-betrayers! They've taken over too much of the world's acreage, they knock these little countries over like dominoes. They're even in this hemisphere. We threw them out of Guatemala, but we failed in Cuba. Tommy, they've got to be stopped, and you and I and every loyal American have got to join the team to stop them!"

I stared at him dumbly. When Finch had said somewhat the same thing I had been flattered to be treated as an intelligent man. It was not flattering to be spoken to like a little leaguer. Yet Frank's intensity and seriousness were disarming, and I couldn't say, "Oh, bullshit, Frank!" It wasn't bullshit, he had only made it sound like it.

"I can tell you this much, Tommy. The Flores regime in the Republic of Santa Cruz has us damn worried. God knows that island was overdue for a decent government, but Flores is acting like he thinks he can get away with some of the stuff Fidel's pulled. We think there's a good chance he's going to take off for left field one of these days, the way Fidel did when he surprised the pants off us. We don't want to be surprised that way again, Tommy." He gave me a long look, purse-mouthed and hard-chinned. "And that's just about the piece of cake as far as our thinking goes."

It seemed to be time for me to say something. "I can't accept the fact that my country is helping a bunch of murderers grab power in Santa Cruz. Cisneros is a murderer. I've seen him do it. He likes it."

"We're not *helping* them, Tommy! We've just got to be prepared to make it look like we backed them all along in case they make it."

"Bullshit," I said.

He assumed a dogged expression; there was so much I didn't know that it might be impossible to educate me, but he would try. "The fact is that you and I don't make policies, Tommy. You and I are just little people. We can't expect to know everything that's going on. We don't have enough information to know what's

best for the old USA. We have to trust the organization. The individual just has to listen to all those
massed brains up there, that's all."

"That's too easy."

"What's too easy?"

"The individual has to leave everything up to the
massed brains."

He stretched. He glanced around us for spies. I
found it impossible to believe that he was first string.
"Tommy," he said indulgently. "How can you know
what's going on in that beard-and-cigar heaven of
Fidel's, for instance? You have to—"

"That what of Fidel's?"

"That beard-and-cigar heaven." He showed me his
teeth so I'd know it was supposed to be a funny. It was
a funny I'd already heard once today. Things seemed to
be closing in all around, like the smog socking in; the
Clipper and Frank Timken, and the *Seguridad*.

"Were you there when they were torturing Gabriela
Bazán?"

A blue vein beat like forked lightning in his temple.
His face was suddenly shuttered. "What the hell do
you mean by that?"

"She said an American was there when she was being
tortured."

"You believed her, huh?"

"I saw what had been done to her breasts. I took her
word they'd used a bottle as a dildo on her."

He hardened his jaw at me, eyes slitted. "The next
question is just how the hell did you happen to be
talking to her?"

I told him. He started up. "She's gone now," I said.

"Gone where?" When I shrugged, he said quietly,
"You did the wrong thing. We'd 've liked to get hold
of that one, Tommy."

"And give her back to the Mexican Security people for some more? Were you there, Frank?"

He clasped his hands together and cracked his knuckles, scowling. "I was there when they were inter-rogating her. There was no torture. Don't put it past a bitch like that to mutilate herself just to sucker you."

"It was a decision I had to make for myself."

"What was?"

"What to believe, and what to do. What was right and wrong."

"Right and *wrong!*" He looked frantically uncompre-hending. He was an unattractive person, he must al-ways have been a lonely man. He stuttered as he said, "Tommy, you don't decide things like that! Tommy, you goddam better . . . level with us! We can get goddam tough!" He managed to make the threat sound inoffensive.

"Tell me something. Do you just sit alone in your office with all this responsibility on your back?"

"How do you m-m-m-m-mean?"

"Do you get orders from someone higher up and pass them along to people like me?"

"Something like that."

"And he gets orders from higher still, and passes them along to you?"

"From pretty high up. Just below Special Group."

"Special Group is the massed brains at the top with access to all the information for making decisions?"

"Well, they sit on top of all the brains and informa-tion I was talking about." He slitted his eyes at me again.

"What if it doesn't really work that way? What if it turns out that certain policies are made at your level? Because the massed brains at the top don't have a clue to what's going on. What if someone in your position

worked like hell to get all the right ingredients programmed—a true son of the Protector, a popular female like Eva Perón—everything gassed up and the
engine idling. Maybe the massed brains would decide
to buy it just because it was all organized and ready to
go."

I had thought I was making dangerous statements,
but he only sighed. He was looking at me worriedly,
but not worriedly enough.

"I don't seem to be getting through to you, Tommy.
It's goddam serious about that Bazán woman. There's
got to be discipline, you can't have every two-bit
stringer making policy decisions. Tommy, a man just
has to have faith that the *very* highly paid, *very* smart
people up top know what they're doing."

I had lost my faith. I extended my legs and looked
down at the blond hairs and dried sweat. "I'm dissent-
ing," I said.

Frank laughed. "I'll tell you something that really
isn't classified, Tommy. At the time of the Guatemala
operation—you remember there wasn't even an attempt to keep a cover on where Castillo Armas' mate-
riel was coming from. A lot of our top people thought
it was bad to operate in the open like that. It could've
been done covertly. Resignations got turned in on that
one. Do you know what good it did?"

"None?"

"None, that's right. So what're *you* going to do?"

"How about another set?"

He stared. Then he laughed again, as though he
thought it an admission that I intended to go along.
We went back out on the court.

This time I made no double-faults, and this time
whenever Frank charged the net I top-spun a lob over
his head. When he tired of chasing down lobs and
began hanging back, I hooked short drives at his feet.

The second set he got one game, the third set none. When we had finished and he was toweling his face, he said, "That didn't take long. I thought you were hitting pretty bad that first set."

"I decided I had to go over your head."

I saw his doubletake, but he decided not to pursue it and we started back toward the club building. He zipped up his jacket, jerking at the tab when it jammed.

"Now, this is important, Tommy," he said. "Get the Velásquez woman to come in for Cisneros any way that seems best. I mean get tough if you have to. This rally kicking off the El Tres de Julio Movement is shaping up fast. You're the only person she trusts, that's obvious. Cisneros has got to have her support, so we have to count on you. You're the only weak link in the whole set-up."

He didn't realize the half of it. The point of no return had been reached in the chilly waters of the Rubicon. "I'm not working for you any more," I said.

He swung toward me, shark's eyes staring.

"Include me out," I said.

(17) TUESDAY, II

MR. Justin was at home, said his secretary. When I
called him there he asked me to come out. "We'll have
Martinis," Herb said in his easy drawl.

At the house in Polanco, Herb was swimming while
Faye lounged in a web chair beneath the striped parasol, and a transistor radio with a chrome aerial blared.
Faye raised a hand for me to shake, Herb came dripping from the pool. There was a small shock of gray
hair like steel wool in the center of his chest. When he
spoke his voice was drowned by a sudden surge of rock
and roll with a beat like ballbearings shaken in a wash-
tub. Grimacing, he switched off the radio. "Swim,
Tom?"

"No, thanks. I've just been playing tennis with
Frank."

He stood with his head inclined to one side as
though listening to distant drums. Faye said, "How are
you and sweet Jenny Gray getting along out in San
Angel, Tommy?" She hooped her red mouth at me
roguishly. "Oh, dear, John Finch is here, isn't he?"

"Good game?" Herb asked, and Faye said if we were
going to talk tennis she would get the Martinis herself.

"I need help," I said, when she left. Herb gestured

me into a metal chair. I said, "You may know that I was recruited to work for Frank awhile back."

He raised his eyes in a stylized flinch. "Sorry, Tom. Frank's affairs are not my affairs."

"You can't tell me the DCM doesn't rank him."

"Do oranges rank apples?" Faye returned with a sweatbeaded pitcher and glasses on a tray, and he said to her, "You'll have to excuse us, hon."

"Oh, I'm used to being bumped from all the really interesting conversations," she said, and slouched off with a Martini.

"All right, let's have it, Tom. I presume this has to do with Senator Herrerro and his daughter."

"I'll tell you something you may not know. His daughter shot him. The émigré movement is going to be *Protectorista,* and she felt strongly about the Protector, and about her father joining forces with Cisneros. The Protector had let his favorite son do the killing when the Colonel's Plot failed—Velásquez among them."

"Unhealthy atmosphere for a growing boy," Herb said. His voice was easy, his eyes watched me levelly. "The child as father to the man shows rather prominently, too." His attention was diverted as two small gray birds descended in a swift arc across the pool, and flicked away through an opening in the hedge leaving a ripple fading on the surface of the water. "Frank knows the daughter shot her father?" he asked.

"I told him. He wants to frame El Chato and his girl friend and the two servants who disappeared."

Herb whistled. "I don't see how they can expect to pull off anything as improbable as that. Though if they can just flutter the headlines with it I suppose they'll feel it's been worthwhile. You really don't want to upset yourself about that sort of business, Tom. We have

men who spend their lives dreaming of ways to make
the other side look bad, and they have their counter-
parts dreaming on us. That's the way the game is
played."

"I've quit my job," I said.

"Which job?"

"Both."

"A little refill here?" He took up the pitcher to replenish our glasses.

"Aurelia Velásquez has given me a couple of things
to think about," I said. "Were we involved in the plot
to kill the Protector?"

"Let's say we certainly wanted him out of there."

"Now tell me how far left Flores is."

"The problem with Flores is that he is being aggressively independent. If he decides to become really
independent it's probable that he'll turn to the other
fellows for assistance. Fidel's rather set the pattern
there." His voice took on a mocking edge. "And we do
not find that a viable solution to hemispheric
problems."

"But the fact is that we are planning to overthrow a
liberal regime we helped create, in favor of a rightwing
dictatorship. I can't go along with that."

"So you quit Armstrong. Was it bloody?"

"I haven't unzipped yet to look."

"And Frank?"

"He stuttered. I couldn't make out what he was going to do to me."

Herb chuckled. "Maybe you're still young enough to
dissent without considering the ramifications of your
dissent. But let me give you some weary old advice.
There will be a certain solution to the problem of Santa
Cruz, but after a number of years it won't matter
much. I felt the same way you do about Hungary. That
if we didn't intercede in the Hungarian Revolt to keep

those brave people from slavery, we could never hold up our heads again. But now Hungary is probably just about as free as she would have been had the revolt succeeded."

Maybe the weary old advice was valid, but it was only facile, only a rationalization in the end. "Herb, can't you protest Santa Cruz policy to some higher authority?"

"I don't have anything to do with Santa Cruz policy."

"But you could do something if you thought it was important enough."

"Spears could, if he were here and not back in the States having his plumbing repaired. I'm only the DCM." Our eyes met, and he sighed and said, "All right, Tom. But I'm not going to do anything."

I sat slumped in the web chair gazing out at the pool and the clipped green grass, the green shade beneath the trees and the splashes of color of the flowers in their beds. It was a nice garden, and a nice house, made possible by a nice position in the foreign service. Herb was proud of his son who went to St. Something School in Connecticut, and of his daughter who attended the American School in Mexico City. And he liked the things. He had a Thunderbird and a Mustang, an impressive accumulation of hifi stereo components, records and tapes; he had cameras and motion-picture cameras, slide projectors and movie projectors, he had skis and tennis rackets and scuba gear and a beautiful shotgun handmade for him in Germany. All of it, of course, was made possible by not protesting to higher authority, by not making waves. Maybe you're still young enough to dissent without considering the ramifications of your dissent, he had said.

"You happen to know someone who moves in pretty rarefied circles," Herb said. "Who walks with Special Group and talks with the president."

"Oh, Finch."

"Don't underestimate him. Finch is big enough to tell your father-in-law to go to hell. I couldn't do that, much as I might like to, and neither could Spears."

"And Frank Timken couldn't," I said.

"What do you mean by that?"

"I think Frank is making the Santa Cruz policy to Clipper Armstrong's specifications."

With the slightest of alterations, Herb's expression became chill. "Shooting from the hip, aren't you?"

"I don't think so."

He poured the last of the Martinis into our two glasses with great attention to the process. "I should think Finch is your best bet if you're serious about this," he said.

I was serious. I felt like a plodding, earnest idealistic jerk. It wasn't my style.

"Do you remember Voltaire on gardens?" Herb said. " 'Il faut cultiver notre jardin.' I'm afraid one of the marks of middle age is an increasing interest in one's own garden.

"Of course," he went on, after sipping his Martini. "Voltaire said that when he was very old. But in a job like mine one gets old in the mind very early." He sounded a little sad. "You're not going?" he said.

I said I had to be going. On the way home I stopped to see Dr. P. T. Ibis.

Ibis paced the sun-drenched black-and-white tiles of his sala, preceded by a bowsprit of thin, dark cigar. He wore a striped red-and-blue shirt, knee-length bleeding Madras shorts, and huaraches decorated with red stones. Around the sala ferns drooped, so vividly green, in the sun through the skylights, they looked like congealed color. High on one wall was a painting of a man in a black tunic with electric gray hair, an arm raised in a curse or a blessing, or maybe a warning—both comical and impressive, like Ibis himself.

Blowing smoke, smiling brilliantly, Ibis stopped and said, "I am so glad you have come to visit me, my friend Murdoch." I doubted it. At the far end of the room, before a TV set, was the young bullfighter Jesús Obregón, shirtless, with a bare, sallow, quick-muscled torso, wide belt, tight white pants. He sat with his fists in his pockets sneering at what he watched on TV.

"And when will we play our doubles match again?" Ibis asked. "I have no exercise, I grow fat."

I said we must play soon again, and wished I hadn't come.

"And how do they progress, your studies in faith?" Ibis inquired, waving his cigar. "Have you made visits to the shrine of Guadalupe? You are tempted to travel on the knees across the stones?"

He flicked ashes on the floor and glanced nervously toward Obregón, who had turned his head toward us, alert and haughty as an eagle. "Yes, yes!" Ibis went on. "Truly to study faith one must visit the great shrines. Guadalupe, Fatima, Tomb of Lenin, Buchenwald—"

"Buchenwald?"

"To see inscription over the gate there, do you know it? 'Right or wrong—My fatherland!' It is faith, my friend!" Behind his steel-rimmed, round glasses, his enlarged eyes were bright and pleased. He kept playing to the audience of the young bullfighter.

"I'd better be going," I said, but he insisted I must have refreshment before I went, and clapped his hands like a pasha. An elderly maid appeared, and she went with Ibis as a delegation to wheedle Obregón into consenting to a whiskey-soda. Roused by this, the matador began to walk up and down, scowling, hands still in his pockets as though manacled there. Ibis became even more phonily jolly, glancing over one shoulder and then the other as Obregón swung past us.

"Ah, what a country is America," he said loudly. "So difficult to have pleasure, so quick to guilt. How often I see the guilt of my American patients that their country acts in the world no longer from honor. I ask if this guilt can be assuaged by passing on the knees across the stones of Guadalupe?"

Perhaps it was what I had come here for, to hear America denounced by this fat creep, like isometric exercises to strengthen the disillusioned muscles of my spirit. I said, "It's like your forehand, isn't it? It's not whether it works or not, it's the principle of the thing."

He gazed at me silently, losing concentration as the matador passed once more, bootheels cracking.

"So similar, the puritan and the revolutionary," he continued. "See the little Cuban. She cannot live her life because a finger must be kept always in the hole in the dike. The terrible illusion that one's duty is to mend the world! It is ultimate madness."

The maid brought the drinks. Obregón managed to free a hand from his pocket to accept his whiskey-soda. He plumped himself down before the TV again. I sat in my leather drum chair trying not to feel part of a triangle.

Sipping tequila from a narrow tube of glass, Ibis said, "This man Finch is dying man. It is in color of the face, knowledge is in the eyes. Why will Madame Gray cling to this man, such a young, beautiful and talented woman?"

"You'd met Finch before," I said.

"In Paris we have known the same people, I did not know him well." He tapped his fat, pink, lower lip. "Last evening it is so difficult to keep this shut," he said. " 'Freedom!' says the great man Finch, 'Freedom!' cries the Cubana—even this splendid person your fa-

ther-in-law speaks in hushed voice of freedom. Do you
know what freedom truly is, friend Murdoch?"

"I was in class the day you defined it," I said. "Freedom is lawfulness without laws."

He pouted, shook his head, glanced once toward
Obregón, and, swinging a fist for emphasis, said, "Freedom is *danger!* Freedom is *disaster! Tragedy!* It is all
things great mass societies try to make laws against. I
tell you this so you will know what risks one must take
to be *individual* man, not masses. *I* take these risks. Do
you, my partner?"

He was drilling close to the nerve, and his magnified
eyes watched me closely and uncomfortably. "Certainly
not," I said.

He laughed and continued: "What a fresh air to
meet this man Armstrong. Your father-in-law takes
these risks, my friend. To be very rich is to be an individual, and men will live in utmost poverty and degra-
dation if there remains one little chance to become
rich, to win the lottery—because this is a way to become an individual. It is America's great weapon in
struggle for the world. And what a man America has in
this Armstrong! Not gray and dying like Finch, but a
titan standing against the sunset of a once great nation!"

The TV sound came up loud, rapid voices arguing in
Spanish. Ibis frowned delicately, and I gulped my beer.
Ibis was not the first intelligent man the titan-against-
the-sunset had charmed out of his socks. The charming
seemed to have been mutual. Time to go, time to go.

"Perhaps you have problem and you wish to speak of
it to Dr. Ibis," Ibis said in a suddenly human voice, as I
rose.

"I'm afraid the individual man must solve his individual problems."

Obregón was on his feet also. Hands buried in his
pockets, he walked rapidly across the end of the room

and kicked a large bronze platter that leaned against the wall. The bronze tolled a dull warning, and Ibis' face flushed into scarlet lumpishness. I said, "And solve his problems in his own, individual way. ¡Adiós, señor!" I called to Obregón.

He bowed. Ibis took my arm and moved with me toward the door. "I give you this advice, my good friend. Remember! No one of us is what he seems, each is only what he must be. Each of us is only a time-space event. Nothing is eternal, not loyalty, not love, not anyone or anything. We move with rhythm of time, we occupy a space upon the line progressing from childish faith in parents and God and country, toward ultimate freedom of individual man!"

At the door his seriousness vanished and he patted me on the arm, shook my hand, and swore he would arrange another tennis match for tomorrow or the next day so we could win more pesos from the rich Americans of the embassy.

I drove home toward the Casa de la Fuente wondering how to separate the bullshit from the wisdom of the time-space event named Ibis.

I nosed the Corvette up to the garage door and stood on the cobbles looking down at its brutal splendor of gleaming red enamel and chrome, an inseparable piece of my own time-space event, complicated mechanism both of freedom and servitude. I smoothed a hand along the long, cool, smooth curve of fender and considered my own individuality compared with that of El Chato Villaneuve, who was obsessed by the ultimate madness that it was his duty to save the world. I was only obsessed with the Republic of Santa Cruz, which I had never seen and didn't want to see.

There was no answer when I knocked on Aurelia's door. I crossed to Jenny's apartment, and she summoned me to her studio, where in a flood of clear light she perched on her stool before the easel. Her hair hung in a ponytail down her back, she wore her glasses, and an unlit cigaret protruded from the corner of her mouth. The canvas on which she was working was a bronze background slashed with harsh black strokes like oriental calligraphy.

"Aurelia's gone off for the afternoon, Murdoch. Something to do with her father's bank accounts."

"Who'd she go with?"

"Young man from the embassy. Poor thing, she spent the morning in tears." Jenny slid to her feet, removed the large canvas from the easel, and leaned it against the wall. "My *critic*al faculties are not a mess, at least," she said. "Sit down, Murdoch. Would you like something—"

"Yes," I said, before she finished. She let her glasses hang from the cord around her neck. She tossed her cigaret into the glass ashtray. First her ears turned pink, then her cheeks. She sat down and propped her bare small wedge-shaped feet on the edge of the coffee table. I wondered if I had always been a latent foot fetishist.

"What will it do for my image if I pour my heart out to you?" I said.

"I'd love it," she said, and so I told Jenny Gray why I had come to Mexico. I told her why I had moved into the Casa de la Fuente. ("What a shit you are, Murdoch.") I told her everything, and it was a relief not to examine each item before giving it security clearance. "I don't have the right to throw the first stone," she said. Her face was bright with emotion, her pilot light had come back on. "Do you suppose that damned island really exists?"

"Somebody ought to stop what's going to happen there. Herb Justin says John Finch is the man."

Jenny was shivering, rubbing a bare arm. "So it's Pompadour under the circumstances," she said, and managed a smile.

"*Maintenant,* Maintenon."

"Why does that crummy, insignificant island have to be so important? Just because that big black girl looks like the Statue of Liberty? As far as I can make out her politics are strictly Genghis Khan. But she *is* against misery and death. Yes, I have to do this, don't I?"

It seemed a very raw moment. Maybe we were on the edge of the great simplicities she had mentioned once.

I said, "I seem to have an inability to talk seriously. I have to communicate what I feel by joking, or sarcasm, or—for instance, I love my country, but it's impossible for me to say that."

"I know," Jenny said, hugging her knees to her chest.

"I saw a man murdered. Right—there. He was murdered by Cisneros. I can say—I disapprove of that sort of thing. I can't seem to say that I'm *horrified.* I can't seem to make the point to the people I've been protesting to that I'm *horrified* at what my country, that I love, has in mind for that miserable little Republic no one seems to give a damn about. But I care more and more."

"I care," Jenny said. Her face was deeply flushed. "But you'd better let me see John alone, Murdoch. I *hate* the feeling that it's you and I against *him.*"

"Maybe he'll agree with us."

Distantly the second-class bus snarled and popped. "Once he would have," Jenny said.

(18) TUESDAY, III

I SAT in the gray flannel darkness of my apartment sipping a highball and thinking up names for new brands of bourbon, maybe a new creative line of work when I got home to Los Angeles: Old Faith, Hope and Charity, Old Morality, Old Cleanliness—next to Old Godliness on the liquor store shelf—Old Brave, Clean and Reverent, Old Patience, Old Oblivion, Old Loser. The brand names seemed to have a downhill inclination. Old Buck Up? I wondered if anything were happening tonight with Old Doc and Clipper, sitting in the dark and watching a show of headlights on a louvred shutter, hearing automotive movement, Old Finch coming home to Old Jenny Gray?

After a while Old Murdoch went out into the patio where dusk lay thickly, as though the dark were heavier than the light, for above the walls the sky was still a smoky green. Burnt orange bulbs glowed at intervals in their grid above the patio, a whiter bulb burned over Aurelia's studio, and her window was a square of light. I knocked. "Come, Tomás."

I entered. Her face gazed at me over her shoulder. She stood before the mirror, so that briefly her features were presented full face and in profile like a Picasso portrait. Her shoulders were bare and she wore a long, black scabbard of a dress. There was a black velvet band around her throat.

The double aspect of her face dissolved as she turned back to the mirror, raising the brush in her hand again. "I have talked much with your friend of the *embajada* today, Tomás."

"Mr. Timken," I said.

"Yes. He will help me have the money of my father which is in Miami. Also the money of Zurich, perhaps. He will help me with this if I will do a thing for him."

"Did he tell you what the thing was?"

She cocked her head with another long stroke of the brush. Her face turned toward me once more in the doubled aspect of amber eyes and proud nostrils, glazed with sadness. She nodded.

I should not have told Pat that Aurelia was concerned about her father's money. She watched me in the mirror as she swept the brush through her hair. "Don't do it," I said.

"Tomás, you must trust me. What I will do is the best thing."

There was a knock and she moved past me to open the door. A man's voice said, "Ah! señora!" and she responded in Spanish to Rodolfo Cisneros, who stood beneath the light outside. His wavy hair gleamed, his white smile was broad, a big-shouldered, narrow-waisted playboy type with a hell of an appraising eye. His shirtfront gleamed luminously in the light.

"Well, it's Sugar Company," he said, and his smile changed. Aurelia took up her handbag and fur from the bed.

"So Santa Cruz will bleed like the bull at the Plaza Mexico on Sunday," a thick voice said. Aurelia only shook her head at me patiently, sadly. "And the little, little girls in the communion dresses," I said. If I was talking to the Dark Angel of Santa Cruz I was talking

to a dark, blank wall. Maybe I was only talking to
myself, Old Too-Little-and-Too-Late.

Aurelia settled her stole on her shoulders and
stepped outside to join the *máximo líder* of the El Tres
de Julio Movement. It seemed the last moment I could
have interfered, and it passed.

In the pool of light within the surrounding dark
Aurelia and Cisneros were two very big, very handsome
people, an unbeatable pair. He took her arm and she
turned away from me.

"An *abrazo* with a monster just for the Miami
money and the Zurich money?" I said to her back. I
had lost my cool. The Protector's favorite son and my
country's choice gazed back at me grinning no longer.
He released Aurelia's arm as I stepped outside. Tension
locked in swift cam action. "You goddam murdering
gooks," I said.

A tic pulling at a corner of his eye, he surged toward
me. I ducked inside his swinging arm and hit for the
center of the white shirtfront, exulting in a fierce
pleasure of contact as the Big Guy grunted with pain
and staggered back.

I went after him and hit him one more time before
someone crashed on my back and pain exploded against
the side of my head. I staggered as Mickey held me,
cursing me, consciousness surging and fading like a
missing engine. Cisneros' face came at me again, and
this time I couldn't dodge the swinging fist. Still I
managed to stand, with Mickey panting in my ear. The
Big Guy swung again, unhurriedly, and senses swooped
away like a descending elevator. Mickey let me go.
Someone kicked me as I fell.

I lay on cool bricks staring up at hovering faces,
Cisneros with a lock of hair fallen over his forehead,
light moving like an electric current along the blued
steel barrel of Mickey's gun. Farther away the face of

the Dark Angel showed only a wooden remoteness. I remembered Ibis' lecture on disaster as freedom, and kicked up at Cisneros' crotch. My foot struck his leg a glancing blow, and Mickey immediately skipped forward to retaliate in kind. I doubled up on shrill pain. The faces vibrated hazily. I understood the word "mad dog" in Spanish.

The three of them withdrew. Just before they were lost in shadows Aurelia looked back over her shoulder at me one last time in that aspect of her beauty that had never failed to please me until now.

I was trying to stanch my nosebleed at the washstand when I heard tires on the cobbles outside, the slam of a car door. This time surely it must be good, gray John Doane Finch, the Great Liberal, the statesman, who walked with Special Group and talked with the President, coming home.

I sat in the dark nursing a slug from the bottle of Old Dissenter, taut as a cheap toy wound to the spring-break point. And finally there was a knock and a call and it was Jenny. The pale triangle of her face showed at the barred gate. "Don't turn on the light, please," she said. "Shall we go for a walk, Murdoch?"

I joined her and we went out into the lane. We passed the square bulk of the postbox suspended on the wall outside my window. The sky was full of unfamiliar stars. "How did it go?" I asked, just to be asking.

"It didn't go," Jenny said.

A path of smooth flagstones was laid in the cobbles, crossing in diagonals from entrance to entrance. The narrow way stretched in a long curve, each section of wall we passed of a different texture—adobe, plaster, brick, light-colored stone. Jenny took my arm.

Her plea to Finch had not gone, and my encounter with Cisneros and Aurelia had been a bloody-nosed failure. The bad guys were ahead. God was on the side of the bigger artillery, or else He was deaf from having spent too many centuries too close to those big guns. A car approached, filling the alley with enormous headlights, and I almost panicked. I flattened myself against rough stone ahead of Jenny, and the car rattled harmlessly past. On the corner was the little shrine in the wall, red flame flickering. "I thought I could swing it," Jenny said. "But maybe there wasn't any way."

"I'm sorry," I said.

We walked over the cobbles, not trying to follow the zigzag path. "He is so afraid of personal involvement in what he is doing, you see," Jenny said. She did not sound particularly depressed. "He was afraid to see how Gabriela had been tortured. He was *very* panicky when I tried to get him to talk to Aurelia about the *Protectoristas*."

The gate in the wall of the old convent yard was open on inky darkness, but once inside the path was discernible, and starlight caught the stone cross. It was the only one of its kind I'd ever seen, a crucifix with Jesus physically incorporated in the cross, His head the top of the upright, His feet the base, His hands the ends of the horizontal beam. Jenny and I sat down on the stone bench facing the cross. I heard her draw a deep breath.

"I asked him to do it for the liberals," she said. "For liberalism. Because he was the Great Liberal. Because it seems more and more nowadays the old dog has lost her teeth. Or else it shows now that she didn't have any to start with. 'For *liberalism*, John!' " she said in a stagy voice, and laughed a little.

She leaned on my shoulder. She smelled of soap, cologne, and turpentine. I put my arm around her and she shivered and pressed against me. " 'For love, John!' " she said. " 'Because I wanted your child and you wouldn't give it to me!' It's so hard to *beg*," she said. At the same instant I moved my arm and she turned her body so that her breast lay against my hand. "He said I was being *female*," she said. "That I was overemotionally involved." Her breast pressed into my palm. "Poor, sick, frightened old thing," she said in a muffled voice. "Afraid to find out your cards aren't high any more."

Her face turned into my neck. I touched her hair. "I was lectured severely on the big picture, which I don't understand," she whispered. "Santa Cruz is *not* of much importance, Murdoch. We are dealing with all of Latin America here. He cannot bring himself to go over anyone's head for a matter of so little consequence. He is so honorable, you see, that he cannot commit an unstatesmanlike act. For liberalism, or love, or *me*. He spelled that out very carefully."

I turned her further and she straddled my leg. Her face moved toward mine, dark depressions of eyes by starlight, damp pale gleam of teeth, lips missing once and then engaging, tongues driving together. Her face twisted away, she panted, and said, "He is *very* angry with me. I said to him, 'But isn't it worse to commit an immoral act than an unstatesmanlike one? Because that's what *we* are doing!' And he said, 'My dear, I'm afraid that morality must often be subservient to the necessity to *exist*.' "

With my two hands I brought her face to mine again, once more the heat and the taut sweet straining, the twisting apart.

"*Isn't* that too bad," Jenny said. "Murdoch, it *ruined* me. Because, could I say—oh, something pompous and righteous? I could not! Because he knows he's lost and if he tries to force anything like this he may find out that everything he has ever tried to accomplish is a *ruin*. Immoral in order to exist," she said, and her

mouth clutched back at mine. Behind her, dim and
pale, was the serene, wide-armed Christ imprisoned
within his crucifix.

Jenny's arms gripped me to her. Her mouth released
mine reluctantly again, her hands hurried my hands.
"I'm afraid—" she whispered. "I'm afraid it's time for
him to die."

Leaves rustled above us. Heat and clarity. "But most
of all he was so bitter over something I'd done," Jenny
breathed. "Something I hadn't known he knew. Something I shouldn't have done, and I'd *never* do again."

I tasted salt, my blood or her tears. "A man?"

"Not a man. That would have been honest, at least.
Come in, come in," she whispered. She laughed in
delight, or release, as before the anthropomorphic cross
we engaged in the ritual of regeneration.

Jenny and I walked arm in arm back to the Casa de
la Fuente in the dark, and I asked where she had
known Ibis.

"In Paris," she said. "He was part of the thing I'd
thought John hadn't known. I can't talk about it."

Taillights became visible as we rounded a curve, a car
with darting gleams of light on chrome stripping
parked before the Casa de la Fuente. Closer, I could
see the chrome-trisected circle in the reddish glow, a
Mercedes limousine. "Who's that?" Jenny said.

"I think Rodolfo Cisneros has brought Aurelia
home."

"My God, did we lose that one, too?"

A little farther along the lane I made out the figure
of a man, pale inhaling glow of a cigaret—Mickey on
duty. Jenny and I passed into the patio. The bare bulb
over Aurelia's doorway was lighted, the square of her
window was not. A voice said, "Oh, it's you."

It was Finch, a shadow like a child's stick figure in

the dim, burnt-orange illumination of the patio. "Have you and your lover been for a stroll?" he said to Jenny.

"Yes, John." She didn't release my arm. There was a scrape of a step behind us, and Mickey drifted between the gate and the side of the limousine, his cigaret tip glowing again, ruby ring reflecting fire.

"My dear—" Finch began in a frozen voice. There was a muffled shout and a crash from Aurelia's studio, a harsh jarring of furniture legs dragged across a tile floor, then silence. Mickey muttered. "My dear," Finch began again. "I am very much afraid—"

Aurelia's door slammed open and a naked man staggered outside, an arm extended to point at us where we stood. He cried for help in a strangled shout: "¡AYUDAME!"

With no attempt to break his fall, he collapsed with a meaty whack onto the bricks where I had lain groaning not long ago. A peg protruded from between his shoulders. "¡AYUDAME!" Rodolfo Cisneros cried again.

Mickey thrust past, his gun pointed at the door which had swung half closed behind his master. He scuttled forward and crouched with his gun probing at the door. This time I was on his back.

He sprawled on his face, my two hands on his gun. It came away easily. When I got off of him he turned over on his back, panic in his eyes, his cheek and chin scraped to raw bacon. He surged up at me with a yell and I had to halt the reflex of my finger on the trigger of his automatic. I swept my arm in a short arc to clout him on the side of the head, and he fell back against the trellis beside the door.

"Aurelia!" I called. There was no answer. Cisneros was groaning with a hard, dry catch in his lungs. In the center of his back was the black blunt handle of a knife. Mickey's hat lay on the doorstep. He stared up at me with his mouth open, panting, his chin dripping blood.

Always facing him, I passed him to push open the door and grope inside for the switch. The room came alight. Huddled on the floor, naked and black, was the Dark Angel of Santa Cruz with her neck impossibly bent. There was no dignity there now. A little blood had stained the bedclothes where she had stabbed Rodolfo Cisneros in their *abrazo*. I turned off the light and backed outside.

"Is she dead?" Jenny asked in a calm voice. Beside her Finch stood at an acute angle against the edge of the fountain, a hand braced behind him as though to catch himself if he fell. Their faces were whitish balloons in the dark.

"Dead," I said, and mopped at the sweat on my forehead with the back of my hand. Mickey had shifted his position to sit against the trellis. He had a bald, freckled head. "¡AYUDAME!" Cisneros panted.

He managed to rise to his hands and knees. He swayed there, his head twisting from side to side. Dark plantations of hairs extended down his back and circled into cowlicks on his haunches.

"Aren't you going to do anything?" John Finch cried in a ragged voice. "My God, you must get a doctor here! You—"

I shook my head, holding the gun on Mickey. His chin and cheek were a bloody mess. He wore gartered socks with intricate, old-fashioned clocks. Finch was bent at the waist as though he'd been hit in the stomach, Jenny holding his arm. "My *dear!*" he whispered. "In common humanity!"

We all watched the dying man swaying in agony on his hands and knees, on the final journey over the painful stones. Hurry up and die! I almost said it aloud. Die for the Republic of Santa Cruz, that Greek tragedy island. Die because Aurelia Velásquez, the tyrannicide, had solved and completed her own fate, and saved her island at least for the moment. I stood gripping Mickey's automatic as though it were a handle to reality. Blood looked black where it ran in a thin stream across Cisneros' back and dripped to the bricks.

"How did she die?" Jenny asked.

"He broke her neck," I said. Two very big, very strong, people locked in sex and then in death.

"Are you going to do nothing to help that man?" Finch said in a choking voice.

I shook my head again. Mickey sat watching me, seated now against the trellis on the crushed plants. I thought of the bullfights I had seen with the bull staggering and leaden, and the perspiring matador willing the animal to accept death.

"*¡Ayúdame!*" Cisneros whispered.

Jenny turned to face someone—Pepita—speaking to her rapidly. Pepita vanished. "I'm cold," Finch said in an old man's petulant voice, and Jenny put her arms around him.

The leader of the El Tres de Julio Movement collapsed. His arms gave way, he fell over sideways. He grunted harshly, his face lost in shadow beneath an arm, the knife handle hidden. It seemed to me that hours passed. His fingers began scraping at the bricks. When this stopped I let my arm supporting the heavy pistol drop. Mickey rose, I kicked his hat over toward him and plucked it up. With the hat on his bald head he immediately looked more dangerous.

"You want to give me that now?" he said, jerking his bloody chin at the automatic.

"I'll keep it."

I heard him suck his teeth. "Okay, blondie," he said, and strolled past me to fade into shadows. Jenny and Finch sat together on the edge of the fountain, her arms around him against the cold. I could feel the pressure of her eyes.

"What now, Murdoch?"

"I'll go phone." As I dropped the automatic into my jacket pocket the Mercedes started and rolled down the alley. Jenny helped Finch to his feet. His eyes stared at me out of his gray face as I passed them.

In my apartment the lamp beside the couch cast a funnel of light over a crumpled cushion and a glass containing a quarter of an inch of Old Mortality. My legs gave and I sat down. My collar was soaked with sweat.

"*Murdoch!*" Jenny's voice cried.

I ran stumbling outside. They were not in the patio, where Cisneros lay dead beneath the light over the studio door. "*Murdoch!*" In the lighted living room of Jenny's apartment, Finch lay on the tiles, his body arched like a bow and Jenny sprawled on top of him with her mouth pressed to his in an obscene and frantic openmouthed kiss. Her face jerked panting toward me: "He's had a heart attack and he can't swallow his pills! Get a doctor!"

She sucked in a breath. Her mouth descended on Finch's blue lips again. Nausea hit me in the solar plexus. On the writing table behind Jenny was Finch's chrome and leather attaché case with the snaps open, his half-frame glasses, a gold pen, and a small blue-leather-covered journal with his name engraved in gold on the cover: JOHN DOANE FINCH.

I had to go back to my own apartment to find Ibis' number. I encountered Pepita abroad again, and told her to go help the señora, the señor was *muy enfermo*.

"*El corazón!*" Pepita cried, and fled. Ibis said he would come immediately.

When I had hung up I sat with my eyes closed contemplating the fact that I had helped to kill John

Doane Finch. I didn't seem to feel anything. I drew
Mickey's automatic from my pocket, handfilling, satis-
fyingly heavy, mechanically beautiful. I had never had
much to do with guns. I tucked it beneath the cushion
of the chair, took up the phone again and rang the
emergency number. Someone would be along soon. On
my way back to Apartment B, I snapped off the light
over Aurelia's door and unscrewed two of the orange
bulbs to leave Cisneros' body in darkness.

I met Pepita coming out of Jenny's gate. Whimper-
ing, she pressed against the wall away from me, at the
same time almost thrusting something at me. It was
Finch's leatherbound journal. Weeping, she sprayed
me with unintelligible Spanish explanations. I took the
book from her, dropped it into my pocket, and went on
inside. Jenny knelt beside Finch, no longer attempting
resuscitation.

"Ibis is coming."

"It's too late." She gazed down into the gray face. "I
suppose it's never pretty," she said. She made con-
stricted gestures, rising, and I helped her to lift Finch's
body to the studio couch beside the writing desk. He
was surprisingly light. In a breaking voice she said, "I'm
sorry I said it was time for him to die."

She busied herself arranging his clothing, arranging
his arms and hands. Ibis arrived, to lean over Finch and
straighten immediately. "Ah, Madame Gray, there is
nothing to be done."

He kept nodding to himself while his eyes behind
the thick glasses darted around the room. Aware I was
watching him, he pressed a hand to the dead man's
chest, frowning. He stepped to the desk and opened
the attaché case, which was empty. "Pills?" he said to
Jenny. "There were pills to give?"

She produced a small bottle, he studied the label,
held the bottle to the light, shrugged and returned it to

her. He glanced swiftly around the room again. "One must not be shocked," he said. "You will telephone the Cruz Verde, friend Murdoch?"

"I'll call the embassy," I said, and left them. I had already called the embassy. In my apartment I took Finch's journal from my pocket. It was filled with a dense, tiny cursive I didn't even try to read in my haste. Now I realized Pepita had been saying she had taken it because Gabriela wanted it. Ibis had been looking for something in Jenny's apartment, Ibis whom she had known in Paris, who was part of the thing she hadn't known Finch knew, that she couldn't tell me about. There had been a scandal in Paris when Finch had threatened to retire and publish his memoirs. I slipped the journal into one of the brown envelopes I kept for mailing reports to American Ventures, addressed it to myself c/o U.S. Embassy, Mexico, D.F., plastered the envelope with stamps, opened the shutters and deposited it in the postbox outside my window.

I had just closed the shutters when Ibis walked in. He strolled a circuit of the room, looking solemn, but looking. He said, "I have given Madame Gray a sedative but I do not think she wishes to take it. Perhaps you will persuade her."

I said I would try.

"Perhaps you will do this now. I will wait here."

"I'll walk with you to the gate, P.T." He offered no argument and I went outside with him. Cisneros' body was not visible. Ibis drove away in his little sports model with the top down.

I was with Jenny when cars began arriving, and I met Frank Timken in the patio. Others were with him. I turned on the light over the studio door. The naked body of the Big Guy lay with his arm stretched over his face and blood congealed on his fingertips where he had scratched at the bricks in his final agony.

Frank glowered down at him. When I turned on the inside light he looked in at the body of the Dark Angel of Santa Cruz. Muscles stood out at the corners of his jaw, and when he spoke he sounded as though he had a cold in his head.

"That goddam big coon," he said.

I lay on the couch listening to the sound effects in the patio. There was movement and conversation, and traffic in the alley making a lightshow on the louvred shutters. Periodically the distant sound of the second-class bus interrupted my concentration on my anxieties: Mickey with his, "Okay, Blondie"; Clipper Armstrong's orders for me to go home, and the information that Eloise had infrared photographs of me engaged in adultery, probably with a twenty-year-old go-go dancer I had pursued in a bar until she caught me one long drunken night; and Finch's journal in the green mailbox decorated with the yellow postman's horn. Mexican mail was sometimes fast, sometimes slow, and sometimes lost.

I wondered about Ibis, about Pepita. Was everyone only a cover, no one what he seemed, all of us conspirators in the general defense, soldiers in one great citizen army or another, and no civilians left? Who was going to pay the taxes? Light blanched the shutters. There was a conversation near my gate I could almost understand. I resisted the impulse to eavesdrop. How would they handle this? Possibly they would have the good sense to do the simplest thing.

Finch had died past the peak of his career, full of honors and heart disease. I did not mourn him, nor Aurelia Velásquez, who had died a heroine. I only regretted that I had not trusted the Dark Angel to deal with her own great simplicity. When I moved to sit in the easy chair I could feel the shape of Mickey's automatic beneath the cushion, the princess and the pea. I considered the pros and cons of getting another drink, and wondered if I were going to have to face Frank again tonight. A woman's voice called, "Tommy? Can I come in?"

I got to my feet as Pat Hepner entered, in a tan sweater and skirt, a creamy polo coat draped over her shoulders. She swung around to present the coat to me for removal. "This damned place," she said. "If you'd moved out when we asked you to none of this would have happened. But I'm not going to say any more about *that*."

"How's Frank holding up?"

She ignored the question, striding like a model around the room. She seemed extremely nervous. "What are they doing with all the bodies out there?" I asked, cold-bloodedly.

"They've taken them away." With a swing of her skirt she turned to confront me. "Tommy, you look awful! What happened to your face?"

"One of those household accidents."

"You poor thing! What a lot you've been through today!"

"Do you want a drink, Pat?"

She wanted a drink but she insisted on getting it herself, and I was happy enough to sit down again and let her be the barman. I told her where to find the *agua purificada*.

She brought me back my highball and sat on the couch facing me in a semblance of great ease, with her tan legs crossed, her shoes kicked loose, and her brightest smile. We sipped our drinks. Conversation did not flow.

Pat was in constant motion, rearranging her hair, re-crossing her legs, turning her head from side to side to present me with a choice of clean-cut profiles. "Do you

mind if I take my shoes off, Tommy? I'm a barefoot
girl at heart."

I did not mind, though I was worried that the evening might progress toward a consummation I devoutly
did not wish. Pat watched me attentively, as though my
face were more marked than I had thought. My head
felt thick and dull. I shook it to clear it. The barefoot
girl was very handsome, but there were too many of
her.

Carefully I set the half-finished glass of Old Mickey
Finn on the floor beside my chair. A chorus line of
gracefully reclining girls danced in my eyes. Pat was in
pursuit of the journal, of course. I could still, with a
great effort, congeal her into one, but I knew I was not
going to be moving from my chair. My body felt as
though it had been soaking for days in some warm and
enervating fluid. "What would you do if I came after
you?" I asked. "Karate?"

No reply.

Her face was stiff and a little frightened, and I de-
duced that I wasn't supposed to have realized what was
happening to me.

"What was it you slipped into my drink, the opium
of the people?" I asked. I squinted ferociously to hold
the image of her face from multiplying. "*You*'re the
opium of the people!" I said.

My concentration slipped a notch and a colony of
Pat Hepners, the one woman gang, frowned in fluttery
blond images to the periphery of my vision. "Do you
know how I know who you are?" I asked. "Because I'm
married to you."

The host of blondes began slowly to revolve, and my
voice vibrated so I could hardly make out what I was
saying. "I'm sorry about that go-go girl, Ellie. And I'm
sorry she wasn't the only one. Unfortunately I serve
women very well, it's a thing I have. I suppose I'm

searching for something, there are certain dissatisfac-
tions I really hate to mention so I won't. But adultery
is a quest, you know." I remember telling Ibis we
needed a new America to sail off to. But of course it
wasn't Eloise I was talking to, it was Pat Hepner like a
sheet of photographic proofs. I said, vibrato, "And
there is considerable doubt that you can adulterously
penetrate something inorganic anyway. For how do you
explain," I said, mentally shooting a fast cross exam-
iner's finger at her, on the offensive at last, "the
absence of sweat glands? The lack of body odor? The
fact that hair no longer seeks to grow in the armpits? Is
it not true that, cut in section, no bowels or organs
would show, but only styrofoam?" I mentally held up a
hand to stem her lies and excuses.

She said something that failed to come through. I
had hurt her feelings. My head was unbearably heavy as
I peered at the myriad Her on the couch. I hadn't
meant to hurt. "I'm sorry, Ellie," I said. "It was a bad
joke.

"But if I could only explain to you how I feel,"
somebody's voice, no longer vibrating but thick as cold
molasses, went on. "You know I hate to talk seriously,
but it seems so important to me that somebody try to
bust the system. Put a monkey wrench in the gears. Get
the blood out of the sugar and the hostages away from
the future. Can't you see?" I said, feeling my voice
running down with relief that I could quit now, sleep
now, the bull die now; running down and down, talking, but saying what? "Can't you see?" I cried in one
last heroic effort. "That we have to invent America all
over again?"

In troubled sleep I was aware of activity all around
me, voices echoing as though people were hallooing in
a great, windy shed, moving about, carrying, lifting—
what were they doing? All the world was searching for

Finch's journal. Very cold, you over there. A little
warmer by the window. No, cold again; quite cold.
That frailest of stringers, Pepita, must have finked that
the Señor Güero had taken the journal from her.
Overthinking as usual, instead of coming to me with a
simple request like, "Give us the journal or we'll kill
you!" elaborate plots had been contrived, with beautiful girl agents and doped drinks. They were all comedi-
ans, only their ultimate power could be taken seriously,
their progresses and failures to be viewed with laughter
and with terror.

There did seem to be a great many of them calling
back and forth within the echoing warehouse. Pat, and
Frank—and *Jenny?* No, not Jenny! Tears of protest
ached in my eyes, ached through my mind. No, I would
not accept that. No, not Jenny. *Not Jenny Gray!*

(19) WEDNESDAY, I

THE alarm that rang me back from wherever I'd been was the popping of the second-class bus straining up the hill into San Angel's Plaza San Jacinto. The sound bored into the fortifications of my consciousness with a persistence and a duration that made it clear something would have to be done about that bus, a Molotov cocktail or a plastic bomb.

It was not the bus, but someone speaking in a rapid staccato close within my head.

I was sitting aching in the same chair, and across from me on the couch was Pat Hepner. Pat stared at me, or just past me, with a stupid expression. It was an incomprehensible tableau, for Frank Timken stood before the table in the dining alcove, coatless, tie jerked off center, sleeves rolled on his wrists which for some reason were elevated to shoulder level, hands spread-fingered as though supporting something large and invisible. No Jenny in sight. But as I came slowly back to consciousness I realized that there was a third party present, who had been speaking in the staccato voice, and by triangulation I fixed the presence as slightly behind my left shoulder.

Out of the corner of my eye I could make out something that looked like a discolored tin can suspended horizontally. It was connected to a black rod, which, further back, entered a larger greasy-looking cylinder. A hand gripped the cylinder. My mind toiled over this evidence, and it was as though I could watch the circuits in operation inside my head, a dim spark moving over a grid of burnt and rusty wires. Someone was standing behind me holding a machine pistol, and the tin can on the end was a silencer.

The weapon was pointed at Pat Hepner, whose stupefied expression was one of fear, and Frank Timken, who had his hands raised. Pat and Frank were American agents, so whoever held the gun was not one. And when the voice spoke again I almost nodded, for although it was harsh, the accent thick and phony, it was familiar.

"You weel give it to me this moment or I will kill you. Thee girl is first!"

Pat folded her arms over her breast. No one looked at me, merely a part of the furnishing of the room. In a choked voice, Frank said, "Can't you understand we haven't found it, for Christ's sake!"

"But he had it," Gabriela Bazán said, behind me. "I know thees!"

I puzzled over why she was trying to disguise her voice, my mind moving through the slow process on the grid again, this time without result. Next I began checking my control systems. Muscles in my right arm fluttered, my left arm tensed and relaxed, my legs tickled as though they had been asleep.

The tin can moved nearer. "Can thees one wake up?" My shoulder was prodded. "Wake up!"

My right hand swung to catch the greasy barrel, jerking it back and up, wrenching it sideways with a twist of my body. It came loose with a harsh squawk from Gabriela. I staggered to my feet holding the machine pistol, and braced myself on the back of my chair while

the room swayed and circled. Facing me was a figure in
a man's suit, a rebozo muffling the bottom of the face,
a gray hat brim pulled down. Gabriela's hands were
held out in a gesture of dismay and surrender. She
stepped backward and leaned against the wall, hands
dropping to her sides.

I crooked the machine pistol over my arm with a
finger on the trigger. I seemed to be in command of the
scene, but not of myself. My legs were quivering, but
the eccentric circling gradually swung to a stop.

"Nice work, Tom," Frank said. I shuffled sideways
where I could face the three of them at once.

Shakily Pat said, "Tommy—it's El Chato!"

My voice still had the reverberating quality inside my
head, as though I were shouting in a sheet metal
hangar. "I'm afraid not," I said. "Let's take off the
rebozo, Gabriela."

In silence she removed her hat and unwound the
rebozo. Her face was drawn with tension. She glanced
coolly from me to Frank, as he came forward.

"You want to give me that now?" Frank said.

"No. Go sit down with Mata Hari."

"Give me that!" He reached for it and I smacked the
silencer against the side of his head. "Oh!" Pat cried, as
he staggered back with both hands clutched to his left
temple.

"What is this?" Gabriela said. "Americans fighting?"

"God damn you, Murdoch! You are way out over
your head in this! You—"

"Sit down! I've been doped and I'm not responsible
for my actions! Down!"

He sat down beside Pat, who hastily drew up her
legs. She was regarding me with awe. Frank studied the
blood on his hand as though it were evidence, grimaced
and pressed it to his head again.

"If you think you're turning my maid over to the

Seguridad again I've got bad news for you," I told him. "She's leaving Mexico for good. She's going back to Cuba to be a schoolteacher."

"Aha!" Gabriela said. Casually she thrust her hands into the pockets of her man's jacket. "A schoolteacher!"

I moved toward her, smiling and holding the machine pistol at ease. I jammed a hand into her pocket over her hand, and captured the little revolver she had there. She hissed at me as I dropped it into my own pocket.

"A two-gun schoolteacher," Frank said. "You naive jerk!"

"A jerk in the hand is worth two bushers like you," I said. "You had your way earlier and how many people died? Now let's try it my way. I don't want any more holes burnt in this one, even if she is a Commie."

All were staring at me. I felt like a drunk unable to face sobriety just yet. Frank said with flattened lips, "You value an individual more than your country's interest, right?"

"I'm accentuating the individual, right. My country's interest is something you say but I don't believe any more."

"If you let that bitch get away you're in real trouble, and you'd better believe it."

"Tommy—" Pat started, but subsided.

"You are going to let this bitch get away?" Gabriela asked.

"Even better than that."

"Tom," Frank said, in a more reasonable voice. "The fact of the matter is we know you stole that journal."

I didn't think I wanted to go into that now. I said to Gabriela, "Go out and open the garage door and get in the car."

"¡Sí!" Gabriela said, and vanished around the corner like a cat in flight.

•

"You let her *go!*" Pat breathed.

I saluted case-officer and cutout with the machine pistol, and started out. All things seemed clear to me, standing out from peripheral confusion, particulars surfacing from abstractions. The orange lights of the patio were still on, forming strange shadows on the bricks just outside my gate. I feinted like a netman in doubles to pull a shot to my alley, stepping back as a burly figure lurched across my path. I slammed the barrel of the machine pistol against his head and he fell with an explosive grunt. I stood over the motionless body panting with surprise at his ineptitude or else my own talent for this game.

I had a glimpse of Gabriela's slimmer figure disappearing. I turned on the entry light. Shattered glasses glinted. I had never seen a blackjack before; this one looked like a streamlined, leathercovered lambchop. A fat man lay unconscious on the bricks, one arm under him, the other crumpled against the wall. He wore a black beret, a dark suit and huaraches. Frank appeared in the hallway as I pulled at Ibis' shoulder to expose his face. He made a labored, snoring sound.

"Here, you can have this one," I said to Frank, and went on out to the garage. I thought Gabriela would have vanished, but the door was open, and when I called her name she said, "I am here."

I squeezed into the driver's seat of the Corvette with metal bruising my hipbones, and jammed the machine pistol down between my seat and the door. Backing out of the garage, I spun my wheels starting down the alley. The exhaust rocketed between the walls.

"I am grateful, Thomas Murdoch," Gabriela said, clinging to the dashboard.

"Were you working with Ibis all along?"

"I cannot answer that, please."

It came on me that I might have been a little too

dashing, that maybe being soft on Commies, or else my antagonism for Pat and Frank, had led me to dubious decisions. I swung out onto Insurgentes. There was no traffic; it had to be well after midnight. Now I began to worry about Frank phoning the Mexican police and the lack of anonymity of the big red Corvette. I cut over to the Avenida of the Revolucíon as a less logical route into the center of Mexico City. Clarity and certainty were withering.

"Go home," I said to the silent figure beside me. "If they catch you it's back to the *Seguridad* for more of the same, and they will probably stick you with the murder of Herrerro. Go home. Go to the provinces and teach school. That's a very popular and patriotic thing to do right now in Cuba, I understand."

"Not very popular with those who have done it," Gabriela said. "You are very romantic, Thomas." And she said, "And what of my *novio?*"

"I remember your story about a girl being brought her brother's eye to make her give information that did not exist. I think El Chato is dead, or—"

"Perhaps you think too much."

"I think El Chato is a fine propaganda device for Cuba. If there were no El Chato it would be necessary to invent him, and if he existed he would have been here tonight instead of Ibis. Where do you want to go this time?"

"It does not matter. Perhaps the Plaza Garibaldi."

"And go *home*."

"All right, Thomas."

"Promise."

"You like me, huh?" she said, and made a curious sound. But then she said in a hard voice, "Perhaps I will go home, but I will not stay there. You are very sweet. You are very sentimental, very romantic. But this is not a sentimental and romantic game we play. I will tell you who that fat doctor is. He is KGB."

"What's KGB?"

She laughed harshly. Then she sighed. "Thomas, to me you are sweet, sentimental, romantic—playing games. To KGB *we* are like that. KGB is your FBI, CIA, all military intelligence and secret service together, only it is Russian."

The Corvette was moving fast down the Avenue of the Revolution toward the *centro*. Involuntarily my foot pressed harder on the accelerator.

"He is Department D," Gabriela's voice continued. "You do not know of this, either. Department D is Dezinformatsiya, which means what it sounds like in English. They work to make United States look bad to the world through bad information. They forge documents, they make propaganda and scandals against you. The doctor wants very much the famous journal of John Finch. He sees me there, he finds out who I am, and he has the power to make me help him. This is where I have been since you took me away the other time. At the house of the doctor. I do not like him, I do not like what I have seen there, and I warn you against him. And, I must tell you that you are in great danger because of the journal of John Finch. This is a very important matter to Department D of the KGB. Pepita says you have it. Do you have it?"

"I don't have it," I said.

Headlights swung out of a side street behind us. I did not accelerate and they came closer, very bright. Gabriela was hunched down in her seat staring at the light filing the rearview mirror. She said, "This *coche* looks like it will go very fast."

With my foot down on the throttle the tachometer needle jumped and the Corvette walked away from the

lights. "Turn here now," Gabriela said, and we
squawled around a corner. "Now again," she said. Immediately we lost the pursuing car, if it had even been
after us at all. We were in a part of town my Grey Line
Tour hadn't visited. "Now we must go to the Plaza
Garibaldi," Gabriela said, sitting up very straight with
one hand on the dashboard. No more headlights appeared.

She directed me, constantly turning, always keeping
off the main streets, until I recognized the old town
area around the Zócalo. I crossed streetcar tracks and
entered another maze of narrow streets. Finally I saw
the giant neon cowboy with the rope, unlighted now.
There was no one abroad in the Plaza Garibaldi. Gabriela sighed with relief as I cruised around the square,
and nosed into the curb where she pointed her finger
like aiming a gun. She said, "Do you kiss this Commie
one last time?"

I leaned over to kiss her one last time in the thick
darkness, and caught too late at her hand extracting her
little revolver from my jacket pocket. She pushed the
muzzle against my breastbone.

"You will tell me where to find the journal of John
Finch which you have taken from Pepita!"

I laughed at her, she cursed me, and headlights
blazed suddenly all around us. A car swept at speed
into the Plaza Garibaldi, and without a word Gabriela
thrust open her door and jumped out. The other car
roared across the square as though bent on ramming
the Corvette, and I started out my own door just as it
veered off and braked with screaming tires, fishtailing
with its speed. Gabriela's running figure was caught in
its lights as doors flew open against their stops. Two
men leaped out and sprinted after her.

There was a moment of silence in which the crack of
running feet was the only sound, and then the silence

blew up in an enormous shattering series of explosions
that my stunned mind could not even comprehend
until I saw in their own headlights the two *Seguridad*
men spin and dance and fall as though jerked by ropes
with a shrill screaming inside the drumroll of the machine gun while Gabriela fled from sight.

The headlights of the police car were snuffed out,
there was the screech of a ricochet and the washpan
thumping of bullets piercing metal. I dropped to the
pavement and rolled up against a low curbing as bullets
stitched across the side of the Corvette above me. A
tire blew.

When the shooting ceased the silence was awesome.
Lying against the curb, I smelled the raw stink of
gasoline.

A stocky figure appeared in the small illumination
from my parking lights. He carried a gun like the one I
had taken from Gabriela, which I couldn't reach now.
There was a flare of a match, a glimpse of a broad,
brutal face. He was big through the shoulders. If it was
not El Chato, he would do until the real thing came
along.

Chato flipped his match out in a long arc. Immediately igniting gasoline flickering bluely around the *Seguridad* car. My gas tank had also been hit. El Chato
would not care much whether I burned or he shot me,
but I thought I would rather be shot. I hunched back-
wards along the curb, rose, and sprinted for cover.

Gabriela's voice said clearly, "No, Chato! *No!*"

It was an interminable moment until I reached the
corner, where I jerked one glance behind me to see the
flames spreading toward my beautiful Corvette.

The phone in my apartment didn't answer. I decided
against calling Jenny Gray. I dialed the emergency
number and told the swing-shift operator I had to talk

to Frank Timken. I was instructed to call back in ten minutes.

I waited in the phone booth in the sleeping lobby of an old hotel sinking into dignified decrepitude near the Zócalo. A brown-faced, tousled clerk watched me from behind the desk. Above his head clock hands split a white circle vertically. As I watched the minute hand imperceptibly moved; five after six, ten after six.

The second time I rang the number Frank was available. He did not greet me like a long-lost friend.

"That was quite a foursome we had," I said. "I thought it was just tennis and it turned out to be the front lines of the secret war. Do you have him there?"

"Who?" Frank said irritably.

"Ibis!"

He didn't answer. Realization scratched a light like a match. I said, "You do know he's KGB, Department D. He was after Finch's journal and he'd drafted Bazán into playing gunman for him."

A faintly whistling silence continued, as though Frank were listening in outer space. Finally he said, "Where do you get your information, Murdoch?"

"Bazán."

"You let her get away, did you?"

"You let Ibis get away."

There was heavy breathing as he got control of himself, and shifted over to the offense. "We know you took that journal, Murdoch."

"Hadn't you better get in touch with the *Seguridad* about Ibis? He's a hell of a lot bigger game than Gabriela Bazán."

"I told you you're way out over your head in this!"

"You were right," I said, and told him about the massacre in the Plaza Garibaldi, while he muttered, "Christ, Murdoch!" and, "Jesus *Christ!*"

In a steely voice he said, "Do you see what you've done? You've led two poor fellows from the *Seguridad* into a trap!"

It seemed to me that if I revealed to Frank that I took anything seriously as was warranted, he had me. "My car is on my tourist card," I complained. "What do I have to do to leave the country without it? It's a wreck."

"Christ, you're *cold*," Frank said. "If the *Seguridad* catches up with you you're never going to leave the country. You get in here with that journal right now and we'll see what we can do about spiriting you out of Mexico."

I told him I didn't have to talk to him if he was going to threaten me, and hung up. I leaned in the phone booth sweating, tired as ashes. What now, Tiger?

Outside the sky was pale green with dawn. I walked empty streets past ancient stone buildings and slabsided modern bank buildings patrolled by cops. I was very jittery about cops. A streetcar whined along a side street, and at the end of a broad avenue there was a glimpse of one of the tilted churches of Mexico City. Behind and above it, floating disembodied was a volcano like a white island on an invisible sea.

I found an early opening café on Tacuba, and over a tall glass of *café con leche* and some sweet rolls that tasted like fine sawdust and sweet sand I considered the probability that Frank was right and I was in trouble over my head. I could get out of trouble by turning over the journal. My spirits rose at the thought of telling the Clipper, who had such a fine eye for a Commie, about his friend the Doc.

When I phoned him at the María Isabel, he said, "Tommy, for Christ's sake can you get over here right

away? How soon can you get here, Tommy?" It was a
cry for help.

In Suite D the geriatric wonder boy was not his usual
ebullient self. He needed a shave and the stubble was
frosted as though he'd spent the night with his head in
the deepfreeze. I wondered what he put on his hair. A
tray of dishes rested on a stand, and he asked if I
wanted coffee.

I was already relenting, but I said, "What do you
hear from your friend the Doc?"

"That son of a bitch."

"That Commie son of a bitch?"

Eyewhites flashed at me. Breathing heavily, he bent
to pour coffee into a blue cup. "That son of a bitch's
really got me, Tommy."

Moving as though he had a sore back, he sat down in
a zebra-striped chair. He crossed his legs and brooded
into his cup. He had forgotten to pour coffee for me, a
shocking indication of his morale. I remembered Gabriela saying that Dezinformatsiya meant what it
sounded like in English, disinformation. Forged documents and scandals and propaganda against the United
States. Such as Finch's journal which might contain
criticism of American policies, such as— "What did he
get on you?" I asked.

His eyes with their different slants gazed back at me
miserably. I pictured him with Ibis among the mariachis, Old Doc and Clipper singing the USC Fight
Song in the Plaza Garibaldi where El Chato hung out,
but also the pimp with the mirror glasses and a little
girl only eleven years old. What do you want, señor?

"Pictures?" I asked.

He ran a hand through miraculously non-graying
curls, sipped his coffee, nodded once. "Can we forget

all the goddam water under the goddam bridge,
Tommy?"

I went to pour myself a cup of coffee. I was embarrassed for him. "I'd better see the pictures," I said.

"You don't want to see the pictures."

I sipped lukewarm black coffee and watched him
dither with his own cup. Finally he made clicking
sounds with his tongue, rose, and marched into the
bedroom. He returned with a sheaf of photographs,
four-by-six black and white. His cheeks were veined
with dark red beneath the snowy stubble as he stood
riffling his thumb through them.

"You know how a guy gets horny sometimes," he
said. "You and I're a lot the same kind of guy,
Tommy."

"How old was she?"

He wet his lips with a slide of his tongue. "It's not
that. Christ, I wish it *was* that."

I put out my hands for the photographs. Still he held
them back. "That clever son of a bitch!" he said.
"Tommy, he's got me by the goddam *balls*. Not just
me, either."

I held out my hand.

"He took me like the original hick from Rub,"
Clipper said. "*Christ*. Who hasn't heard of the routine!
Get some hick in the whorehouse chasing a naked babe
with his pecker flapping and everybody watching
through peepholes." He stopped to clear his throat.

"I don't know what you'll think of the old Clipper,"
he said as he handed me the first photograph. It was a
shot of Mister Jelly Roll with a girl in a white lace dress
on a loveseat. The lace suggested a communion dress,
but it was not a little girl wearing it. Clipper's hand
covered the girl's knee, his face her face.

He passed me another. In this the girl's features were

visible; black, high-coiffed hair, dark-lipsticked mouth.
The arrogant face was tantalizingly familiar. Clipper
had stripped to polka dot shorts, and a roll of waist fat
showed. In succeeding photographs the scene became
one of action as Clipper, sans polka dots and majestically flapping, chased the girl past a bed, the loveseat, a
corner table with a vase on it, both participants with
laughing faces, and the girl's clothing gradually dwin-
dling to bra and panties. She had smooth, muscular
legs. Once Clipper caught her against the table, bending her over it to kiss her, but she escaped and the
chase continued. I was uncomfortably reminded of my
own televised adventures in the tower bedroom. The
familiarity of the whore's face continued to bother me.

"You don't get it yet?" Clipper said heavily. More
photos were more of the same. He held back the final
three or four. "Don't you get it, Tommy?" His mouth
turned down with misery and distaste, he said, "It's a
son of a bitch in *drag!*"

He passed me the last pictures, all climactic. It was a
son of a bitch in drag, all right.

"Do you know who this is?" I asked. He didn't
know. "He's a matador named Jesús Obregón."

"Tommy, if these get out everybody'll think I'm
queer!"

Laughter gripped my gullet. I couldn't keep it back,
holding the photos in one hand, coffee slopping onto
my knee from the cup in the other. He shouted at me.

I went to stand looking out the window. The pristine
islands still hovered, but the Valley of the Anahuac was
fading into its tan cocoon.

"Tommy, these are frames from a *movie!*"

He would be a star on the gay smoker circuit. I
looked through the photographs at each showing of the
face of Jesús Obregón. Clipper was the comedian of the
piece, but Obregón's expression was another matter.

Neither phony nor conniving, it was merely private. I handed the stack back to Superrube.

"You've got to get me off the hook, Tommy." He said it pathetically, but I thought he might not be the broken man he seemed. I had learned never to underestimate my father-in-law. "How about a drink?" he said, slapping his hands together as though we had just made a deal. "That's what we need."

He strode across to the sideboard. "You'll fix it for me, won't you, Tommy?" He sloshed whiskey into a glass.

"What did you mean, not just you?" I said.

"What's that?"

"You said Ibis had you by the balls, but not just you."

He straightened to attention, his hand holding his dark brown drink like his hat against his heart. "I mean my country, Tommy. That Commie son of a bitch can get at my country through this thing. That's what we're working against, here. It's not just for me."

"What if I can make a deal?"

"You're the only one that can, Tommy."

I didn't know what he meant.

"You're the only one that can make him the deal he wants," he said. "He's got it in his mind you stole something of Finch's, Tommy. He'll deal for that."

"You're kidding," I said.

"Tommy, I knew Finch well enough—*you* knew him well enough—to know he wouldn't write anything that would hurt his country."

"If the KGB has that journal it won't matter what Finch wrote."

We stood staring at each other for a concentrated moment. "You're kidding," I said again.

He nodded dully. "I guess you're right, Tommy."

He turned away from me with his shoulders sagging.

"I sold that sugar stock," he said. "You were taking it so hard there. I did it for you, Tommy."

"Make anything on it?"

"A few bucks," the Clipper said. He sat down again, sipping his scotch and gazing at me with cloudy eyes.

"Will you back me up if I can make a deal with Ibis? It may cost you a few bucks."

"He doesn't want money."

"I think he might."

"Pay blackmail the rest of my life," he said.

"That's the trouble with photographs, you can never be sure you've got them all the way bought. Unless you're dealing with an honest businessman."

"How the hell can a Commie be an honest businessman, for Christ's sake," the Clipper said disgustedly. He seemed tired of the international crap.

I went to phone Ibis. I knew the number now, and as usual he answered immediately. "Come to see me, come to see me, my partner Murdoch," he said in his jolliest voice. "And we will talk over this matter like tennis players and gentlemen."

"What'd you say that bullfighter's name was?" the Clipper asked as I was leaving.

Dr. P. T. Ibis wore a bandage like a skullcap covering his right temple, and his left arm in a muslin sling. He had on a purple shirt with white cord lacing, greenish Madras shorts. On his feet, which seemed to have too many toes, were his fancy huaraches. His glasses glinted genially in the sunlight in the sala, and I had no intimations of being surrounded by KGB death squads.

"Well, friend Murdoch, so now we meet as our truer selves, eh?"

"How's the head, P.T.?"

"Ha! Ha!" He touched a finger to his skullcap, he illustrated that he could raise his slinged elbow. "To throw the ball in service will be difficult for a little while."

"Broken?"

"A dislocation of the shoulder only. Well, well, last night was unfortunate. One cannot attend to two projects with complete attention, one is unlucky who must depend on allies. And as has been said it is not whether one wins or loses, but how one plays the game. You have played well."

From the wall above the sun-filled ferns the man in the black tunic gazed down, arm raised over us. I said, "You mean I played well, but you won?"

"Ha! Ha!" Ibis said, ushering me to a chair. We sat facing each other across three feet of tiles. Ibis' bare knees looked like pink grapefruit. "Of course I win," he said. "I am a student of the mind! Your father-in-law, who is a giant of a man, has this small Achilles' heel. He has fears of his manhood. This is a commonplace in these great, strong American men. I have won by a masterpiece, yes—it will be an example for textbooks."

"I was surprised to learn you were a Communist, P.T. You never seemed the type."

"But I am secret agent merely! I have been agent for Americans also—it is where I have learned of the journal of John Finch. Some think I am an agent of America still—and perhaps I will be again!" He laughed fatly, nodding. "No, friend Murdoch, not a Communist, a professional. One is paid for one's services."

He took off his glasses and began to polish the lenses with his handkerchief. Naked, his eyes were pink, fleshy and squinting, like a pig's eyes.

"I think Clipper Armstrong will pay a hundred thousand for those negatives," I said.

Ibis laughed and flipped his fingers in a gesture of more. "I know your father-in-law Armstrong has unlimited money, but I am afraid he would rather commit suicide than give much to me. There is resentment, eh, not merely admiration for masterpiece?"

"He said something about a goddam Commie queen."

"Ha! Ha!" Ibis said. "Do you think five millions?"

"Suicide."

"How much will he give, the ultimate figure, do you think?"

I had no idea. I sat looking into his solemn face, his mouth arranged into a pretense of a grin. Probably, as a businessman, he was as sharp and just about as honest as the Clipper.

"My friend Murdoch, I do not know your limitations, but I urge you to think in the very largest figures. This concerns us both very much."

"Both of us why?"

"Because we will share it!" He rearranged his arm in the sling, his face bunched with intensity. "My friend, you and I stand at this moment in such power that what we can demand in money is limited only by the ability of our minds to grasp our position."

His addressing me as his partner had taken on a new meaning. I cleared my throat. "I don't understand."

"Listen! I know what my employers will pay for journal of John Finch. You must determine what Armstrong will pay for photographs. These two figures will be combined, each of us to have one half. Will Armstrong pay two millions?"

"Is that what the KGB will pay?"

His eyes swam at me. The palms of my hands were sweating. "And Armstrong?" Ibis said. "Maybe he will pay three?"

I began to laugh.

"You must listen!" Ibis cried. "What is the sum of two millions of dollars? Merely the price of U-2 airplane! But can you understand what a man can do with two millions? Stretch the mind, my partner! Millions multiply. It is the advantage of capitalism that money procreates itself. Two millions can quickly become ten, twenty. Then!"

"What then?"

"Your mind will not absorb this," Ibis said unhappily, tossing his good hand into the air. "My partner, everywhere is collectivism on the march. Everywhere Malthus and Marx triumph. Even in America where socialism must be called something else. Accommodation must be made for millions of new humans on this planet each year, new laws, new restrictions on freedom, fewer and fewer options. Soon individual will be extinct! Already no more kings, soon no more titans of capitalism like your father-in-law, presently no more poets, artists, nonconformists, no more individuals. Only masses, robots of state! How can we hold back this flood? We can hold it back for ourselves, my friend. With two millions, with ten or twenty millions and the imagination of an unlimited mind, one can be a king with his own kingdom!"

He peered at me, his lips working over his teeth. "My partner, the one way left to be a great individual is to be very rich. We have in our hands means to this greatness!"

"I'm afraid I wouldn't enjoy it," I said. "I'd feel guilty."

Ibis made a sound of infinite disgust. "The tragedy is that what you say is true!" he cried. He slammed his fist on his knee and leaned back in his chair, his face a hectic red. "Ha! you are loyal American boy!" he continued. "Are you loyal also to your father-in-law Armstrong, who exploits you? For he is not America, friend Murdoch. He has no loyalty to anything but money increasing itself."

"That sounds a little party liney," I said.

There was a sound of steps and the subject of all this came into the sala. Clipper wore dark glasses and a pale blue double-breasted suit. His clean-shaven face was stony.

"Welcome, my dear Armstrong," Ibis said. "The employer comes to see how the negotiations proceed, eh? We have agreed upon a figure."

"Yeah?" Clipper said.

"It is three million dollars," Ibis said.

"You've got to be kidding," Clipper said in a bleak voice. The dark glasses turned toward me, his big chin jutted. He moved his shoulders restlessly inside the double-breasted jacket, put a hand in his pocket and stepped toward Ibis, scowling.

"But what is this?" Ibis said. "Do you think one would not have oneself covered in case of danger?"

"I want those goddam negatives," Clipper said through his teeth. He swung furiously toward me. "After all I've done for you! Three million bucks!"

"I'd thought we were talking two million," I said.

"For*get* it!" He faced Ibis again. "You told me the deal you'd make, Ibis!"

Ibis sighed. "Yes," he said. "Yes, my dear Armstrong."

I sat in the leather chair and watched Clipper remove his hand from his pocket. In a conciliatory voice he said, "You told me yourself it doesn't matter what's in that journal, Tommy, the Russkies would make up what they wanted to, anyway."

"That of course is correct," Ibis said, nodding.

"I'm going to make it goddam worth your while, Tommy," the Clipper went on. It was as though a demonstration had been arranged to follow Ibis' lecture on him. America first, after Clipper Armstrong. And he would be thinking he was going to have his way, as usual.

"Go fuck yourself," I said.

Ibis laughed. "That is, of course, more socially acceptable than what is revealed in motion pictures."

Clipper shouted wordlessly. Ibis said, "We wish the same consummation, my dear Armstrong. Why do we not have it?" Without moving he appeared all at once to be standing much closer to Sell-out, both of them gazing down at me, Department D of the KGB and the Great Linebuster, in thick glasses and impenetrable dark ones.

Ibis said, "You will remember what was done to brave little *Cubana*, friend Murdoch. There was no imagination there."

"And you have imagination, P.T.? What about you, AC–DC?"

"What is most important is that *you* have," Ibis said. He nodded and smiled, and said to Clipper, "He is very brave, your son-in-law?"

"I don't think so," said C. E. Armstrong.

"Just torture me copasetic, will you?" I was having a problem with shortness of breath. Clipper produced a revolver and showed it to me, and Ibis began to laugh.

"Come, come, come! Let us please discuss this matter as three friends. Please, the armaments make conversation so difficult!" Ibis was still chuckling when Jesús Obregón came in, carrying a sword.

The matador had on a gray felt cap pulled down to his dark glasses. He wore a beige jacket with a purple foulard scarf knotted around his throat, and black and white checked pants. The sword, which he carried like a cane, had a scarlet cord wrapped around the hilt and a little way down the blade, which was bent at the tip—a bull-killing sword. He strutted into the sala, posing like a dancer. With graceful moués of his body he crossed the tiles to Ibis, paying no attention to Clipper and me.

Ibis retreated, speaking rapidly in Spanish, until he backed into the TV set. Obregón profiled with the sword raised like a duelist. I thought it surely a joke, as Ibis lifted his sling to cross his arms in front of his body. He screamed as the bent tip of the sword cut past his fat forearms. The sword encountered some obstruction in a visible hesitation, until with a surge of his shoulder Obregón sent it home.

The fat man crumpled and Obregón stepped back, jerking the sword free. Ibis rolled onto the floor face down. There was a bloody hole in the back of his purple shirt.

I sat stupidly watching Obregón wiping the bloody blade on a green Madras buttock, one side and then the other. Clipper was holding his revolver limply, the barrel pointed down. His face glistened like spoiled fish.

My mind began to operate again. "Are you responsible for this?"

"Christ! I only sent those prints over to him, in case—"

Obregón dropped the sword with a clatter and swung dramatically toward us. He spoke in Spanish to Clipper; I understood the gist of it.

"He wants you to help him hunt for the negatives. But you're not going to find anything here."

Clipper fumbled the revolver back into his pocket while nodding with overemphatic friendliness to Obregón, who stood slim and square-shouldered, with a hip cocked like a fairy David before the dead Goliath. Blood was puddling out from beneath Ibis' body.

With a peremptory gesture Obregón strutted off

toward the interior of the house. I left for the outer
light and air, and Clipper trailed behind me into the
soft San Angel sunshine. Breathing deeply, I watched
Big Shorty lurch against Obregón's purple Porsche. He
leaned there retching, a corseted, crooked, sell-out old
man with dyed hair, his glamor collapsed around his
feet like overalls in an outhouse.

"It's got to be tough when you're in the bigs," I
said.

"Tommy!" he called, when I started away. "Hey,
Tommy!"

I didn't know if I had the strength to make it on foot
to the Casa de la Fuente, but I had enough not to look
back. I had lived too long the friend to eagles, too close
to the big guns; now the handwriting was on the wall,
the blood in the sugar (*Do Not Deny!*), the bell was
tolling for crappy little Caribbean Republics no one
gave a damn about, but also for the America I loved.
Coming up from error, the individual man was all
strung out in space and time on the rocky road leading
to the disaster that was freedom. I stumbled, swinging
a foot too low over the cobbles.

A honk startled me, and I leaned against a stone wall
to let the car pass. A gray Chevrolet drew abreast,
Frank Timken leaning across the seat with a glare
decorated by a patch of white adhesive.

"Where the hell do you think you're going?" he
almost shouted. "We been looking for you! Don't
think you're going back to that place of yours!"

Clipper sat in the center of the back seat, stony-faced
behind his dark glasses. It would be Armstrong's luck
to be picked up immediately by an obliging public ser-
vant, while Murdoch stumped along the weary way.
"Why not?" I asked Frank.

"You think the *Seguridad* doesn't have it staked, for

Christ's sake?" His wall eyes peered hostilely at me.
"You're coming downtown and we're getting everything sorted out!"

I slid in beside him, leaned my head against the seat
and closed my eyes as he made a grunting project of
backing and turning around. "Those negatives have to
be somewhere, Timken," Clipper Armstrong said.

My head jiggling with the motion of the car, I
listened to C. E. Armstrong briefing his staff on a
problem he had, which he wanted cleared up. I was no
longer a part of that staff, but Frank's voice tugged at
its forelock when he spoke; Yes, Massa. On Insurgentes
he swung into the curb behind a parked taxi which we
were to take to the María Isabel. He assured Clipper
that everything possible would be done, and warned me
to stay put.

When I said I didn't intend to go to the hotel with
Clipper, Frank looked as though he would come after
me with Mace and a riot gun. Clipper laid a hand on
my shoulder. "Come on, Tommy. There's someone
come to town you want to see."

I got into the taxi with him; Daddy Warbucks had
sent for Little Orphan Annie.

She rose from the couch as we entered, and her voice
with its immediate husky little echo made the hairs at
the back of my neck prickle. "Hello, Tommy," Eloise
said.

She was the most beautiful woman in the world. In
her summer-colored silk dress that clung to her in
delight, with her lightly browned arms and ripe round
legs, the cloud of fair hair crowning her smooth forehead, the violet power of her eyes and her pale ribbon
of a mouth smiling uncertainly, she was all the beautiful girls in the slickpaper magazine advertisements of
the means, ends, and products of America, Coca-Cola

and menthol cigarets, new model V-8s and prefab swimming pools, borax furniture and toothpaste, foundation garments and blended whiskey, all the labor-saving and the luxurious, the meretricious and the marvelous, the quality and the crap. "Hello, Ellie," I said.

Clipper Armstrong had moved to stand spraddle-legged against the valley of Mexico, watching this conjugal scene unsmiling, and I felt the pressure to kiss my wife as a husband who hasn't seen his darling for ten days should certainly do, a reluctance to kiss her just because of that Armstrong pressure and because all at once kissing Eloise had become a matter of immorality-in-order-to-exist. But I stepped toward her, and felt her soft hands brush my cheeks and then the hairs at the back of my neck she didn't need to stimulate because the sound of her voice had already erected them. "Mmmmmmmmmmmmm*mmmmm!*" she murmured.

"How's Meander Hills?" I asked, stepping back. She said it was marvelous, absolutely marvelous, beautiful. She had lost weight, probably she had done some time at the sybaritic reducing spa she frequented, that cost like a moon shot. Her expression of uncertainty had vanished, and now she was sure of herself again, and sure of me, for she knew she was the only woman in the world for Tommy Murdoch. When I computed how long it had been since I had been in contact with a bed, my knees buckled with exhaustion and I sat down.

Clipper Armstrong's expression had relaxed. "Timken told me that wagon of yours got totaled, Tommy. Don't worry, we'll get you another one just like it."

I shook my head at him. Eloise sat down beside me, legs close together, back arched, breasts on display. She had the style to transform Pat Hepner's affectations into a polished work of art. I shook my head at her father.

"Drink, Tommy?" he inquired a little anxiously.

I kept shaking my head. No more of his expensive cars and no more of his expensive liquor. There was a stiff moment as father and daughter ignored my bad manners.

"Say, I'll bet you're tired, Tommy," the Clipper said. "Say, you really look beat. Ellie, why don't you get Tommy in bed before he conks out?"

Obediently she took my hands in hers and stood up. She said all the right things, but she was doubling in my eyes like Pat Hepner in her duplicity. I was tired, all right.

I said, "Ellie, how about going to bed because we want to and not because he wants us to?"

"Tom-*mee!*" she whispered. When I rose she put an arm around me. Moving toward the bedroom, our hips bumped pleasantly, while Clipper watched us flanked by the distant snow-capped peaks like some fantastic T-formation quarterback. "Don't feel bad about the Corvette," Eloise whispered. "I'll make him get us a Lambo. I love Lambos!" She stood over me as I sat on the bed, S-shaped with fatigue.

Gazing up into the lovely, promising and compromising violet shimmer of her eyes, I said, "Do you think if we loved each other we could get along without Lambos and Meander Hills and the penthouse, and just some job where I could stand what I was doing?"

"If we loved each other you wouldn't even think of trying to make me unhappy," she said. I was fumbling with my tie. "Here; let me help my darling," Ellie said.

How beguiling it was in the soft bed, in the lush and responsive arms of the Dominant Apparatus, the Establishment, the Affluent Society, the *E Pluribus Unum*. I cruised over the lovely hills and valleys, the plateaus and mountaintops and deep forests, grazed the fertile plains and delighted in the busy centers of industry and

the arts. And with the organismic balance restored, I
lay awake beside my sleeping wife and considered the
copasetic side of American life, the Corvettes and
Lamborghinis and country clubs, the fancy money, the
consenting adulteries; plenty of bucks and plenty of
fucks, and what do you want, Murdoch, milk for all the
babies in the world? It was so very comfortable, so very
pleasant, in Clipper Armstrong's bed, in Eloise's arms,
but how did it compare with love on a bench in an old
convent yard, desperately seeking beneath a stone
crucifix, the mind and heart totally engaged? Maybe
you were never aware of the crossroads of your life until
you had gone past, on one highway or the other.

I could hear voices in the other room, the time had
come, and I rose and dressed and stood looking down
on Sleeping Beauty for a long moment before I went
out to join the men. Frank Timken was with the
World's Tallest Dwarf, dark glasses on, Clipper's liquor
in his hand.

"Say, I guess you're wanted over at the Embassy,"
my father-in-law said. He winked at me: "When you
come back we'll hash over a little project I've got going
for you."

He looked worried when I didn't say anything to
that, and Frank and I left for the Embassy, where
Finch's journal had to be disposed of, like atomic
waste.

(20) WEDNESDAY, II

THE stars and stripes on an eagle-headed staff, and a framed photograph of the President flanked a smiling Sandy Brody. He rose from behind his desk as Frank and I entered, a heavy man with graying reddish hair, a tweed suit, a pipe. I had met him with Ibis at Herb Justin's, weeks, months, years ago.

"Well, Tom, how're you hitting the ball?" he asked, as we shook hands. He appeared to hang very loose compared with uptight Frank Timken, whose superior I guessed he was, and who now stalked around the desk to occupy a post at Sandy's right hand.

I remarked that I'd heard Sandy had gone to Washington, he said it had seemed advisable to make a trip back down, and gestured to a chair. "Sit down, sit down, please, Tom."

I sat down and sorted through my emotions, none of which I liked. I felt very irritable, with a hard anger like a pressure in my sinuses. Frank and Sandy seated themselves, Frank cracking his knuckles, Sandy blowing smoke. Everything seemed phony.

"We really can't understand you, Tom," Sandy said, still smiling. "You set yourself against us all the way. If a marriage—of convenience, certainly—could have been arranged between Cisneros and Aurelia Velás-

quez, an almost bloodless coup would have been possible in Santa Cruz. He had the old *Protectoristas,* and
she had all the conservative element—and the *campe-
sinos.* It was a perfect setup."

I totted up the mortalities in the preliminaries of the
almost bloodless coup; eight. "If you're giving me
credit for spoiling your perfect setup, thanks," I said.
"But I have to defer to the Dark Angel. She loved her
country, you see."

Frank started to bluster, but Sandy halted him with a
damping motion of his hand. "Tom, it does seem that
you've had an excessive faith in your own judgment.
Which was really pretty *bad* judgment. That little
Cubana conned you, Tom."

I had admitted the possibility to myself.

"And that chauffeur in Jalisco," Frank said. He
looked like the Tin Woodman of Oz with his chin
stuck out at me. "Conned again," he said. "There is no
question that he was an agent of the red Flores—"

"Why don't we skip that?" I said. "I don't believe
it."

Sandy looked amused. "You refuse to believe it,
Tom?"

I nodded. "And if you proved he was a Flores agent I
still wouldn't believe he was a red. Because I don't
believe Flores is a red. And if you proved *that,* I still
wouldn't believe the Republic of Santa Cruz doesn't
have the right to elect the government it wants."

The two of them stared at me each in character—as
the good-guy cop and the bad-guy cop. But my speech
had been a phony too, only for show. It wasn't my
style to keep a finger in the dike, or to try to cure the
world. They could have what they wanted as soon as
they relaxed the pressure. Didn't they understand that?

Sandy said, "Are you trying to blackmail us, Tom?"

"I don't think I have to. I'll bet Santa Cruz policy is

being reexamined anyway. C. E. Armstrong having disposed of his sugar stock. And one thing and another. Right, Frank?"

Timken's face turned pink and pale in blotches, and Sandy said smoothly that C. E. Armstrong didn't dictate American policy.

"I thought he did there, for a while."

Sandy's voice had a hard crust on it suddenly. "And neither do you. We want that journal of Finch's."

"I don't have it," I said.

There was a digestive silence. Frank rose and leaned on the desk with his big-knuckled hands spread flat, glaring, while Sandy applied a match to the bole of his gone-out pipe. There was time for me to wonder why I had said that.

"We're worried about the *Seguridad*, Tom," Sandy said, eyebrows tucking together to show how worried he was. "There are several matters they want to question you about—Herrerro, the Velásquez woman and Cisneros. And of course those two security men who were shot down from ambush."

"The *Seguridad* can play pretty rough," Frank added.

I restrained myself from asking if he often got to watch them at play. Time to de-escalate.

"You know, there's an entirely different legal system down here," Sandy continued. "I'm afraid without any—*insulation*—you might find the harassment extremely unpleasant."

"They'd be sure to beat it out of me that Ibis was a double agent, for instance."

My ace-in-the-hole was met with a poker-faced silence. Sandy went on again, not quite so pleasantly. "This matter of harassment is something not much understood by people who have never been exposed to the negative side of life. The crude hassling of the cop

on the beat, the highway patrol, sheriff's office, welfare
people—" He shrugged with his hands. "And it gets
much more sophisticated on up the economic ladder.
For instance, Internal Revenue, and so many regulatory
agencies, and—"

He stopped, dramatically, for another try at lighting
his pipe. The rasping flare of the match snarled along
my nerves, and all at once I was shaking with rage.
Their estimate of me was insulting, their methods were
clumsy, they were stupid men.

"Don't you ever find that threats have the opposite
effect from what everybody wants?"

"You'd better believe we're not just threatening!"
Frank shouted.

I got to my feet and demanded to know if I was
being detained.

Sandy made a lot of business with his pipe. Frank
had moved a step back. Neither of them spoke. I stood
facing them in a show of righteous indignation, and
said I wanted to see the DCM.

My emotions kept beating against my better judgment like panicked birds against a cage. I watched the
pinched white line like a purse string, that had pulled
tight around Sandy's mouth. It relaxed, and he smiled
again; everything was okay now that he had thought it
through and we understood each other.

"Fine, Tom. Certainly. Go see Herb."

I went to see if I had any mail first. The cute Mexican
clerk in the mailroom sorted the letters from the M
pigeonhole, and then searched the bin of packages and
oversized envelopes. "Yes, yes, here is a big mail for
Mister Thomas Murdoch."

My adrenalin count was running up toward the red
line as I took the envelope containing John Finch's
journal into the men's room. I locked myself in the stall
farthest from the door and took out the pebble-grained,

blue-leather journal. JOHN DOANE FINCH. I
thumbed through what seemed hundreds of pages of
tightly knit script, and my eye was caught by a poem
with a long quotation in front of it, and the title, A
MARINE'S HYMN:

I spent thirty-three years and four months in active service
as a member of one of our country's most agile military
forces—the Marine Corps. I helped make Mexico and
especially Tampico safe for American oil interests in 1914.
I helped make Haiti and Cuba a decent place for the National City Bank boys to collect revenues in. I helped
purify Nicaragua for the international banking house of
Brown Brothers in 1909–1912. I brought light to the Do-
minican Republic for the sugar interest in 1916. I helped
make Honduras "right" for American fruit companies in
1903. In China in 1927 I helped see that Standard Oil
went its way unmolested.

During these years I had, as the boys in the back room
would say, a swell racket. I was rewarded with honors,
medals, promotions. Looking back on it, I feel I might have
given Al Capone a few hints. The best he could do was to
operate his racket in three city districts. We Marines operated on three continents.

Major General Smedley D. Butler, USMC

Thirty-three years I fought for the Corps,
Collecting tithes for the National City,
Starting the flow for Standard Oil,
Lending a hand to the Brothers Brown,
Filling the bowl for American Sugar.

Thirty-three years for the U.S.A.,
Turning the valves for Standard Oil,
Sweetening the taste for American Sugar,
Bilking the spics for the Brothers Brown,
Filling the till for the National City.

Thirty-three years of active duty,
In Nicaragua for Brothers Brown,

In Haiti for the National City,
In Honduras for United Fruit,
And also in China for Standard Oil.

Thirty-three years I fought for the nation,
Growing bananas for United Fruit,
Collecting the rent for National City,
Cleaning up for the Brothers Brown,
Exploiting the natives for American Sugar.

Thirty-three years of honors and medals,
Thirty-three years of worthy promotions,
Thirty-three years of running the rackets,
Thirty-three years of lining our pockets,
Thirty-three years of the fat of the lands;
Thirty-three years, thirty-three years.

Other titles caught my eye as I paged on:

AUSCHWITZ

The advice of the Bishop of Osnabrück to Dr. Lucas,
who was troubled by his role as prison doctor at Auschwitz,
was that an immoral order should not be obeyed, but resistance should not go so far as to endanger one's life. One
reads this and sneers at the "good German" mentality. One
is sneering at mankind, for rarely does resistance go so far
as to endanger even one's standard of living. I perceive in
myself this dichotomy between high-minded utterance and
simple selfishness, but am capable only of the perception
with its attendant guilt. My Jenny, however, would without
hesitation throw up worldly goods and life itself for truth,
and perhaps it is the women who will save the world while
the men engage in their endless hypocrisy.

MOBY DICK

We sail on the mad ship *Pequod*, captained by mad
Ahab, in search of the red whale. All will perish in the
quest. Why is it more comforting to die in common
catastrophe than in lonely but honorable dissent? It is because the world is governed by old men whose obsession

with death is essentially the fear of its loneliness. It is not so terrible to perish in the warm company of all mankind.

GNP
Only the Gross National Product has its patriots. America has been abandoned by those to whom she gave too much wealth and comfort, and so the fear of losing them.

The last entry in the little book was headed:

JENNY
You say that you will leave me, for I will not act. I have chosen to work within the administration rather than in opposition to it, in hope that I could accomplish some good. Or perhaps in rationalization, as you suggest.

Your indictment is simple and damning. Powerful commercial interests may be dictating the formation of policy toward the government of the Republic of Santa Cruz, combining with and taking advantage of paranoid elements in our own administration. We will aid in the installation of a reactionary regime. And this is wrong, you say so simply. And I, who have chosen to accommodate myself to this sort of thing, have become corrupt, you say.

No plea of ignorance is possible. I should have known exactly what was happening, of course. Previous parallel situations have educated me, but by now I have found that I can only function by not accepting what I know in my heart to be true. Immoral in order to exist—that unfortunate phrase of mine that so offended you.

I have been sent here with certain responsibilities and powers, and while I work to build—not even that, only to preserve—something which has been, and still might be, of value, agencies with concentrated power but apparently no responsibility, work to destroy. They have narrow objectives narrowly coordinated, narrow loyalties, a narrowly pragmatic morality, and a total ruthlessness.

So it has been for many years, and until now I have managed to ignore it. But if what is planned in the Re-

public of Santa Cruz succeeds—and I do confess I know
roughly what is planned—the whole frail structure I have
been spending my last years and resources patching together, will collapse. Our credibility in Latin America will
vanish. I have lied for the last time to the world, my
country, and to my own self.

Dearest Jenny, I was not angry with you. I have been
destroyed. It is difficult to acknowledge that fact with
grace.

He had written it while Jenny Gray and I made love
on the stone bench in the convent yard, straining
together as though something could still be won if the
contact were deep enough. It had been a mistake to look
into the journal of John Doane Finch; what now?
Department D of the KGB wanted the journal to turn
into Disinformation. Sandy and Frank probably wanted
to destroy it. If I turned it over to Herb Justin, as had
been tacitly arranged, he would pass it along to them.
It might not be a world-shaking document, but I didn't
think the backroom boys should have it.

Waiting to see the Deputy Chief of Mission, I had
the scrotum-tightening sensation, here in this little bit
of America in a foreign land, of being on enemy
terrain.

Herb was standing before his desk when I entered,
cool and reserved. "Help!" I said.

"You really must do what you are urgently required
to do, Tom." He cocked his head at me, he jingled the
change in his pocket; he was a position and not a man.

"Or I'll be pursued and harassed to the ends of the
earth?"

"They can be very unpleasant. You could get twenty
years in a federal pen if you've signed the loyalty oath,
you know."

"I haven't signed it. Are we being fucking monitored, Herb?"

He flushed. He shook his head.

"Talk to me then! I don't think the sons of bitches have any right to what they say they urgently require. How about smuggling it home in the diplomatic pouch for me?"

Lips drawn into a rigid line, he shook his head once. But something in his face shone rawly past his cool, the man, not the position, as he said in a thick voice, "I'm not free to make that decision, Tom."

I almost shouted at him that no one was ever free to make decisions. The decisions had all been made and determined before we were born, and I was as preconditioned and Pavloved, as trapped and hung-up, as anybody. But somehow, somewhere, somebody had to make a move. I stood looking at him contemptuously, and then I walked out with the journal still in my pocket, heavy and uncomfortable.

Outside the DCM's office I saw the elevator doors open. A woman and a man with a briefcase came out, pausing a moment in conversation, and behind them in the elevator was Jenny Gray.

She held the door. In half a dozen quick steps I was inside with her, and the door slid closed behind me. Her hand gripped mine for an instant with fingers sharp as talons. Staring into her eyes, I said, "Do you work for them too?"

She stepped back from me. The glow went out of her face. With a jar the elevator started upward. "All right," she said. "I used to. Never mind how, they recruited me to spy on the man I loved. Because he might have written something damaging to the administration. Because he had a heart condition. Because he might die—and someone might get the journal. I've been the guardian of his journal." I glanced from her face to the floor indicator. "And of course I failed," Jenny said. "Because he died. And somebody got it."

I produced the battered envelope and handed it to her. With a gasp of shock she stuffed it into her purse. I held my finger on the button as the elevator halted, and with another mechanical twitch we began to descend. Jenny's eyes were fastened to mine.

"It ought to be published," I said.

"You and I, Murdoch?" she whispered. "We—"

"Jenny, I've got a wife. And my life, that I like—that I used to like. That I have to try to—fix."

It took all my will to face her eyes, like Herb Justin facing mine. Her pilot light blazed up in contempt, her mouth twisted. "All right, Murdoch," she said. "I'll get it to Emily Finch, it's hers by rights anyway. We de*test* each other, but at least she's on the side of the angels."

She slumped into the corner of the elevator, eyeing the indicator needle above the door, her purse clasped to her breast like a schoolgirl's books. She closed her eyes tightly for a moment. The elevator halted at the ground floor. I felt as though I had been whipped with padded ropes.

"Have a *good* life, Murdoch," Jenny said. She hurried out past a crewcut young man with his arms full of looseleaf binders, heading for the steps to the street. Muscles shaped like inverted hearts caught in her calves with the length of her stride.

"Up?" the young man asked. I rode up with him, changed elevators and rode down again, to separate myself in time from Jenny Gray. No one interfered when I strolled through the lobby, down the steps and out from under the white lampshade and back toward the hotel. It was hard lines to see Jenny once more when I reached the corner.

She was in a *cocodrilo* with the jagged yellow line

along the side, a driver with a plaid cap, the cab halted
in a line of traffic waiting to turn onto Reforma. I stood
on the curb and watched the guardian of the journal
staring straight ahead with a set chin and her black-
rimmed glasses on.

Freedom was a disaster, as Ibis had said, the individual man's costs were much too high, and the time-
space event that was Thomas Murdoch hurt like hell.
It was not so much that my eyes were newly opened, it
was that I could never close them again. And so I could
never work for Clipper Armstrong again. And my
prophetical soul was almost certain how my wife would
respond to my ultimatums; but not quite.

Jenny gave no sign that she saw me. In due course
the traffic was unstoppered and her taxi moved on
along, turning out onto the boulevard. When I
couldn't see it any more I started on across the street
toward the hotel. It was my own journey across my own
painful stones, maybe in penitence, and probably in
faith, but certainly because I recognized the bed I had
made. I didn't have to lie in it. I had to try to make it
over again.